Masterson

". . . an engaging novel that takes its inspiration from history."
—*Chicago Tribune*

"The author knows the West and its history . . . like all of Wheeler's works, the novel is based on meticulous research."
—*The Denver Post*

"There is something for every reader who enjoys a good story in *Masterson*: romance, intrigue, and a glimpse of the past, of legend and the past as it was." —*The Billings Outpost*

Masterson is classic Wheeler. He is among the top living writers of Western historical novels—if not the best—highly recommended." —*Tulsa World*

"This is classic Wheeler, a solid story about real people told with wit, compassion, and a bit of whimsy."
—*Publishers Weekly*

". . . Wheeler shows his storytelling magic with an insightful look into the soul of a man with his new novel. . . . Wheeler's novels rise above the genre." —*El Paso Times*

Dark Passage

". . . an entertaining frontier adventure . . . told in terms as ruggedly beautiful as the mountain country in which it is set. A Western Writers of America Golden Spur Award winner, Wheeler has a sharp eye for detail and writes prose worth savoring." —*Booklist*

"All of the details and characters ring true . . . the pacing is impeccable . . . never a false beat." —*The Missoulian*

RICHARD S. WHEELER

VENGEANCE VALLEY

Pinnacle BOOKS
Kensington Publishing Corp.
http://www.kensingtonbooks.com

PINNACLE BOOKS are published by

Kensington Publishing Corp.
850 Third Avenue
New York, NY 10022

This novel is a work of fiction. Names, characters, places, and incidents are either the product of the author's imagination, or are used fictitiously. Any resemblance to actual persons, living or dead, or events is entirely coincidental.

All Kensington titles, Imprints, and Distributed lines are available at special quantity discounts for bulk purchases for sales promotions, premiums, fund-raising, and educational or institutional use. Special book excerpts or customized printings can also be created to fit specific needs. For details, write or phone the office of the Kensington special sales manager: Kensington Publishing Corp., 850 Third Avenue, New York, NY 10022, attn. Special Sales Department, Phone: 1-800-221-2647.

Pinnacle and the P logo Reg. U.S. Pat. & TM Off.

First Pinnacle Books Printing: September 2004
10 9 8 7 6 5 4 3 2 1

Printed in the United States of America

One

When Hard Luck Yancey found the pebble, he knew at once what it was and how it might transform his life. It was a curious pebble, dark and heavy, pocked and pitted and twisted. Its color was not far from black. He hefted it, licked it, studied it minutely, and then looked for more like it, wedged against a pink granite boulder on the slope.

It was black gold, telluride gold, but it looked nothing like gold and would have escaped the attention of an untrained eye. It was what prospectors called float, a tiny bit of mineral that had eroded from someplace above, maybe miles away, some mother lode that had outcropped somewhere. Finding the source of float was probably the main task of prospectors, and a daunting one.

Yancey peered about, studying the vast and inhospitable grade, corrugated by innumerable gulches, choked with cedar and juniper, silent in the sun. Far below lay an arid sand-bottomed valley with a dry streambed. Above, the slope was capped by a naked ridge radiating out from Table Mountain. Off to the north and east the peaks of the San Juan Mountains confused the horizon.

From where he stood, the whole panorama seemed utterly devoid of human life, but in fact he was only a mile or so from a mining town huddled at the crest of this vast slope. The town was named Yancey, after him, the discoverer of a huge silver bonanza up there. He could not see the town because of a dull, anonymous stratum of pink granite that blocked the view.

He turned the nugget around, absorbing its appearance so that he might spot its kin. Then he began a sharp-eyed hunt up and down the shallow gulch, sometimes fighting his way through nettlesome brush, looking for more of the black pebbles. He found nothing. He didn't really expect to. Float was seductive and treacherous and maddening. He did not know how the gold had arrived there. It might have been carried by an animal, dropped by a bird, discharged from the earth by a burrowing creature. But most float simply broke away from some outcrop somewhere, and over aeons of time was transported by gravity, sun, rain, snow, wind, or even quakes, to where it now lay.

There was no guarantee that other float would lie in the same gulch, so he crawled up a shelf and dropped down into the neighboring drainage. An hour later he was convinced that no black gold existed there. He tried various other gullies, and the tiny divides between them, pausing especially at places such as the upslope side of boulders, where a heavy pebble might be arrested.

No luck. Still, he knew that black gold came from *somewhere,* and that somewhere was the focus of his dreams and hopes, and he intended to find it. He saw not another mortal in this juniper jungle, only some ravens circling above. Slowly he made his way uphill, sweating in the autumnal sun, arriving at last at the massive stratum of red granite that seemed to divide the slope into two segments. Above was gray limestone, which rose toward the arid ridge where he had found the carbonate silver ore. But that was another world, and another story.

The chances were that the float had eroded from an outcrop in this very granite, probably a quartz vein. But he saw nothing, only the anonymous, smooth-grained, fractured, and jumbled wall of hard red rock that showed not the slightest sign of treasure. He walked along the wall, examining segments of it with his trained prospector's eye, studying the uppermost reaches, the middle range, and the lower parts, paying particular attention to the pebbles that formed talus at its base, and any fracture in the wall.

Nothing. He hadn't expected it to be easy. Tracing float was one of the most maddening occupations engaged in by mortals.

Still, he had hoped for at least one other sample, some small confirmation that he was on the right track, something to suggest that the presence of black gold on that silent and jumbled grade was more than the freakish result of a passing animal or bird. He also kept a sharp eye for silvery pebbles, because telluride gold was actually silvery deep in its rocky tomb, and darkened only when it was exposed to the elements. But he found nothing.

Tomorrow he would return to his clerking job at the hardware store far above. But this Sabbath he had spent, as he usually did, exploring alone. When the sun dipped behind the distant snow-tipped peaks and darkness threatened to entrap him in a maze of juniper brush, he surrendered and wearily toiled upslope toward a notch in the granite escarpment, clambered up that notch, his heart thudding with the effort, and found himself in another world.

Here the slope was less steep, and an astonishing city of two thousand souls huddled under the drab ridge, its board-and-batten buildings weather-stained and gray. Along the ridge itself the headframes of half-a-dozen mines jabbed the cobalt sky. It was not a place where a town should be, and the entire mining camp seemed poised to tumble down that gray slope.

He had acquired the Hard Luck moniker as a result of three calamities. The last and worst disaster had befallen him only recently, but Hard Luck figured he had learned something. That's how he dealt with tragedy: If he had learned something, he could make use of it in the future.

The whole town of Yancey City, and the mining district itself, was named for him. He had located a magnificent body of carbonate silver ore on a high ridge south of the San Juan Mountains, started up the Minerva Mine, named after the goddess of wisdom, and set out to get rich so that he could marry well, since he was as plain as a cucumber.

The raw town soon blossomed just below the Minerva headframe, the whole of it perched on a slope so steep that its buildings were partly dug into notches in the hillside, and half supported on stilts. Eventually, some level streets were scraped into the side of that slope, but those were the only places a person could stand without leaning uphill.

The exception was the hospital run by the Sisters of Charity of Leavenworth, located on two acres well below the town in an intimate little plateau notched in a gulch. The flat was watered by a miraculous spring of sweet cool water, which not only supplied the hospital but the entire town. It was the sole source of water for miles in any direction.

It had taken a lot of doing to start the Minerva Mine in a place so lonesome. But Yancey had patiently hired twenty-mule teams to drag the mining equipment up there and start blasting. Everything from heavy timbers to woven cable had to be dragged up there by ox or mule power. He had just as hard a time keeping miners hired. No one wanted to live on a windy ridge, thousands of feet from a spring, scores of miles from the nearest burg, without a level inch of ground in the whole place.

But he persevered, dragged prefabricated buildings up there, put them on stilts, found a good blasting crew, and began driving a shaft. Soon enough the promising mine turned into a bonanza. Not twenty feet in, the silver ore had become fabulously rich and so valuable that Hard Luck could afford to send it to the mill by pack mule and still come out way ahead.

Word of the big silver strike swiftly filtered through Colorado and all the mining camps of the West, and in no time every inch of ground along that ledge was claimed, sometimes by two or three people, which kept the courts entertained. The hard gray limestone of Table Mountain disgorged its silver ore, the town bloomed, and soon half-a-dozen mines, all in a row, lined that alpine ridge, their headframes stark against blue sky.

It all started well enough. To the right of the Minerva was the Poco Loco, belonging to Alfred Noble and his Rhode Island Syndicate, while to the left was the Good Times, sole property of Gustav Moran, a seedy little bag of tricks with a wounded look in his face.

What Hard Luck's neighbors lacked was scruples, and next thing Hard Luck knew, he was being dragged into the nearest federal court to defend against apex suits. The mining law of the country permitted the discoverer of a mineral vein to pursue it wherever it wandered, provided that it apexed, or surfaced, on his claim, no matter whether the vein found its way into neighboring claims. This made mining lawyers rich, and made the entire mining industry the vassal of powerful law firms. And it broke Hard Luck Yancey.

Moran and Noble had the means to engage nefarious lawyers and butter up fat judges, and soon Hard Luck was fighting a novel double apex suit, never before known to mining law, which claimed that the vein actually surfaced twice, on either side of the Minerva, and that Hard Luck was therefore stealing ore that belonged to the Poco Loco and Good Times.

The judge found for the plaintiffs, declared that Hard Luck owed his neighbors $273,000 for the value of ore stolen from them, and additional damages to the tune of $130,000 for damage to the neighboring properties.

Noble and Moran swiftly attached the Minerva, soon owned it, and Hard Luck was once again euchred out of his property. Like that wretch Henry Comstock, who had sold off his claim for a pittance only to learn he had given his name to a bonanza, Will Yancey had more than once seen a fortune slide through his fingers.

But while poor Comstock drifted from mining town to mining town and never amounted to anything, Yancey always managed to start again. Yancey didn't think the name Hard Luck was very accurate; it wasn't hard luck that cost him the Minerva, but neighbors as crooked and ruthless as mortals ever get. So, with each loss, Will Yancey studied on the matter, learned something, and filed away his knowledge for the future. Someday, he figured, he'd be smart. He knew how to discover ore; what baffled him was dealing with ruthless and unscrupulous men. If he could figure that out someday, he might hang on to his discoveries.

That was the thing about Yancey: He was a quiet, mild, bookish sort. While other prospectors were wandering the hills without knowing galena from fool's gold, or nitric acid from moonshine, Yancey was delving into texts about minerals and geology and chemistry.

While the rest were poking at worthless limestone with picks and shovels, Yancey was learning about hydraulics, explosives, amalgamation, and stamp mills. The result of all this was that Hard Luck Yancey was the most learned and able of all prospectors, and kept finding ore in places that had been passed over by hordes of ignorant sourdoughs. He kept his secrets to himself, quietly studied the brooding hills, and somehow knew or intuited what lay deep within them.

To support himself for now he worked part-time in Mulholland's Hardware Emporium, where his mastery of all things mechanical made him a valued employee. He lived in a modest board-and-batten cottage, its rear notched into the slope, its front propped up on stilts like most every structure in town. It was the same cottage he had built soon after he started up the Minerva, and far more modest than the elaborate rock eyries erected by the mining moguls who watched car after one-ton car of silver ore emerge from their mines each shift.

The moguls had even tried to take that cottage from him too, but the town's miners themselves had threatened to walk out if they did. Hard Luck was popular among them; he had been a fair and kind employer who paid the going rate of three dollars a day, but saw to it that the drifts were properly timbered and safe.

So Alfred Noble and Gustav Moran contented themselves with stealing a mine, and did not squeeze Hard Luck any further, though they claimed that Yancey still owed them $78,000. Noble even offered Yancy a job as shift boss, knowing how well he got along with the hard-rock miners who descended into the bowels of Table Mountain each shift and worked in utter darkness save for the pale light of a few lamps. With a foreman like Yancey down there, labor problems would vanish.

But the main reason the miners defended Yancey was that he had donated the ground for the hospital. Any mining town needs an infirmary at the very least, and a hospital if possible, because mining crushes flesh, snaps bones, scorches lungs, burns, cuts, blinds, deafens, chops, breaks, and bloodies men. Yancey saw the need, surveyed the little flat, then turned it over to the Sisters of Charity of Leavenworth, who otherwise lacked the means to set up shop in Yancey, Colorado.

Just ahead of full dark, Yancey reached his weathered cottage, lit a lamp, pulled the black gold from his pocket, rubbed it, and dreamed. Maybe this time he could make his pile without losing it to ruthless men.

Two

Hard Luck Yancey really wanted one thing from life, a sweetheart. In every moment of his adult life he had suffered this yearning. He had no explanation for it; he simply knew that once he found and won the right girl, everything would be perpetual spring. He had been set upon this earth to be a good husband and father. He had been born to kiss his bride, share a long life together, and raise a family.

He knew most men had this natural urge, only his was more intense. For him, the right girl meant a lifetime without ever being lonely. He thought maybe it was the loneliness that drove him. He had always been lonely because he was a little different. In Ypsilanti, where he grew up, the third son of a logger, he burrowed into books.

He had an owlish look about him, a curved beak of a nose, big dark smudges of eyes, and a noble brow that stretched up and up and up and seemed to contain a huge brain. One glance in the looking glass reminded him how strange he looked. The girls ignored him. He was plain, slow to speak up because he measured everything he uttered, and his voice was soft as velvet, so people had to lean close to hear him.

Back there in Michigan he had graduated with honors from the normal school and set his cap for Miss Mandy, the girl who shot fevers and lightning through him whenever he saw her. But Mandy hardly noticed. He got a job clerking in Pendleton's Dry Goods Emporium, and thought to win her attention when he sold Mandy some good percale or calico, but she never gave him a second glance. Then one bleak day he discovered that Mandy had eloped with a fat whiskey drummer with curly red muttonchops who had plenty of greenbacks in his purse, and the last Will Yancey heard, the couple was settled in Atlanta.

He drew a grave lesson from it, as he always did: It took money to get a girl. Especially if you were reserved, shy, and homely as a stump, the way Yancey was. Clerking would never get him the money he needed to fetch a wife; he could work until the age of thirty and maybe save a thousand dollars if he was frugal, and that wouldn't get Yancey more than one toenail of a bride.

But there was a whole West full of mines and people were getting rich from minerals, and he saw the chance in it. He would prospect. Being a man who studied before he acted, he read all about prospecting and mining and gold and silver, then caught the Union Pacific west, and then some stagecoaches, and outfitted himself as a prospector.

He didn't do badly. Book learning proved to be more useful than he had imagined out in the wilds, and in some ways he was brighter than veteran prospectors who had all the intelligence of fire ants. He had won and lost several paying mines, and had gained knowledge from each victory and disaster. Someday soon, he knew, he would make some money and then he could get married. Even such an odd duck as himself would find a sweetheart if he had a pocket full of double eagles.

He wasn't making much progress in the alpine burg of Yancey, perhaps because there were so few women in town. He could almost count on his fingers the number of superintendents' wives and daughters in town, and they, plus a few score of miners' wives, constituted the whole of the town's proper women. Of course there were some shopworn ones in the Knights of Babylon Club, and the Sandwich Islands Saloon down on Gulch Alley off Copper Street. The dearth of females was so bad that he took to watching the arrival of the Cunningham and Charter Stage Coach, which arrived twice weekly at four o'clock, its eight-horse team exhausted by the tortuous climb to the C and C Stage Office on Mineral Street. But all he saw step down from the Concord to the flinty street was sewing machine drummers and stock brokers in brocade vests, and others of that ilk.

So he endured, ordered an occasional mining or geological tome from distant Denver, read by the yellow light of a coal-oil lamp, and spent his rare free daytime prospecting. The whole district was mineralized; he could do no better than to hunt right there, and someday he would find what he was after, and get rich and get married.

Meanwhile, Hard Luck kept an eye on the local mining, looking for a chance to get back what had been euchred from him. There was some activity up at the Minerva Mine that Alfie Noble didn't want anyone to know about. His syndicate was driving an exploratory shaft straight down from the silver-bearing seam to see whether the whole geologic formation might repeat itself farther down. But now they were into the granite.

Hard Luck knew that because he prowled the tailings pile of his old Minerva Mine at night, between the two shifts. There was a night watchman around sometimes, but the old duffer's task was to keep miners from pilfering ore, and he never wandered in the direction of the huge mound of tailings that were being dumped in a gulch just west of the town. Eventually the tailings would reach the Knights of Babylon Club and bury it, but that wouldn't happen for a while, at least not until they built a church in Yancey, which might be never.

Hard Luck had dressed in dark clothes, poked and probed the pile by the light of a gibbous moon, pocketed samples of the granite, and knew exactly what was happening in the bowels of the mine that had once been his own. The close-mouthed miners said little in the saloons because Alfie Noble didn't want gossip, but that didn't slow down Hard Luck. He knew that for some reason the syndicate was blasting deep into the granite that underlay the limestone. So they weren't looking for carbonate silver anymore.

Had they an inkling there might be quartz gold in that granite? Hard Luck didn't know, and could only guess that yes, they did. There was little reason otherwise to bore a shaft so deep, and through rock that would never yield carbonate silver ore. That was what had inspired Hard Luck to begin probing the rough slopes below the town. And what had led to his pocketing of a little piece of float that could herald a fortune—for the one who found the mother lode. He thought maybe he might, being more patient and better versed in geology than the run of men in the town.

At the break of dawn the following Sunday Yancey headed through the quiet streets, then onto the arid slopes, negotiated his way down to the juniper-choked gulch, and began hunting for more float. That was a long, lonely, disheartening day that yielded nothing. But the Sunday after that, a cold day that forced him into a thick wool coat, he was poking around directly below the hospital and found a second piece of black gold, this one larger and wiry and pocked, but just as dark and anonymous as the first piece. He found three more pieces, one of them the better part of an ounce, and knew that he was at last on the trail.

When he drew a line from the site of his first discovery to his last, it ran roughly toward the great granite shelf that underlay the hospital of the Sisters of Charity.

The following Sunday, a brisk October day with a tender sun, he probed the jumbled and tumbled granite escarpment that formed the bed of the little flat where the hospital stood. Now he was close to people and might be discovered, so he masked his work with a picnic basket half full of clippings of shrubs. Let them think that the prospector had turned into an herbalist.

Indeed, just above where he was studying that red rock was a favorite trail of the sisters, who took the air by circumnavigating the little flat, sometimes reciting from breviaries. But no one noticed. He poked and studied, scraped away talus and debris with his pick-hammer, widened his search to neighboring areas, and felt rising frustration: The mother lode was still eluding him. Even more frustrating, he was on the very property he had deeded to the sisters for their hospital, ten acres in all, though only two of them were level enough to support habitation.

Then, along one gully, the very one that carried off the springwater, he discovered more of the black gold, indeed in the space of five minutes, seven shining pieces of it. The burbling water was eroding it from somewhere nearby. Two hundred yards above, the spring gushed from a fracture in the limestone that overlay the granite, tumbled into a pool carved in the granite, and flowed into a weed-choked cess in the slope. And somewhere between where the spring was and the point where the water vanished was the mother lode, its riches steadily plucked from rock by the passing stream. And the most likely place was directly under the whitewashed wooden hospital, along with a small convent house for the five sisters.

Hard Luck Yancey scarcely knew what to do. His mind

teemed with possibilities and objections, his brain fevered at the thought of a fortune a hundred yards away, a fortune not his because he had deeded the land in fee simple to the sisters, reserving no mineral rights. Who would have thought that gold lay under that grassy meadow below the rough town above?

There might well be a fortune, unless the black gold was being eroded from a small pocket of little value. But it really would be the sisters' fortune, not his. He held black gold in his hand, nubbins of it, pocked, pitted, twisted, lustrous, especially when wet. It didn't look like gold; it looked like fragments of iron. But it was gold. He had done his own private assays in his cabin, using the small assaying furnace he kept there for just such purposes. Tellurium could not be separated from gold by any method other than roasting at high temperatures, so he roasted a sample, and ended up with a button of gleaming yellow metal. It was gold, the answer to his dreams, the very metal that gave power to his hopes. Gold! He had exulted, smiled, felt a vast affection for this mining district named after him.

But now he despaired. The mother lode wasn't his. It properly belonged to the sisters' order, and the deed was no doubt in the lockbox of the motherhouse in Leavenworth.

And suddenly it hit him: There was the syndicate, in the form of Alfie Noble, drilling deep in the very granite that had locked a fortune in its cold bosom, and suddenly Hard Luck knew why the syndicate was drilling a shaft from its silver works into the granite four hundred feet below. Someone in the company had also found float, and now the syndicate was going to steal the gold from the Sisters of Charity.

Three

Alfred Noble, the Friend of the Working Man, began and ended each day with a smile on his face. The smile at bedtime was the same as the smile at dawn, but frayed a little, plastered on his somewhat puffy countenance as bona-fide evidence that he was at peace with all of mankind.

He had smiled at Hard Luck Yancey while Noble's lawyers were eviscerating the discoverer of the silver ridge. He had smiled at the widow of a Cousin Jack miner who had died when he fell down a shaft, as he handed her a funeral check for $37.50. He had smiled when his bank, the Yancey Merchants' and Stockmen's Association, foreclosed on Peter Mathes when Mathes caught consumption, and smiled when he donated three Yancey District carbonate-ore samples to the Rocky Mountain Detective Association for use as evidence against pilfering employees.

For Alfie Noble, a smile was goodwill, and the more goodwill he could spread in a day, the more he fertilized the world. He always smiled at his wife, Gertrude, who kept a teetotal house and eschewed coffee as well. He and Gertrude had no children to smile at. He himself was ardently teetotal, and sorrowed when his miners squandered their fortnightly pay envelopes in the saloons of Yancey, depriving their penurious wives and families of bread for their tables.

But being teetotal was a weight on the nerves that required periodic relief from Dr. Borden, so whenever Noble was too much on edge or burdened by his heavy responsibilities, he checked into the Sisters' Hospital, actually St. Vincent's, for a day or two so that Dr. Borden could administer the medicinal cure, an hourly half beaker of a vile-tasting brain elixir and blood-thinning tonic called Wildroot that soon calmed frayed nerves and settled his unruly stomach. Noble did not inquire just what went into the elixir; Dr. Borden simply grinned cynically, dosed his patient, and sent stiff bills.

The sisters were a little snippy about it, but let the doctor admit and discharge his prominent patient at will. At least they made three dollars a day from it, and the smiling mine superintendent sometimes tipped them two bits, which they put into the Funeral Fund.

This day Noble was smiling extra hard because his hired mining geologist, Ambrose Hodgson, had reported that the syndicate silver mines were reaching the end of their life. In a few months, unless new ore was uncovered, the Minerva, the Poco Loco, the Good Times, and all the rest along the ridge would start to shut down, mining some overlooked low-grade for a few weeks and then quitting altogether. Yancey City might hang on for another month, while operators frantically looked for ore, but within half a year, the metropolis on the ridge would be another wind-rattled ghost town, like scores of others all across the West.

Noble had begun a long-shot exploration, hoping to find another and parallel seam of carbonate ore straight down, as sometimes happened, and had contracted with some independent miners to drive a shaft. But now the independent outfit was thirty feet into anonymous pink granite, ordinary country rock with a slight sheen, and Noble knew in his sorrowing bosom that Yancey City was doomed; the syndicate would pay a paltry final dividend, put its last shipment of greenbacks into pay envelopes, and close the window.

Yancey, a town of three thousand people of which eighty-five percent were male, boasted seventeen belles of the evening, one concert hall, twenty-one saloons, twelve tonsorial parlors, five blacksmiths, and twenty-nine square blocks of creaky plank structures notched into the slope. It would swiftly diminish to a handful of cranky old-timers determined to die there, and would soon burn. Old mining towns usually burned up.

The life of Yancey would last six years and five or six months from the date of Will Yancey's discovery claim to the grim day of exodus, when hundreds of wagons would carry a whole city down the mountain, leaving only a strange and strangled silence.

That was too much to bear. Noble didn't much care about the fate of the miners, but the cessation of those dividend checks was a fate worse than leprosy. In its heyday the Minerva alone paid twenty-five percent per annum. The Poco Loco paid seventeen, year after year. The rest of the mines on the ridge, all part of the syndicate now, paid fifteen or sixteen percent.

That was as much as a man could endure. He would go to the hospital and place himself in the care of Dr. Borden, an epileptic surgeon from Fall River, Massachusetts. Noble kept his hospital gowns packed in a Gladstone for any emergencies, so he plucked up his convalescing bag, as he called it, and descended from his handsome mine office, with its velvet-flocked magenta wallpaper and chased-brass spittoons, down the precipitous grade, past the doomed city, and at last to Spring Road, where the water wagons, great dripping casks on wheels, drawn by cashiered percherons bought cheap, lined up at the miraculous spring to fill up and carry the precious liquid up to the housewives and barkeeps above who bought it for two cents a bucket.

Within, he found Sister Carmela at her usual roost inside the door. The miners called her Sister Drill Sergeant, which evoked a beatific smile in her. She was, in fact, built like a Beefeater, and were it not for her the hospital would not have risen. She'd arrived three years before, with four timorous sisters and not a cent, having been summoned by Hard Luck Yancey, who'd pleaded with the motherhouse in Kansas to set up a hospital for the miners.

Sister Drill Sergeant soon organized that whole male community into work brigades. Let a miner get off shift, weary and grimy and ready for a mug of ale, and he was naught but the raw labor for Sister's project. But in the space of a month the weary miners built the hospital, whitewashed it, hammered down a shake roof, added a convent house for the sisters, and the place was in business. Yancey had an infirmary, and it had been occupied, sometimes to overflowing, every day since. No mining camp was more blessed than Yancey. There were miracles daily: lives spared, limbs repaired, pain relieved, sickness healed, childbirth made safer, and all because of the hospital.

"Sister, I am suffering neurasthenia once again, the usual, and need a day or two of rest," Noble said. "The burdens are so heavy."

"We don't have any room, but I'll put you on a cot in the corridor, Mr. Noble."

"No room?"

"The last cave-in, you know."

"Yes, that was terrible. And how are the men?"

"Why don't you go see?"

"I, ah . . ."

He was not eager to see the mangled results of poor timbering in the Poco Loco. One dead, three crushed, seven with respiratory trouble from the dust, one with a head fracture, two recovering from amputations.

She stood like a bulldog before him. "Now, if we had the new wing done, we could accommodate you, Mr. Noble. Perhaps you'd care to contribute?"

"It's a splendid project. Send someone up to the office one of these days."

She eyed him. "Let me summon Dr. Borden. Perhaps he can treat you at home."

"Ah . . ."

Sister Drill Sergeant smiled. "I'm sure Dr. Borden can administer the Wildroot Tonic in your own home. Or your wife?"

"Perhaps if I take a bottle with me . . ."

Sister Drill Sergeant nodded, and within moments a blue bottle of the tonic appeared, greenbacks changed hands, and the transaction was done. Noble did not entirely know the contents, nor were they printed on the label, but he did know the tonic was a handy fire-starter, useful when a cold flue was keeping a newly laid fire from burning in his stove, and it also had a little tincture of opium to soothe away the pains of body and soul. He believed its tart taste was derived from juniper berries.

He thought to offer kindly advice. "You know, Sister, the new wing might not be a good plan with all the uncertainty afflicting the world."

She stared up at him, her unblinking brown gaze drilling straight into him. "Why?"

He didn't really want to say anything about the condition of the mines and regretted his impulse. "Ah, you know how mining towns are, up and down."

"You're telling me that the mines are failing?"

"Not at all, not at all. Lots of ore down there, and we're exploring. In fact, fifty percent of our budget is exploration."

"Failing," she said with an awful finality.

"No, that would be an entirely false interpretation."

She laughed, and Noble wished he had kept his mouth shut.

"I tell you what, Mr. Noble. Deeds speak louder than words. If you finance the new six-bed wing, we'll know the mines are fine. If not . . . ." She shrugged.

"Why, Sister, the mines will be fine, but I would simply suggest a temporary postponement. There might be a little dip in the local economy, we may lay off a few score miners for a while, and you wouldn't be needing those extra beds. Now, in time, the mines will be stronger than ever. We're estimating three to four decades of life. But there might be a little hitch. . . ."

"Drink your Wildroot Tonic, Mr. Noble."

She rose suddenly, a vast eruption of black and white fabric, and pumped his hand.

He nodded and hastened into the cold sunlight, tonic in hand. He had let loose the awful truth and regretted it. It worried him. The tonic worried him. Gertrude would sniff it and pour it away. There was, he knew, a tad of ardent spirit in it, good as a medicinal kidney purge and salutary for his lumbago.

He comforted himself with the knowledge that Sister Drill Sergeant wouldn't blab about the future. She was an executive, like himself, and well aware of how sensitive certain information could be.

Maybe he could dip into the Wildroot in his office, just a little, and no one would notice the difference. He hiked his way upslope, dodging water wagons heading to the spring, smiling and panting because of the steep grade, passed the huddle of board-and-batten structures that comprised Yancey City, not a permanent brick or stone business building in the entire town, not even his bank, so deep was the distrust of the mines above, and arrived, all out of breath, in his office a half hour later.

He collapsed into his swivel chair, wiped sweat from his brow, and uncorked the Wildroot Tonic, a beatific smile spreading across his pink cheeks.

That's when Galway, his shift foreman, burst in and laid a sample of orange granite on his desk, this one laced with milky quartz along one side and something silvery threading through it.

"Gold," Galway said. "Telluride gold at four hundred seventy feet."

Four

Sister Carmela slumped into her straight-backed wooden chair. There were no easy chairs in St. Vincent's Hospital, nor would she have any.

The mines were failing. The harder Noble smiled, the worse he lied, and this time he'd been smiling like an undertaker during a plague. It would be painful to let go after she had struggled so long. She remembered the awful sight of a jerry-built town, a collection of shacks really, huddled below a string of headframes along a lonely ridge, all of them looking like gallows, and how faint of heart she and her dear sisters in the Lord had felt when they first beheld this desolate place one twilight long ago.

She remembered meeting Mr. Yancey himself, who ushered the sisters down to the postage-stamp flat where the hospital would rise. It was an oddly sweet corner, verdant with willows and aspen, notched into an arid slope. And that's all there was. An almost level patch, thick grass, a purling spring, and no sign of a hospital, much less a convent.

"Here's your deed. Carved out of the town lot company's holdings. Ten acres, free and clear, deeded to the Sisters of Charity of Leavenworth."

"Mr. Yancey, but we need a hospital building," she

had said, surveying the little meadow. "Not to mention a place where we might, ah, find repose."

In response, Will Yancey escorted the sisters upslope to the narrow main street, Mineral Avenue, notched into the hillside, and then straight into a gaudy saloon jammed with miners just off shift. The rank odor of sweated flesh and stale ale nauseated Sister Carmela. No sooner had she set foot within this odious place than a startled hush settled.

"This is Sister Carmela," said Yancey quietly. "She and the other sisters in the wagon outside have come to give us a hospital. This is what the Sisters of Charity do. Just as they have done in many mining camps, such as Virginia City, Montana. We'll build the hospital for them. Every man here, every man in the other clubs. Starting now. And we'll build a home for these dedicated souls as well."

"Now?" asked a miner.

"Now. Get shovels, picks, wheelbarrows. We're going to lay up a foundation using rock from the tailing piles, and we'll do it in the moonlight. And then we're going to saw wood."

That was the start. Amazingly, the burly miners filed out, but not before downing the tepid contents of their mugs and tumblers, and soon a gaggle of them was trudging down the slope to the Spring Flat, as it was called.

That was a September day three years ago. By the first of November, a crude hospital and adjacent house stood, and she had discovered that her name had become Sister Drill Sergeant for reasons that were plain to all the males in the camp. It didn't embarrass her; she would have her hospital one way or another.

Soon they had secured the services of Dr. Borden, and found others to help out. One was Slow Eddie, a bachelor miner bashed in the head by falling rock, who was not quite right after that though he seemed bright enough. Slow Eddie kept the place going, not only as an orderly who could carry patients, but also as the man who filled the stoves, cleaned the floors, emptied the thunder mugs, cooked some of the meals, and ran errands.

Now she thought of all those miners who had been rushed into her twelve-bed hospital, bloody, wounded, sobbing, unconscious. Some lived, some died. They had all been cared for, their pain eased with laudanum or Dover's powder or belladonna, and prayed for too. Hundreds and hundreds of admissions; beds filled and emptied and filled again; sometimes filled to overflowing, cots in the corridor. Women bearing children, children bitten by snakes, but rarely the very old because there hardly was anyone in Yancey over the age of forty.

And always the miners, men crushed by fallen rock, pinned by an ore car, blinded by a blast, choked by noxious gases, deafened by a premature charge, mauled by a hammer. They had arrived bloody, moaning, comatose, sawn into parts, choking, blue in the face, wild-eyed, weeping. And the sisters had summoned Dr. Borden, laved the wounded, administered opiates, held hands, wept with widows, prayed for each and every soul.

Sister Drill Sergeant indeed. She was that. She had no authority but her stentorian voice and the will to get things done, which she employed to full effect whenever necessary. Little by little the building was improved, whitewashed, furnished, rendered proof against brutal winter storms that swept that high ridge, and wherever there had been improvements, Sister Carmela's hand and will had been the driving force.

Now she stared at her trim white hospital, with good glass in its windows and stoves in every room, with at least one sister on duty at all times, and wondered if it had all been for naught. The town was doomed. She and her sisters were dedicated to acts of charity performed in the service of their Lord, and especially nursing the desperate. Everything she and the sisters did was tied to the mines. If they failed, the hospital would fail. If the mines shut down, Yancey would shut down. There was no excuse for a town huddled on top of a lonely ridge, save for the mines.

She had always thought that two things could fell the place; failing mines, or a failing spring. The bountiful spring gushed sweet and pure water from a seam in the rock just above the meadow. It tumbled off a ledge into a pool. The water had been ample for the whole city as well as the hospital, and she thought maybe the water was blessed, or even miraculous, because so many of her injured patients drank it, sighed, and seemed to start on the road to health. Some iron pipes brought the cold water right into the hospital, thanks to a gift from the syndicate that had shoved poor Hard Luck Yancey out of his mine.

No sooner had she thought of the quiet man than he walked into the hospital, peered about owlishly, his gaze finally settling on Sister Drill Sergeant.

"Mr. Yancey?" she said.

The man fumbled with his felt hat, a hat very like the ones worn by the miners while working in the bowels of the earth.

"I guess it's nothing," he said, and started to back out.

"Mr. Yancey!"

This was the ritual. Hard Luck always had to be coaxed. He had been that way ever since the syndicate had euchred him out of everything he possessed. She had never heard him whine about it, but she knew it had crushed something inside of Yancey.

He dug into a pocket and extracted some curious pebbles, very dark, pitted, twisted, lustrous. These he dropped into her hand.

"What pretty little things," she said.

"Black gold."

"They do look a bit like gold."

"Black gold. Telluride gold."

She studied the heavy little stones. "Gold? Mr. Yancey, you're taking advantage of a poor sister."

He frowned. "I was poking around down below, on the slope, and found these. They're called float. They've broken out of a lode, or seam, somewhere above. Float's what prospectors look for, it's a trail we follow up to where the mineral is."

"And where did this trail lead you, Mr. Yancey?"

"Here."

She studied the innocuous dark pebbles that were about to change her life. "You'd better explain," she said.

"Right under this hospital, unknown to anyone until now, is a seam of telluride gold. It could be just a small pocket, or it could be an outcrop that leads back into a bonanza deep in the mountain, and under the city. You've gold under you. It apexed here. That's a word for cropping out here on your land. So you own it."

This amazed her. "We own a gold seam, a lot of gold?"

"I just don't know."

"And what are we to do with it?"

He grinned. "Pray, I guess."

She waited for more of an explanation.

"Some people, they're going to take advantage of you if they can."

"How?"

He smiled owlishly. "Just about every way there is, Sister."

She rubbed a finger across the pitted lustrous surfaces. "I'm not sure this is a good thing."

"I have just filed claims on both sides of you, along this granite escarpment. Regular mining claims, two hundred by six hundred."

"You what?"

"Might be a bonanza for me, maybe not, maybe nothing there. Where the spring creek runs back of the hospital and falls over the granite ledge, that's where the black gold outcropped. It's all yours unless the syndicate decides it's all theirs. The mining law gives all the breaks to the outfit that owns the place where the mineral crops out—that's you—but by the time the mine company lawyers get done with you, you'll think that the gold outcropped in the bottom layer of hell first. Believe me, I know."

She peered at him. "Why did you come here? You could have kept it secret."

"Guess I'm a fool, Sister."

"I don't really want gold under this hospital. We've worked so hard. . . ."

"Oh, the syndicate will offer to move you off of here, you can bet on that, or maybe just mine under you, or maybe just take it without even talking to you. Gold does that to people. But I guess what you'll be hearing is that you should move the hospital, and maybe they'll even pay you a little for the gold, but I guess that you won't see any royalties."

"We are religious, Mr. Yancey, and we're caring for the sick, not trying to manage a gold mine."

He smiled, not responding.

"Are you really saying someone will find ways to take what lies under the hospital?"

He nodded. "I hope I'm wrong. I think you'd better do a few things. File a discovery claim to document that the gold seam apexed on your land, and hire a lawyer."

The more Sister Carmela listened, the deeper her dread.

"What about you, Mr. Yancey? What's your interest?"

"Oh, I was beat out of a bonanza once or twice, but I learned something each time. Maybe I've learned enough this time."

She started to hand the pebbles back, but he shook his head. "You keep those. When you're ready for a walk, I'll show you where the seam outcrops. It's there, behind some brush."

"Let's go now, Mr. Yancey."

He led her behind the hospital to the icy spring creek, and helped her down a short sharp grade through brush, which caught at her heavy skirts and white nursing smock. There, at a horizontal fault in the pink granite, lay a strange seam, thirty yards wide, several inches thick, of lustrous quartz laced with something dark. She marveled. A few years earlier, several hundred miners had erected a hospital only a few yards from a bonanza and never suspected what lay at their feet.

Five

Alfie Noble was so happy he forgot to smile. The first assays from the bottom of the shaft in the Minerva Mine were spectacular: eighty-five troy ounces of gold to the ton of ore, telluride gold in quartz matrix with a copper and silver byproduct. The ore seam was thin, barely six inches, and five of those were low-grade. The bottom inch, and that's all it was, contained threads and nodules of silvery gold so heavy they could be plucked out of the quartz by hand.

The shift foremen weren't so enthused, and one came to discuss matters.

"Mr. Noble, that shaft's two hundred feet below our bottom carbonate level, four hundred seventy feet below grass. Air don't clear out; it's toxic, hangs there after each blast, chokes the men working in the bottom of a little hole. Can't put a crew in there more'n fifteen minutes or they croak. We ain't mining down there until we blow air in," said Pollard. "If I was you, I'd bore in from the hillside below the hospital, run an adit, take ore out horizontal, drain mine water too. Maybe that seam outcrops down there. It'd be cheaper and better than trying to mine granite down the longest rat-hole I've ever worked on. Blowers cost money. Where'll we get the cordwood for the boilers? There ain't enough wood to do the job, and not a seam of coal anywhere near."

Noble appreciated the advice. That's why he had veteran Cornishmen as shift bosses. They knew the trade.

"Drift with the seam, and try some crosscuts too, until I look into it," he replied.

"You got some way of getting air down there?"

"We can use some bellows and wooden pipe. Put a mine mule to work. The men won't mind, not if they get bonuses."

Pollard snorted.

That afternoon Alfie Noble took a stroll down through town and its ramshackle buildings, down the barren grade to the hospital, past the rushing spring that poured life into Yancey, Colorado, and then he ventured onto new turf, the arid slopes and gulches below the hospital, dotted with chaparral, broken by granitic outcrops. He kept an eye on the headframe of the Minerva, wanting to stay directly downslope from the great mine. He came at last to some new cairns marking claims, and was filled at once with wild suspicion. He would look up these in the claim book kept in the Yancey Town Lot office.

But as near as he could tell, the gold seam ran below the level of the hospital, so he prowled along the pink escarpment, pushing brush aside, chasing off lizards, but found only the blank, bland slightly lustrous granite, much fractured by the elements. He knew he was still on hospital property, but just a little lower he would be on unclaimed land. The syndicate could begin an adit there, run it right under the hospital, and eventually connect with the shaft from the Minerva.

He smiled. It would be easy. He'd buy the land, move the nuns to new digs up in the town, and start mining.

A great euphoria swept through him. Rich ore, in the nick of time, right there, in the great Minerva Mine. Oh, wait until the syndicate started hauling this treasure from the bowels of the earth! It would all be downhill too. They could chute the ore to the distant valley floor using gravity instead of fighting it, as they would have if they used the shaft. Everything was perfect. That ore would make mining barons of the six partners in the syndicate.

Filled with sheer joy, he labored up the steep grade, feeling his heart pound. The faster his heart pounded as he toiled up the slope, the headier were his dreams.

He ignored the hospital for the moment. The sisters hardly mattered. He would need to get some measuring tape and some muckers borrowed from the second shift and have them raise some cairns and measure out two claims, which would just about cover the sisters' ten acres.

When he reached Mineral Street, his armpits were soaked and his legs wobbled under him. He mopped his beet-red face with his white kerchief, which Gertrude always provided, and made his way past the weathered and sun-blasted saloons, hardware and dry-goods stores, the greengrocer, and the harness maker, to the land office, Yancey Town Lot Company, which acted as agent for the federal government's Mining Bureau, registering claims in its ledgers.

The gaunt clerk recognized him. "Ah, Mr. Noble, you look a bit tired," the man said.

"I'll be all right, just climbed five hundred feet is all," he replied. He wiped his sweated forehead. "I could use some water."

The clerk leapt to supply it, filling a tumbler with the cool stuff, dipped from a speckled blue pail.

"There's nothing like Yancey water, is there, Hodgkins?" Noble said, recalling the clerk's name. "We have the finest water in southern Colorado."

"And the only water for five miles," the clerk replied. "Now, what can I do for you?"

"Any recent claims filed below town?"

"Yes, in fact, there were a couple filed just a day ago," Hodgkins said. "Hard Luck."

"Hard Luck Yancey?"

"One and the same. Here." He shoved the ledger toward the mining superintendent.

There indeed were two new claims, lying on either side of the hospital, along the granite ledge. Noble felt as if he had been punched in the gut. But it didn't matter. He would file claims just below the hospital land, where he intended to bore to the vein of gold, and Yancey's claims wouldn't count. But he wondered what Yancey knew, and how he knew it. Rank suspicion bloomed in Noble's head. Had someone been whispering? Was Yancey bribing someone? Noble wished he had driven Yancey clear out of the district.

The next days were so busy that Noble quite forgot his quart of Wildroot Tonic sitting in a locked cabinet in his office. He ordered a mule-powered blower for the shaft, discharged the independent contractors, and put his own miners down there, running a drift along the gold seam. In time he would do some crosscuts to see how wide the seam was. He added a shift, wanting around-the-clock progress. With every blast, he had ore brought up for assay, and was heartened by the fine values. This was a bonanza for sure!

He consulted with mining engineers and shift foremen, who were unanimous in their support of a new adit, started below the hospital, which would permit the ore to be brought to daylight far below town. The more he contemplated this, the more he eyed the hospital, which would make a fine mine headquarters on the only level ground anywhere near. Yes, he would move the sisters elsewhere and take over that building, and eventually abandon all the upper works, which were running out of ore. The Minerva would move bodily from above town to below it.

Of course he had to talk to the sisters, buy their land for as little as possible, and maybe outfit one of those claptrap stores on Mineral Street as a hospital. That posed no problems. The sisters would no doubt enjoy living in town rather than below it.

The day came when he simply had to deal with Sister Drill Sergeant, so he dusted off his three-piece suit, blackened his boots, swilled some Wildroot Tonic, which sandpapered his throat and tickled his larynx, then topped his bald bean with his bowler, and headed on his mission of charity: He would tell her that he would put the sisters in better quarters.

He found Sister Carmela soothing a miner's wife, holding her hand while her husband's thumb was being amputated by Dr. Borden.

"Ah, Sister, a word with you?"

"Yes, but later," she said.

"Ah, it's good news for you."

She stared at him, absorbing his vast and unctuous smile, and nodded reluctantly. "He'll be fine, I just know it," she whispered to the distraught woman.

"But what if the doctor has a fit?"

"You've heard him explain it, I'm sure. He has his attacks maybe once a month, they last only a few minutes but leave him bewildered for an hour. What are the odds, Mrs. Karnos, of having anything like that strike him in the middle of surgery?"

"Maybe this'll be the time it happens," she said.

"It isn't. He usually has some premonition, and he was in fine fettle today. I'll talk to Mr. Noble here for a moment and then we'll just wait out the surgery together."

The gaunt woman nodded and seemed to shrink into herself.

Sister Drill Sergeant led the superintendent to a private alcove.

"Yes?"

"That's a fine thing, sitting with that poor woman, Sister Carmela. A fine thing."

She waited silently.

"Ah, I'm interested in improving your quarters, starting over, new hospital, right in Yanceytown, where you can be close to your customers, ah, patients."

"You what?"

"Well, you see, your work is so important, you need a real hospital, not this little place outside of town. What I'm proposing is that I purchase these acres from you, along with the structures, and situate you in a remodeled building right on Mineral Street, going from twelve beds to twenty, and more comfortable too. Let's call it an even trade: I'll buy this land, you and your lovely colleagues will get a bigger hospital and personal living quarters." He didn't know whether to call them a convent, but it didn't matter. "That should be appealing to you, and a token of my bona fides."

Sister Drill Sergeant stared at him, hands on hips. "Just like that, Mr. Noble, an offer that generous?"

"Just like that. It's in me to benefit the town of Yancey if I can, and I earnestly wish to do so."

"We will take it under advisement," she said.

"Why, what is there to consider?"

"We will place the matter before Our Lord, Mr. Noble."

"I see. When may I expect a decision?"

She only smiled.

"But Sister Carmela, it's a simple matter, some charity on behalf of my syndicate, and you'll have swell new quarters."

"It's Sister Drill Sergeant," she said.

Six

Sister Carmela gathered her colleagues about her before evening prayers, after the day's labors were done. They met in the twilit, shadowed common room around a trestle table lovingly built by the miners. Only Sister Isabella was not among them because she herself was fevered. Carmela gazed tenderly, mostly tenderly anyway, at graying, patient Sister Mary, and shy Sister Margaret, barely beyond her novitiate, and Sister Elizabeth, hearty and loving, a favorite with the patients, who always managed a kind word for everyone.

She held out both hands, clasping those to either side, until their clasped hands formed a ring of love and trust and faith.

"Mr. Noble stopped in today with an offer. He proposed to give us a twenty-bed hospital in town, in exchange for this land and our buildings."

She saw the pleased expressions on the faces of the sisters, and waited a moment.

"I told him we'd take it under advisement," she said.

"What a dear man. I hope we don't wait long; a hospital with more room in town would be a blessing," said Sister Elizabeth.

"But it's not for us to decide. It's for the Reverend Mother and the bishop," said Sister Mary. "We're here to serve."

Carmela smiled wryly, and tossed three small dark twisted pebbles on the table, where they rattled across the bare wood.

The nuns stared, not comprehending.

Margaret picked up one of the nuggets. "What strange little things," she said, rubbing her finger across its pitted surface.

"Gold," said Sister Carmela.

"Why, it isn't."

"Black gold, known as telluride gold, Mr. Yancey told me. He gave these to me. He called them float, the little bits that break away from an outcrop, the mother lode, and are carried off by natural forces. Together, those are about an ounce. Ten or twelve dollars before smelting."

"Gold! What curious things. We must thank him for them," said Elizabeth.

"Well, I have, and I also thanked him for showing me the outcrop. He took me straight to it. It's down in the gulch where the spring creek leaves our land. A thin line of gray quartz in the red granite, hidden by grasses, mostly under the little rivulet being washed year after year, century after century." She let her colleagues absorb that. "And he believes the mother lode lies directly under these buildings, and only a few feet down. We're quite probably sitting on a fortune."

No one spoke.

"We may have built our hospital on a river of gold."

"Is it truly ours, Sister?" asked Mary.

"It is. This ten acres was deeded to us from the Yancey Town Lot Company, and we own it entirely except for the spring. You remember that Mr. Yancey gave it to us. He was the owner of the Town Lot Company when he wrote the motherhouse asking for a hospital. The Sisters of Charity own not only any mineral under our ten acres, but also the right to pursue the vein, which outcrops here. That's in the mining law he told me all about. If we choose to have it mined, the gold is ours wherever the seam may lead."

"I suppose we should rejoice," said Margaret with an odd question in her voice.

"I think I understand Mr. Noble's sudden generosity, God forgive me," said Elizabeth, laughing.

Carmela smiled. Elizabeth had a way of making things bright and clear.

"We could move into town and have a good hospital close to the miners, enough beds enough for this city," Sister Carmela said. "And let go of the gold, which may or may not be valuable."

"I don't think we have the authority. . . ." said Sister Mary, who preferred to be told what to do so that she might faithfully follow.

"Our mission is to serve, not make money," said Margaret.

"But the money would help us serve. . . ."

"We might become so . . . well, this could be a curse on us, not a blessing," said Margaret.

All the implications of a hospital and their convent resting on a seam of gold began to permeate them all, and the more they weighed it, the more uncertain they became. Mary wanted to bring in the bishop and the motherhouse and leave it to them. Margaret worried about the mission being corrupted. Elizabeth saw an asset that might be turned into precious sustenance for all the work of the order.

But no one knew what to do.

"Let us do this much," said Sister Carmela, their superior. "Let us abide and see. I'll put off Mr. Noble. Whatever we do, we won't trade our beautiful meadow for anything. Not now. Not until our paths are illumined for us. Let us begin now, in the chapel, to discover Our Lord's will."

She dismissed them with a nod. She didn't know what to do. They didn't either.

After evening prayers she headed over to the little hospital where Slow Eddie was stationed. Dr. Borden had retreated for the night to his bachelor flat up in Yancey.

"Everything is quiet, Eddie?"

He stared, almost a full minute, which was his way. "Yes, Sister. But August Murchison's fever is worse." Somehow, he always delivered what he needed to say, even if it took a long time for words to rise to his tongue.

"I'll look at him," she said.

She was doubling her hours because of Isabella's sickness, and would work through most of this night.

August Murchison was a young Texan who was one of the independent miners in town, working for whoever wanted day labor. He had not been a miner long, and made his way mucking up ore after a blast. He had been in the shaft being dug at the Minerva Mine too soon after a blast, seared his lungs on the harsh gases lingering down there, and caught pneumonia. Now he was deathly sick, his eyes caught in black holes, his breathing a wheeze.

She found him awake, staring up at the whitewashed planks above, but barely aware of her presence.

She lifted his hand and held it, feeling its clamminess. She ran her hand over his forehead, shocked by the heat. The man was burning up; his breathing was labored and liquid.

"Eddie, I'll want cold compresses," she said. "We must get his fever down."

Dr. Borden had thought the man might last a day or

two more, but wanted to be summoned if Murchison was failing.

"Eddie," she said quietly after Eddie brought her the water, "please tell the doctor."

Slow Eddie froze, absorbed that, nodded, and retreated into the quiet night.

She dipped towels into a pail of cold springwater and laved the young man again and again, layering cold cloths over him, changing them, cooling him. But this man only stared, some soft surrender in his eyes, and she knew the flame would soon go out.

She wondered if he had any relatives, a wife, a living family back in Texas, brothers or sisters. She wondered if he had been baptized, what his faith might be, for those things were important.

There had been so little information when they brought him. A name, an age, twenty-eight, a boarding-house address, no next of kin. The West was full of these drifting young men, finding themselves, losing themselves.

"Thank you, Sister," he said perfectly clearly, sighed, and died. The snuffling through his nostrils simply stopped.

She listened at his chest for the beat of life and heard only silence. Felt no pulse. Found no breath clouding a mirror. She made the sign of the cross over him, desolated. Everyone she lost was a defeat, and there had been so many defeats lately, as if those mines above were exacting a terrible price for violating the good earth.

She watched a moment, collected the wet towels, drew a soiled sheet over him, and slipped away. None of the other patients seemed to know, but maybe they did. Something had left the ward, never to return, and whenever that happened the others usually knew.

She withdrew to her desk, where a single coal oil lamp shed light, and made the notation in her ledgers.

When Dr. Borden appeared, she saw at once that he had been preparing for bed and had tucked his night-shirt into his black trousers.

"Sister?"

"Gone," she said.

He sighed. "I thought he'd go through the night." He walked over to the bed, in the near corner of the ward, and sought a pulse, found none, and pulled the sheet over.

They left the silent ward, aware that one or two patients were staring, and retreated to her lamplit alcove. "He didn't leave a widow, did he?" the doctor asked.

"No, he was alone here, like so many."

"I hardly knew him; hardly know any of these people. The mine steals life from them. His lungs were ruined. His chest sounded like a consumptive's last gasp. He was doing shaft work, down in the bottom of a hole. You'll take care of things?"

"Yes," she said as he filled out a small form, dipping her pen into an inkpot and scratching words with it.

He looked beaten. A town of three thousand needed more than one doctor, but he was the only one who came to this forsaken ridge, and she knew why: No place else wanted a doctor with the grand mal. She knew a little of his story too. He had always wanted to be a doctor, but no medical college would accept him, not with epilepsy, yet he persevered, taught himself, apprenticed to several fine doctors, and finally was able to pass the examinations.

He was a doctor, but who wanted him? He was a physician and surgeon, and he practiced between seizures, which sometimes terrified patients. But mostly the miners considered him a good sport, helped him up after the devil had flung him to the floor, grinned, and told him they'd be back later, when he felt better.

He was tired, a lone physician without relief, awakened all hours of the night, his life never his own. He had no wife; who would marry such a man? But he was exceptionally good, she knew that. He had courage and the compassion born from his own terrible suffering, and somehow the sick of Yancey were attended, the wounded were bound, the terrified comforted, the ones in grievous pain were relieved, and between the sisters and Dr. Borden, the ridge-top mining camp offered help to those in need. And precious help it was too.

The doctor trudged into the jet-black night. Sister Carmela found Slow Eddie, and he quietly lifted the lost patient out of his deathbed. She changed the sheets, listening to the rhythms of the other patients, while Slow Eddie summoned an undertaker named Ellwood, who would take the lost miner up the slope to a certain parlor on Copper Street.

She grieved.

Seven

Word of the gold strike had leaked out, but Alfred Noble didn't mind. The town of Yancey seemed to rise up on its haunches and howl.

Peabody, the editor of the *Yancey Weekly Miner,* published a speculative piece under a banner that said GOLD STRIKE.

While the Rhode Island Syndicate, owners of the Yancey mines, would neither confirm nor deny it, Peabody explained, information from within the company indicated that a rich seam of telluride gold had been opened at the 470-foot level of the Minerva Mine, and was assaying at over two thousand dollars a ton.

The ore wasn't that rich, but Peabody had gotten most of it right. Noble poured himself a shot glass of Wildroot Tonic, which he had found salutary to his health and well-being, and examined the daily reports from his shift bosses. He was working three shifts in the bottom of the Minerva shaft, and their task was to follow the seam in both directions. The miners had progressed about ten feet downslope, toward the valley, and eight feet into the mountain, finding an unvarying vein of good quartz, of a width not yet determined.

Noble sent coded wires to his investors, no easy task because Yancey had no telegraph and the flimsies had to be carried to Silverton for transmission, and in return received hearty congratulations. Even Gustav Moran, his associate supervisor, was showing his crocodile smile.

But there remained the problem of extraction. That deep shaft and the drifts extending out from it had to be pumped full of fresh air after each charge. Miners working in cramped quarters had to fill ore cars and push them into a cage that would lift them nearly five hundred feet. There was plenty of country rock, hard granite, to dispose of even before the ore could be loaded. All of which meant that the project was slow, behind schedule, and extremely costly because firewood had to be hauled great distances to power the boiler that ran the engine that lifted the hoist. And telluride gold was less valuable than other kinds because of the difficulty in reducing it.

He gave the Sisters of Charity three days, barely able to contain his impatience, and then approached them once again.

He knew when it was best to approach Sister Drill Sergeant: first thing in the morning, before the cares of the day had worn her.

He blacked his shoes, dusted his suit, and smiled his way downslope, nodding at everyone on the busy streets. Somehow, word of the strike had galvanized Yancey City, and people beamed back at him.

Sister Drill Sergeant was busy admitting a fevered woman, so Noble waited nobly until the small things were out of the way.

"Mr. Noble, you've come about the offer?" she said at last.

"Why, yes. Have you decided?"

"No, we've decided to do nothing for the moment."

"Sister, I could be purchasing a building for your hospital and putting men to work on it right now. Think what it would mean to Yancey."

"We are content to stay here, Mr. Noble."

He could see straight off that he was making no progress. "Would it help if I talked to some of the church people who decide these things?"

"I think they would abide by what we, here, choose to do, Mr. Noble."

"Well, surely you know how much a good hospital means to all the people in this fine city."

"We might move, Mr. Noble, if we could receive half your profits from the gold strike as well as the hospital."

He stared, nonplussed. "I'm afraid I don't follow you."

"I'm talking about the gold that outcrops here and underlies this meadow, Mr. Noble. Perhaps it's the same seam that you've tapped from the Minerva. It appears to be. Mr. Yancey believes it is, and says that we're at the right level."

A cold foreboding stole through him. "Ah, you seem to have some information that has escaped me."

She stared at him, a certain pucker on her lips that suggested that Sister Drill Sergeant would not let herself be trifled with.

"Come," she said, and led him out the rear door of the building, across a windswept field, down to the gulch where the spring creek ran. She did not hesitate to clamber down the rocky grade, through marsh grasses to a red granite ledge, and then she pulled away the grass and showed him the vein, gray quartz he identified instantly.

"It outcrops here," she said. "Under the mining law, it's our privilege to pursue this vein wherever it may lead, and it appears to lead toward the Minerva, doesn't it?"

Noble smiled furiously. "Well, you could knock me over with a feather," he said.

There were fragments of quartz littering the grass. "Take some," she said. "Compare it with yours. And then we'll talk."

Noble stared at the wet rubble lying underfoot as if it were a nest of rattlesnakes.

She smiled, picked up some quartz, and handed it to him. "Here, have it assayed."

He accepted it. "Have you known about this for long?"

"A few days."

"How did you learn of it?"

"Mr. Yancey," she said.

Alfie Noble had never smiled so hard as he did just then. "Ah, how did he find it?"

"He called it float. He found some float down the slope from here and traced it to this place."

"And filed those claims to either side."

"Yes, but he came to us with his discovery. He came right to us and told us, and showed me the seam of gold. What a fine man, Mr. Noble. How many men walking this earth would do that, treat us kindly and fairly like that? Asking nothing for himself. Most men would be scheming to take it from us."

Noble gargled his saliva.

"I'm glad he filed claims to either side of us. Maybe he'll be rewarded," she added.

Alfred Noble's heart was trip-hammering, but he ignored that and smiled broadly.

"I can't believe it's the same ore," he said for the record. "Not the same. Ours is entirely different. This may well be a small pocket. This granite seems to be mineralized, and pockets of gold ore may be scattered about."

She addressed him in her usual no-nonsense manner. "Well, here it was, all the time, just a few feet from where a hundred miners built our hospital for us. Our Lord has put a treasure into our hands, so we might further our work, which is to care for the needy in His name. Don't you think it's a blessing unheard of? So great a gift?"

Noble smiled until his lips ached. "Now, about our arrangement. I'm not even going to talk about a fifty-fifty division of profit on what's probably just a pocket ledge. But I'm prepared to offer you the twenty-bed hospital and quarters, and five hundred dollars. This is just a nuisance pocket, and I'll have a couple of men dig out this ore and be done with it in a week."

"Then we can't do business," she said.

"May I remind you of something you know but this town doesn't? We're running out of the silver ore, and Yancey City would be shutting down in a few months but for the gold. If you prevent us from mining our gold . . . You won't have any reason to operate a hospital here, because there won't be anyone here."

"Yes, that's a consideration, Mr. Noble. I've been thinking about it. We've been seeking guidance. What to do with this gift given us by God. What is His will? Who are we to squander His great gift to this order, this blessing upon our ministry? That's why I propose fifty-fifty. It's our gold, I believe, actually the Lord's gold, revealed to us by a most kind and charitable gentleman who is remembered in our prayers. But we're nursing sisters, not a mining company. I thought you might be interested in a fair arrangement in which we, the owners, and you, the mining company, share equally in the profits. But I see you're not a bit interested. I'll inform the motherhouse and our bishop that you're not planning to accept my offer."

She stood there, solid as a Beefeater, her checkered gingham nursing apron fluttering in the breeze, her gaze direct, unblinking, and forceful.

He hated her then, and smiled all the more. She thought she owned his gold, the syndicate's gold, and if she persisted, there would be a fight, and it didn't matter that she was garbed in a habit. There would be a brutal fight, and the sisters would discover what sort of man he was, and what resources he could bring to bear. One thing he knew: The gold seam was going into the syndicate's pockets and there would be no partners. If it took lawyers and financial inducements to selected parties, gifts to bishops, and other means, he would employ them.

He smiled broadly and nodded. "I'll consult with my partners and we'll see. Maybe we can come up with something quite satisfying for us all," he said.

She nodded, and they clambered out of the gully and strolled toward the hospital.

"You really should stop to see some of your men," she said. "James Yurovich is doing quite well, you know. He's the one who was hit on the shoulder by falling rock. We might discharge him today if Dr. Borden says so."

But his mind wasn't on the miners. It was on that damnable quartz seam half under water, spreading back into the mountain, running through the blackness of rock under Yancey, underlying the entire silver carbonate works of the Minerva Mine, flowing onward deep underground, carrying in its narrow vein a fortune, enough to make every man in the syndicate a millionaire many times over. He saw it all in his mind's eye, saw what needed to be done, and had no hesitation about doing it.

"Won't you come to the ward, Mr. Noble?" she asked. "Your men would treasure a visit."

"Some other time," he replied.

Eight

Bad day. When Hard Luck reported for work at Mulholland's Hardware, Clarence Mulholland fired him.

"I'm sorry, Hard Luck. It has nothing to do with your performance here. You've been a good and faithful clerk. It's the syndicate. Alfred Noble told me you had to go."

Yancey nodded. The syndicate accounted for two thirds of the business.

"I don't know what's in Noble's craw, Hard Luck. He said if I didn't do it, he'd start his own hardware store."

Clarence looked so distraught that Yancey thought the man would start blubbering. But then the owner recovered, took his former clerk back to the elevated cage at the rear where Mulholland could keep a paternal eye on customers while doing his office chores, and counted out twelve dollars for six days' labor.

Yancey stuffed the greenbacks in his pocket and headed into the pale sunlight. This was old familiar ground. Noble must have found out about the seam of quartz under the hospital. Probably Sister Drill Sergeant had told him the whole story. And no doubt Noble had also discovered the two claims Yancey had filed on that granite escarpment at either side of the hospital grounds.

One thing about Alfred Noble: He never wasted a minute.

Hard Luck drifted back to his weathered cottage, only to find a notice tacked to the sagging door: This building, it informed him, was being attached by the Rhode Island Syndicate to service debt totaling $74,872, awarded the syndicate for ore taken from claims rightfully belonging to the Poco Loco and other mines. He was to vacate by midnight. The San Juan County deputy sheriff would see to it.

Hard Luck read the notice, crumpled it, and tossed it into the dirt. He poked around his forlorn cottage to see what was missing, and found everything present, though it had certainly all been examined and misplaced.

He was so angry he felt stiff with rage, as if it had stuffed his body and had no place to escape. But that would pass someday. He had covered this ground before. It was the same old dilemma for which he never had found an answer: How could he deal with ruthless and powerful men? Now he was being hounded out of town for helping the sisters.

He didn't know where to put his stuff, especially the books. He had a proud collection of them, mining and mineralogy and smelting and geology and a whole array of poetry, especially British. It was a dilemma, all right.

Noble wanted him out of Yancey, that was clear. With Hard Luck gone, and no one to advise the sisters, Noble would soon enough have the hospital grounds and the seam of ore, and there would not be the slightest objection from any quarter.

Yancey fumed impotently. There wasn't much he could do for the moment. The syndicate owned the sheriff's deputy, Ralph Dillon, a pleasant enough fellow who kept good order but understood who had power to hire and fire in Yancey, Colorado.

He thought of the Widow Kearney. Maybe she would store his books and a few things. She ran the Clover Club, on Silver Street, a favorite resort of the miners. She and her husband Kelly had arrived during the boom months, built the club on a tough slope, with their apartment snugged under the club and opening on Gold Street, the next one below.

They were almost ready to open for business when Kelly was crushed by a billiard table he was trying to jimmy into the club. That was before there was a hospital or a doctor. Hard Luck had seen the need and begun his campaign for both.

Now the club was run by Adelaide, his widow, and she had a steady trade, including Hard Luck. Within it rested two billiard tables, and the walls were lined with tables and chairs. One could order any sort of beer or ale, but also coffee and a simple meal, usually soup and spuds. Adelaide presided over the kitchen by day, and employed a trusted barkeep by night. The foundation had settled and the rear of the club was a foot lower than the street-front entrance, so all the billiard balls tended to roll downhill, which made the games entertaining, if not unique.

But what drew Yancey to the Clover Club was Adelaide herself, a woman of considerable education who could recite Tennyson while filling a mug with ale. Maybe she could find space for his possessions for a little while. The books anyway. He didn't really care about the rest except for his prospecting tools.

Part of Adelaide's success could be ascribed to her striking looks. Her raven hair and burning blue eyes always impressed males, but she had never shown any interest in any of them since her widowhood. Hard Luck had pined for her, but she had never pined back, and since the syndicate had ruined him, he was just another impoverished male sipping soup at her counter. Still, she had a wry quick smile for him whenever he visited, which was often.

Hard Luck always thought that finding the right woman would be like tracing float to the mother lode. You would find one bit of gold, then another, and not know where it came from unless you were canny enough to scout it to its source. Take Adelaide. She was always tossing him a nugget or two; she was the only other soul in Yancey who cared about poets, and sometimes she gave him a poem she had copied from a book she had ordered from Denver. Sometimes her bright smile was the best nugget of all.

He made his way downslope from his dreary cottage to Silver Street, a block below Mineral, and pushed through the tall double doors into the club. It was early, but he didn't have anywhere else to go. The Clover Club was strange in the morning, with glaring sunlight burning through its small windows, making it a harsh place to be. He preferred the buttery glow of the coal-oil lamps in the chandeliers at night.

"Will, so early," Adelaide said. She was alone, rinsing bar tumblers. She always called him by his real name, and that was another nugget, as far as Yancey was concerned.

"Yes, too early . . ."

Without asking, she pulled a speckled blue pot off a small range in the corner and poured a cup of coffee.

"Fresh," she said. "I guess you take it. I hardly ever see you here this time of day."

"Well, today's different," he said.

There must have been something in his voice, because she stopped wiping tumblers.

"Noble's pushing me out of town. He's attached my cabin, and got me fired at the hardware."

"Oh, Will . . ."

"It has to do with the gold."

"You see this?"

She handed him the new edition of the *Yancey Weekly Miner.*

GOLD AT 470 FEET, read the headline. The rest of it was about the discovery of telluride gold ore at the bottom of the Minerva Mine shaft, which the syndicate had been deepening for months.

"According to Superintendent Alfred Noble, the strike is substantial and potentially profitable if an adit can be started where the hospital now stands and the ore removed by that means. He emphasized that telluride ore is less valuable because it is hard to reduce, and that hoisting it to the surface through the older Minerva works would greatly reduce its value.

" 'But with the cooperation of the Sisters of Charity, who own the hospital acreage, we will proceed with a new tunnel well below town,' he said. 'We estimate forty years of reserves here, enough for generations to come; employment for every miner in town, and maybe more in the near future.' "

Yancey grunted. Forty years? Maybe four if Noble was lucky.

"The silver mines are now several years past their prime, and the future of Yancey was uncertain," Noble went on. "But the syndicate is pursuing an aggressive discovery and development program, at great cost and risk, that will pay off in time. The main thing is to begin the bore below town and move our operations down there. Of course, the company is preparing to move the good sisters into Yancey City, where a larger hospital is being readied for them. We expect to complete our negotiations with the order in the immediate future."

Yancey grunted. Sister Drill Sergeant must have caved in.

"The move will be good for the community," Noble went on. "The hospital will be closer to those who need it. The company will acquire the spring in the process, and will continue to provide water for the entire city. There will be a slight charge, because of the difficulties of maintaining an adequate water supply," Noble said.

Yancey read it all again, there on the front page of the weekly. He discovered Adelaide staring solemnly at him.

"Noble doesn't let any grass grow under him," he said.

"Will, why's he doing this to you?"

"I'll tell you. I found some float and got lucky and traced it to the mother lode. Know where? Smack under the hospital. I told the sisters about it, showed it to Sister Carmela even. And I filed claims on either side of the hospital, the whole granite escarpment there."

"Will! You didn't!"

He smiled thinly. "So I'm causing trouble for Alfie again, and he's decided to move Hard Luck out of town just as fast as he can pull the levers."

"Will, I don't want you to go. Is there anything I can do?"

"Yes, that's why I'm here so early. Could you stow my books for me? And maybe other stuff?"

"You don't know how small my little place is, Will."

"That's right, I don't."

She smiled wryly. He loved that smile. "I'll find room for your books if you'll let me read them."

"The Geology of the Colorado Front Range? Sure, Adelaide."

"No, the poetry, the novels, the histories. Those are what interest me."

"You know the answer to that," he said.

She brightened, as if he were doing her a favor and not the other way around. "Will, why did you even tell Sister Drill Sergeant? You could have kept it a secret and found some way. . . ."

"Her land, Adelaide. The sisters own it clear, including mineral rights. I have no claim to it. I wanted the sisters to know before Noble snatched it all from them. I've been checking the tailings up at the Minerva for weeks, seeing what they're up to, and when they showed pink granite with some quartz, I began to look around.

"That's when I found gold float, maybe half a mile below the hospital, and it took a lot of hunting but I got to the source, and it didn't belong to me. That seam outcrops there, Adelaide; they've got a right to pursue it wherever it may go, even into the Minerva Mine. I told them so. And now you know why Noble is pushing your old friend out the window and why Hard Luck is on the run."

Adelaide did an odd thing. She lifted the corner of her apron and dabbed at those bold blue eyes.

Nine

Hard Luck loaded a wheelbarrow and ran his books downslope to the Clover Club. Some people stared. He knew they had never seen so many books. He had more books than all the rest of the town together. He arrived at the club during lunchtime, and Adelaide was too busy to help him.

"Down there," she said, opening a door at the side of the club, a door always closed. Miners were staring. They had never seen a man enter Adelaide's apartment below.

"He's delivering some things," she said tartly, and dished up some of her antelope stew.

Yancey caught an armload of books, descended the gloomy wooden stairs, entered a snug flat well lit by windows overlooking the slopes below. This was her nest. He wondered where to put his armload of books, and decided to stack them in a corner out of the way. That done, he paused to absorb Adelaide Kearney's rooms. There were only three: a parlor, glowing in the noonday sun; a kitchen and dining area; and a bedroom, its door tightly closed. It was better than most quarters in Yancey City, and seemed more permanent than so many mining camp digs. It was not just tidy, but organized and decorated. There were tintypes of her husband on a table, and other photos in oval frames, and

Yancey paused to study the man Adelaide had lost. Young, insouciant, handsome, everything that Yancey was not.

He felt as if he were intruding on her privacy, and yet found himself lingering there in the sunny parlor, absorbing every little thing from the sewing basket brimming with skirts and blouses and white things that needed attention to the *Harper's* magazines neatly stacked on a side table.

He tore himself away: He had no business there except to bring his books to this safe harbor, but his ache to sit down in one of the horsehair chairs, make himself at home, almost overpowered his good sense. Reluctantly, he found his way back upstairs, hauled several more armloads of his books down, and finally closed that stern door that forbade patrons in the club any access to her sanctuary below.

The lunch crowd had thinned. A few miners shot pool. A pair of them played checkers at a table and sipped java. This was more than a saloon; it was a refuge and home for lonely bachelor miners. There was more served at the Clover Club than spirits and beer and stew, and that was why it prospered and why Adelaide stayed on in an unattractive, windswept, and desolate town.

"Whatcha gonna do with them books, Adelaide?" asked a burly Finn who worked the second shift.

"Light stove fires," she said.

"That's what they're good for," he said. He dipped some of her bread into his stew and lapped it up.

Hard Luck settled at her counter, and she placed a bowl before him without his asking.

"Got everything?" she asked.

"All that I care about."

"What're you going to do, Will?"

"I don't know. Maybe borrow a shotgun and hole up until they drag me out of my house."

Her face clouded, and she reached across the counter and touched his hand.

The Finn paid his four bits, jammed his felt hat down, and vanished into the glaring sunlight. They watched him go.

"You could sleep on my billiard table," she said.

"I might, thank you."

It would mean staying awake until three o'clock or so. Hard Luck was no night owl, preferring to rise before dawn and bunk early. He was different from everyone else in town, he thought. They hated to go to bed, and hated to get up, and Yancey City didn't even come alive until mid-afternoon. The syndicate ran a day shift that quit at six, and a night shift that quit at two in the morning, and most of the saloons burned lamp oil until near dawn. The Clover Club was no exception.

She fixed him in her steady blue gaze: "You let me know. And if you have trouble . . ."

"I won't."

"What're you going to do, Will?" she asked again.

He shrugged. He had no idea.

"Will? Don't go."

"I won't, if I can help it."

Yancey thought he knew where he could bunk, at least for a day or two. The sisters had built an apartment for Slow Eddie off the back of the hospital, and there was room enough in it for him to stretch out. Not that Yancey needed anything most of the year; he had spent plenty of nights under the stars, wrapped in a bedroll, when he was prospecting. But he wasn't as young as he was then.

He started to pay, but she shooed him away, and he

tucked his purse back into his pocket. It felt odd, not having anything to do or any place to go.

She smiled him to the door, and then he was out on the glaring mountaintop street, in a town that bore his name but where he was now an outcast and a vagrant.

He collected his prospecting tools from his cold cottage, and a sack of clothing, and hiked down the precipitous slope to the green meadow. Above, everything was harsh, arid, bright, barren, and brown. There, where the hospital stood, it was quiet, serene, green, and moist. He paused to look at the spring, which tumbled noisily from the red granite ledge into its pool below. A water man was piping some of the liquid into his wagon while others waited.

Yancey understood that spring. It gushed out from the very base of the limestone, the very point where the much-fragmented and stratified limestone rested on the massive granite that had thrust up under it. The water from one side of Table Mountain above, percolated through the limestone, hit that floor of solid granite, and pushed its way out at that place.

The water man noticed Yancey standing there. "Syndicate's charging us three dollars the wagonload starting soon as they get this from the sisters," he said. "I'll have to triple my price. Six cents a bucket in town."

Yancey nodded. "Syndicate knows how to extract the last penny from whatever it owns," he said. "And whatever it doesn't own."

The man laughed darkly.

Yancey hiked across this small, level paradise, his boots stirring the thick grasses, and then he set his burden down outside the apartment built for the orderly.

He found Sister Drill Sergeant in the ward, helping the doctor change a dressing on a comatose miner Will knew slightly.

He waited until she was free, and then asked if he might bunk there a night or two.

"If Slow Eddie agrees, it's fine with me," she said. "What happened?"

"I guess the syndicate wants me out of here."

"Because you told me about the ore, and because you filed claims."

He nodded.

"You could work for us, Will. I can't pay you cash, but I can feed you and you'd have a roof over you."

"Hospital's about to move up to town, isn't it?"

"No, we've decided this is where Our Lord put us, and this is where we'll continue our mission."

"For how long?"

"For as long as we can serve by nursing those who need it."

"I may not stay long, but I'll earn my keep, Sister. I'm glad to have a place."

"You of all people, Will Yancey, will always have a place."

He found Slow Eddie cleaning ash from a stove.

"All right if I use that other bunk for a while? Sister said to ask you."

Slow Eddie smiled, gazed at Hard Luck for what seemed forever, and then spoke. "Yes," he said, and went back to shoveling out ash into a bucket.

After putting his duds in the place, Hard Luck drifted downslope to the edge of the granite escarpment, and then clambered down to the shelf below where he had built his claim cairns. He was not surprised to find a notice tacked to a juniper bush next to a corner marker. "This claim has been attached according to the replevin statutes of the State of Colorado." It was signed by Deputy Dillon. He checked the claim on the other side of the hospital grounds and found it similarly marked. Well, Alfred Noble wasn't missing anything.

There probably was nothing but granite in there, but it didn't please Hard Luck any to have his claims attached.

He remembered he had over a hundred dollars in the Yancey bank. He knew what he would find there, but getting it out was worth a try. Noble might have forgotten. He hiked up the grade, reached the bank, and asked for his money.

"Ah, Mr. Yancey, that's not possible. The account has been attached by, ah, the bank."

Yancey nodded. There was little point in picking a fight with the teller. The syndicate wasn't content to steal his mine; they wanted every last cent. The ancient bitterness welled up in him. He wondered how many times he had been mad in recent years, mad and helpless against ruthless men. He had dealt with anger before, but now when it surged through him, he let it boil past him. Somewhere along the road of life he had learned that anger didn't do much good. Where did it get him?

Someone had told him, "retribution is sweet," and he had tried that too, plotting revenge, scheming to hurt his tormentors. And where had that gotten him? He had wasted a piece of his life trying to hurt those who had hurt him. But he still didn't know how to deal with ruthless people, and wondered if he ever would.

He guessed he hadn't accumulated much wisdom, but at least he tried to focus on what was helpful, and let the rage die away. There were lessons to be learned, if he could only learn them.

He trudged downslope in the late afternoon, paused at the spring to watch the icy water tumble into the hollow below, scooped out of granite through the aeons of time the springwater tumbled there. He had always cherished the spring, and when he had formed the Town Lot Company with several partners, he'd insisted that the spring be held as common property. Now the syndicate was claiming it.

Green moss grew along the sides, nurtured by the spray of the tiny fall. Thick brush battened on the spray that showered the edges of the pond. He dipped his finger into the pool, finding the water refreshing and almost icy. He stared at that steady, reliable flow of cold, pure water that nurtured the whole town, watered every home and business, supplied the mines with all that they needed for their boilers, and supplied the hospital with fresh, healthy water.

It was there because the water could not penetrate the seamless granite that stretched under the limestone. Yancey wondered what would happen if that granite were fissured and loosened by the blasting that would begin as soon as the syndicate pressured the sisters to move up the hill.

The thought interested him.

Ten

Alfred Noble studied the shift and assay reports with increasing delight, but also with increasing itchiness. The drilling had proceeded thirty-seven feet in the direction of the Sisters of Charity hospital, and the seam of gold ore was thickening steadily. Not only was it thickening, but the values were richer, and it was assaying at two thousand dollars the ton. If that trend continued, there would be bonanza gold directly under the hospital. And that was the irritating part. But that could be dealt with. The nuns just needed a little push.

It was a pain to haul all that granite and the quartz ore up the Minerva Mine shaft, 480 feet to grass. Firewood for the boilers cost money. He had to pump air down there or the miners would choke and not produce. He wasn't worried about the choking, but he did want production. It would be so much better to drive a horizontal tunnel, an adit, starting in the slope below the hospital, following the gold seam that Yancey had uncovered, straight toward the Minerva diggings.

He summoned Gustav Moran, who supervised the mines for the syndicate. He had thought of walking over to Moran's office, but decided against it. Let Moran come to him. The greasy gentleman needed the air anyway. Noble often thought that if Moran were roasted over a good charcoal fire, a few pails of fat could be rendered for the betterment of the world.

"You want me?" Moran asked.

Noble flashed his most dazzling smile. "Look at this," he said. "Ore's getting better every foot we drive toward the hospital."

Moran studied the reports and grunted. "I'm glad you have something going, because my silver is fading fast. I could just as well close one or two of those mines because we're breaking even and nothing more's showing up."

"Silver, Gus. I have forgotten all about silver. The only thing on my mind is gold and nuns."

"That figures."

"I'm thinking of starting up a bore below the hospital right now. Doing the preparations anyway. We've got to divert that runoff from the spring."

"It's on their land."

"It's our land, or will be. That fruit will drop in a matter of days."

"How?"

"A little persuasion. I'm about to tell Sister Drill Sergeant—ah, Gus, what a perfect name the miners gave her—that either she moves her hospital into town or we shut down the mines and Yancey City can go to hell."

"I don't think that'll budge her, Alfie."

"It's Alfred, Alfred, Alfred Noble, and don't confuse me with the dynamite man."

"Yeah, sure, Alfie. She's got religion, and religion don't budge."

"What are you saying, Moran?"

"They're listening to Jesus, not us."

Noble contemplated that, smiling extra hard. "We'll

see," he said, and waved his colleague off. "We'll see who they listen to."

Noble donned his black suit coat, even though the sun was fierce, and headed downslope once again, passing through the ramshackle town and along the hairpin-curve road to the hospital below, which basked serenely in the morning sun.

He hunted the hospital and found no sisters at all, but only Slow Eddie at the post.

"Where's Sister Carmela?" he asked.

Slow Eddie, once Noble's employee, stared blankly for thirty seconds, then a minute. "They're in the chapel," he said.

"Well, fetch Sister Carmela."

Slow Eddie digested that. "Not until after Mass. There's a visiting priest. Wait there," he said. "Maybe go see the miners."

Alfie Noble settled in a hard chair. He didn't want to visit the ward. Two men had almost suffocated from bad air and toxic gas. Their lungs were heaving when they were brought up to grass. Now they were here, getting sicker rather than better, their lungs ruined.

He waited restlessly, thinking he should go out and look at that seam. Why did the sisters squander daylight in that chapel? They could be working. Noble sprang up, paced, studied Sister Carmela's tiny office, peered out upon the grassy meadow that sloped gently south to the lip of the granite, and beyond that the vast hazy valley an infinity away. It amused him that he was sitting directly over a fortune. Not fifty feet down lay hundreds of thousands of dollars of gold.

At last he heard a stir, and then the blocky figure of Sister Carmela appeared, a whirl of white and black habit.

"Mr. Noble? You wish to see me?"

"Indeed I do," he said, following her into her cubicle.

She rounded a small desk and faced him with a faint smile.

"Have you decided about moving?" he asked.

"We will stay here," she said. "The water is good and blessed and healing. This is where we were rooted, and this is where we will continue our mission."

"You don't have enough beds."

"Maybe we would if the mines were safer."

That steamed up Noble to the point where his smile distended his face, but he didn't respond to it.

"It's the gold," he said.

She remained silent.

"It's just a pocket, you know. This granite has small pockets. Not anything to count on. If your order was thinking to finance itself with this . . . well, you'd only be disillusioned."

"This is a healing place, this small meadow with its cold water. Our task is to heal, and we've chosen to stay here, Mr. Noble. But thank you for your offer of a larger hospital."

"But . . . you could do so much more in town. . . ."

She began rounding her little desk to escort him to the door.

"Wait," he said. "I'll see about paying five hundred dollars cash for the gold seam, and the twenty-bed hospital in town, and of course your new convent there. That's as much as the syndicate can offer and still stay in the black."

"You might talk to us in a year or two, Mr. Noble."

"There won't be a year or two. Either we acquire this property, or we'll shut down the mines. We can't operate at a loss. If we shut down, it'll be very soon because the silver is playing out."

That gave her pause. "What will happen then, Mr. Noble?"

"The town will empty in days. Have you ever seen a mining town when the mine shuts down, Sister? It'll be a ghost town in two weeks. I'm afraid that's what we must do if we can't buy this property. And then what? The hospital won't have patients and you won't have any reason to stay either."

"And if you do shut down, and the people do leave, and we do sell to you, then what?"

"We'll start mining again. But only if we have this property."

She smiled wryly. "I don't think we'll sell, Mr. Noble. I think you can mine that gold profitably, just as you are now, from the Minerva shaft. I don't think the mines will cease operating; I don't think this town will vanish. I do think the need for our hospital will be greater than ever, and that's what we're here for, to help and bless the needful in the name of God."

"Is this the opinion of your motherhouse in Kansas?"

"It is our view here. We would appreciate any help you might give us, including a new wing for six more patients, as you have discussed. I suppose that covers our business then, doesn't it, Mr. Noble?"

He smiled balefully at Sister Drill Sergeant. "Might I have the privilege of polling the other sisters? I'm wondering whether they really feel about this as you do."

"No, I cannot grant you that."

"May I talk to your superiors?"

"Permission is not mine to give, Mr. Noble. Would you join me in the ward now? Dr. Borden is here, or will be any moment, and I think you would like to see how the men are progressing. At the moment, every patient here is employed by your syndicate. Three are in the silver mines, and the rest have been injured in your new gold works. Seven of our twelve beds. Often their wives and children fill the others."

"Ah, some other time, Sister."

"I'm hoping you'll at least spend a moment with Mr. McGuire. He's the one whose lungs . . . we're praying for a miracle."

"You do our praying for us, Sister. I wish I could spare the time."

The nun accompanied him to the door, somehow looming larger than she really was; a big woman, bulky and commanding. No, domineering, domineering over all those other nuns who followed along, doing whatever she said.

Sister Drill Sergeant indeed. A tough nut to crack, but he would crack it.

He stepped into a quietness broken only by the trill of songbirds. One never heard them up in Yancey.

He had no choice. Laboriously he climbed the steep slope, dodging the water wagons careening around the hairpin curves, and headed straight to the stagecoach office. There he bought a ticket to Silverton on the afternoon stage.

Back in his office he dictated some very special geological reports intended to impress certain people who weren't in the mining business, collected some town-lot papers, sent word to Gertrude that he would be gone two or three days, sent word to Gus Moran that he would be in Denver a few days, sucked from his bottle of Wildroot Tonic to steady his nerves, and then dictated a letter to the *Yancey Weekly Miner.* In it he said that the telluride-gold reserves could be profitable, but only if an adit could be driven from the slope below town, and he urged all miners, businessmen, and others in Yancey to support the development of the gold works in the Minerva, and hinted that the company might have to abandon mining and leave the ore for future development if it could not be profitably worked.

That done, he looked to his travel kit, which he always kept with him, and walked down to the stage office, where he would catch the stage to Silverton and the railroad to Denver, to twist the arm of the bishop, smiling all the way.

Eleven

Adelaide discovered the books stacked neatly against one wall of her parlor, and instantly grew curious about them. There were more than she had seen in one place in Colorado; more than she had imagined were in all of Yancey City.

She was tired. Long days in the club wore her out. She poured water from the rose-tinted porcelain pitcher into the washbasin, laved her face and hands, unlaced her shoes, and settled into her favorite chair, the one with a view out the small windows with the whole hazy valley spread below.

She always worked through the supper hour, but then left the club to her barkeep, Glenn, and headed down the stairs on aching legs to the haven of her apartment. It worked better that way, and spared her the unwanted attentions of lonely miners clinging to the evening, their eyes following her, hoping to find favor with her.

She had no favors to grant them. If they wanted favors, they knew where to buy them. Now the soft moonlight burnished the great valley with silver, making it appear even more lonely than it did when the sun blazed down on it. She did not like Yancey City. It was just another mining camp that would blow away the moment the mines failed. The huddled buildings, ready to slide three thousand feet downhill, didn't make a town;

the overwhelmingly male denizens didn't make a community with neighborhoods and schools, nor did they live in real homes. It was nothing more than a temporary town that would die a sudden death someday soon.

These places were called camps for good reason, and there wasn't a soul clinging to that precipitous slope who didn't plan to leave eventually, with as much boodle as he could carry. And one day Yancey City would be nothing more than hollow wooden shells, and the day after that it would burn to the ground and old-timers down below would point at the ridge and tell their friends that once a big town had flourished there.

She thought she had married a poet who would gravitate to poetical places, like the Isle of Capri. Instead, Kelly was as wild as a hare, always chasing rainbows, always saying they'd get rich in the next camp, mining the miners, and then they could retire to some date groves in California. Yancey was their fourth mining camp in six years, and his last. She buried her poet lover on a windswept hillside over the ridge, with no one attending save for the little undertaker, who was actually a cabinetmaker.

She was trapped there with a brand new club, struggling to make enough money to escape, sometimes not making enough to pay her hired help, but sometimes enough to put a little in the bank, where it would be safe until she could take it out, take it away.

There she was, a new widow, and a thousand miners thought she needed their attentions and comforts. She didn't. She wasn't interested in any of them, and especially the stiff-shouldered ones with money. They were all practical men, but she was always looking for the odd peacock, the bird of paradise, the gaudy parrot. She liked most of them, though; they were tough and hearty, and full of jokes, and could sip ale slowly and enjoy life and not go wild. The raucous ones she sent away to the clubs where there was faro going all hours of the day and night, or a roulette wheel, or a variety show.

The only one in Yancey City who interested her at all was Yancey himself, and only because he had the heart of a poet and tenderness in his gaze. She didn't imagine she had any romantic interest, not with Kelly so recently buried, and in any case if she ever found another man, it would not be a solitary one who wandered the back country looking for minerals, or one who inhabited mining camps. It would be one who would write sonnets in Singapore and weave a wreath of daisies in Tibet. A minstrel who could charm the emperors of China. She had seen more of mining camps in six years than she had ever wanted.

But the club was prospering. A certain sort of quiet miner came to it for a few mugs of ale after his shift, and all their four bits and six bits added up to a living for her. For the moment that was enough; soon she would sell the Clover Club and for once make her own life, free from Kelly's wild schemes and dreams.

But she had loved him, her own magical Kelly Kearney.

After doing utterly nothing for the better part of an hour, she lit a coal-oil lamp and headed for Yancey's books, curious about his library. The books a man collected were windows on his soul, and she was curious about Yancey's soul. What manner of ideas animated her hard-luck friend? They were all a-jumble, having been wheelbarrowed there, but it was plain that Will Yancey favored modern poets and an occasional British novelist. The rest of those books were formidable texts dealing with geology and mineralogy and chemistry, as well as smelting, milling, and assaying.

She knew she would never kiss the lips of a man whose passion was rock.

She opened one, discovering well-done plates showing stratification, erosion, faults, igneous extrusions, lava flow, river flow, water tables, glacial kettles and moraines, all enriched by thick and obscure text she couldn't fathom. Another dealt with chemical tables, minerals, field assays, vegetative clues to the underlying minerals, and more along those lines. Whatever else Yancey might be, he was a master of a science, and he understood the very earth upon which he stood in ways that eluded most mortals. No wonder he kept finding minerals where most prospectors saw nothing at all.

She wished he would take her for some long hikes into the San Juans some day, and show her how the earth was made and what lay within it. She sensed that she would return to her rooms, after a hike like that, and never view the ground under her feet in the same way.

Maybe she would get up the nerve to ask him sometime, if only she could leave the club long enough. Perhaps a Sabbath afternoon. The mining never ceased except on Sundays, and in some of the mines it continued even then. She had heard it had to do with the boilers. It was hard and costly to build up steam after the boilers had been idled a day. Firewood was desperately scarce in Yancey City, all of it brought six or more miles by cart.

Yancey's mining books were dog-eared, and he had not hesitated to mark passages that meant something to him, or fold the corner of a page for a bookmark. So he had studied them seriously, not caring about the books so much as their contents. The marks on those pages suggested to her that he absorbed it all, missed very little, and intended to put what he discovered on those pages to good use. He had won several fortunes from the earth, only to lose them to perfidious rivals who didn't have a tenth of his skills. But what he took from books he kept.

The poetry was even more of a window on his soul. She drew the coal lamp close so she could see in the gloom, and studied those titles. She lifted one from the stack and marveled, for here was a morocco-bound edition that seemed brand-new, unblemished. It was a collection of Alfred, Lord Tennyson's poems. Curious, she dug out all of the poetry from that incoherent jumble, and discovered that each collection of verse was as carefully preserved as human design could achieve, and preserved in spite of the rough passage of Yancey's life and times.

She found a fine gilt-stamped edition of Longfellow, and another small cloth-bound volume of Samuel Taylor Coleridge, and another of Robert Browning, done in costly leather, gilded titles announcing the contents. There were two, no, three editions of the poems of Dante Gabriel Rossetti, and she fathomed that Yancey was a man of deep and tender feeling. All the poetry books were limber and much read, but also preserved against abuse, as if they were richer than gold.

She loved Rossetti herself, and would have lingered on those sweet and romantic pages, but curiosity drove her to see what else this lonely prospector was carrying in his kit. George Gordon, Lord Byron; John Keats; William Wordsworth; William Cowper; Thomas Gray; Robert Burns; James Russell Lowell; Christina Rossetti—there seemed no end to his collection. She found no Shakespeare and none of the other early poets, and wondered at it.

What brought such a man to such a place as this? And how could this passion for verse, so evident in his library, reconcile itself to those formidable works of science and technology? Or did they need to reconcile themselves? Rock and poetry. Perhaps he saw the good earth as the ultimate poem, the song of God's ordered universe. The more she examined his library, the more of a sweet mystery he became to her. Thank heaven he didn't care about women; if he did, she couldn't bear it.

The next noon, when he wandered in, she served up her daily stew special, and paused.

"I've been looking at your titles," she said.

"And now you know more about me than I do."

"Would you take me hiking and show me the world, the world you see, not the one I see?"

"Hiking?"

He seemed so surprised, she regretted her forwardness. But she nodded. "Sunday? I'm free."

He laughed. "I thought it would be the poetry that caught your eye. You really want to learn some geology?"

"I would like nothing better."

"Well, I like hiking, and this is some of the most interesting geology in Colorado."

"Will, I want to learn about the earth. The faults and strata and upthrusts and riverbeds. I want to know a fault when I see one."

"I know a lot of faults," he said, "mostly my own."

She smiled wryly. "I'll be waiting," she said, and hustled off. Noons were always busy.

She could not imagine why she had been so forward. It wasn't him, she assured herself. She merely wanted to venture into a world of science, a world of rock and mineral, that few women had ever penetrated.

She had not been outside the camp for almost three years; ever since Kelly's death she had toiled in her club, trying to get ahead, put a little by, but she had saved only two hundred dollars. Now, at last, she would see something of the surrounding world.

It was odd how the thought of a Sunday hike far from Yancey City fired her imagination.

Twelve

Upon arriving at the American House, the best hostelry in Denver, Alfred Noble swiftly made inquiry about matters unfamiliar to him, being some vague species of Protestant so long as it didn't interfere with his true religion, getting rich.

He discovered that there was no bishop in the young state, but there was indeed a vicar, or deputy, the Reverend Oliver Longbranch, at St. Mary's. Thence did Noble hasten, wearing his cheerful smile and a suave air, guaranteed to have effect among men of the world.

This wouldn't take long. A half-hour interview, or a fine lunch in a gaudy restaurant, would do it. This was Denver, the braggart city, after all, brash and forward and progressive.

He embarked from the hack and tipped the driver handsomely, being in an exuberant mood. An ornate church loomed before him, and beside it a building that no doubt was his destination. He entered there, found his way to an office, and there indeed was the vicar, a man of quiet demeanor, with a fixed gaze through rimless spectacles, long gray hair, and a black crucifix on his bosom. A clerical amanuensis armed with a notepad rose and vanished as Noble entered.

"Sir?"

"I believe you are the Reverend Longbranch?"

"I am."

"I'm Alfred Noble, from Yancey, a mining town out near Silverton."

"Yes, I know of it. We have a mission there."

The vicar waved Noble toward a wooden chair, studying Noble amiably. "Indeed, your name is familiar to me. I believe you superintend the mines there."

Noble was pleased. It would save him some explaining. "You stay abreast of matters," he said.

"Yes, I am in touch with Sister Carmela of the nursing order there. Perhaps you know her?"

"Why, Mr., ah, Reverend, that is exactly what brings me to Denver."

The vicar, plainly curious, waited for more. Noble had been honing his little presentation all the way from Silverton, as the Denver and Rio Grande passenger train rattled over canyons and clung to the edge of bluffs and traversed alarming trestles.

"The Sisters of Charity, sir, are doing a magnificent work in our isolated little town."

"I am glad to hear it, Mr. Noble."

"They have relieved pain and suffering, and all with selfless love of humanity. The miners and their families, men of all faiths, worship at their feet."

The vicar smiled wryly, and Noble wished he had chosen another metaphor.

"I should say, Reverend, that the sisters have won the esteem of everyone in town, including my company, the Rhode Island Syndicate. With few resources and a tiny hospital, and only one doctor in town, they have nursed the broken, comforted the afflicted, blessed our entire little village."

The vicar smiled, his fingers absently thrumming against the polished desk. "What may I do for you?" he asked.

"Why, it's what my company can do for you, sir, that brings me here. The hospital run by the Sisters of Charity is below town, on a flat, not very accessible. It's small, only twelve beds, one ward, and often so full that the sisters must put patients on cots.

"Our plan, Reverend, is to move the hospital into Yancey City, expand it to twenty beds, including a separate women's ward, and build a convent house next door for these lovely women."

"I see. That is certainly a generous plan, sir."

"It would bless our little community, Reverend. The hospital would be immediately available to suffering families. It would be but a moment from the time an injured miner is brought up to grass, to the mine head, I should say, and the help he would receive at the new hospital.

"Our plan is to move the sisters as swiftly as possible and begin work on the new hospital the moment arrangements are completed. We can purchase any of several existing buildings in Yancey City, and have them ready in days.

"We've come to let you know that my company will throw itself into this as soon as a deed of sale may be negotiated. I've been looking at the records of the Yancey Town Lot Company, which we now own, and find that the land, ten acres in all, was given to your Church, in trust for the order. So what I'm here for is to arrange for the sale."

"I see. And Sister Carmela approves?"

"Yes, for the most part, but the sisters there are a little, shall we say, hesitant, not having the authority to make commitments of that sort. And so our project languishes. I'm here to speed things along."

"I have not heard from her; most odd, wouldn't you say? What exactly has she told you about the sale?"

"Why, Reverend, you know how the worries of the world affect women. She thinks perhaps it would be best to stay there, and my encouragements have not at this point changed her thinking, which is why I am here, so that we may proceed directly."

"She opposes?"

"Oh, no, Reverend, she simply believes that the time is not ripe, or something like that. I'm sure she'll come around. But time is of the essence."

"Why?"

"Because, sir, the silver ores are diminishing, and unless we can develop new mineral resources, the mines might come to the end of their useful life."

The reverend frowned. "I'm afraid I don't follow, Mr. Noble. You want to move the sisters to a larger hospital just when the mines are showing signs of exhaustion?"

This was the tricky part, and Noble maneuvered carefully. "We are actually about to expand our operations, which is why we wish to expand the hospital as well. There will be more miners and their families coming to Yancey. The silver carbonate may be diminishing, but our explorations have turned up telluride gold at a deeper level. The ore is much harder to extract, and harder to reduce, and we are taking measures to make the mines as economical as possible."

The reverend stared, and Noble wondered whether all this was sailing right past him.

"What we want is that land where the present hospital stands. It is located well down the slope, and we want to drive a tunnel there that will reach the new ore. It is much cheaper to mine ore horizontally than lifting it out the shaft to the mine head hundreds of feet above. But the sisters, of course, are pursuing other and saintlier matters, and their hearts are in the love of their patients, and so the matter hangs. But you surely understand the economics. . . . "

"In other words, Mr. Noble, you want me to urge them to sell of the hospital land, and in return receive a deed for a city lot or lots, with a larger hospital and a convent. And once you remove the Sisters of Charity, you will use their former place as, I imagine, a new mine head."

"Exactly! I knew you'd understand it at once."

"And yet the sisters hesitate. Now, why is that, and why have they not written me?"

Noble laughed softly. "There's a bit of ore, a small pocket, recently found near the hospital. Probably could be dug out by a couple of men at a net profit of a hundred dollars. My geologists think that such pockets are common in that strata, but meaningless. But you see, the sisters think maybe they should stay put, that the hospital rests on a fortune, and nothing I have said can change their minds."

The vicar's mien changed subtly. "That puts a different light on it, doesn't it?"

"What I'm hoping, sir, is that we can proceed with this straight off. Now, I am prepared to purchase that ten acres for five hundred dollars, which will dispose of the idea that they will receive nothing for their little pocket of gold, and the contract will guarantee the sisters the twenty-bed hospital and new quarters in Yancey one month from the date we execute the sale. They can use the five hundred to furnish the new hospital, or for whatever else they choose."

"Have you been in touch with the motherhouse in Leavenworth, Kansas, Mr. Noble?"

"No, and I don't suppose it's necessary. When those five sisters arrived, the miners themselves pitched in and built their hospital for them." He laughed softly. "And in record time too, thanks to the most admirable Sister Carmela, whom they called the drill sergeant, all in good humor of course."

"Yes, Sister Drill Sergeant. She refers to herself in that manner sometimes." The vicar smiled.

"So, you see, the building is not a consideration with the motherhouse. It's a local matter."

"And what about the spring?"

Noble realized that the vicar knew more than he expected.

"The spring will remain the property of the Yancey Town Lot Company, for use by all residents."

"And your syndicate owns the town lot company, I take it."

"The spring is no problem; the water is plentiful."

"And the sisters would have to buy water from the carriers, I believe?"

"Well, we can handle that, Reverend. I'll make sure their water is free to them. After all, a hospital ought to receive free water."

The vicar thrummed his fingers against the desktop again. "Of course this all may be a great blessing for the order and their work, but you'll understand if I contact Sister Carmela, and the motherhouse of the Sisters of Charity, and of course do an independent survey of the property by a competent geologist."

"I understand, but I was hoping we might shake hands on a sale this very day. You know, Yancey City depends on the mines."

"We're never so much in a hurry as that, Mr. Noble. Our Church has never rushed into anything, but maybe, if everything is as it should be, we can find a mutually satisfactory agreement. But it will be up to the sisters."

Noble debated the issue with the vicar a while more, but could not hasten matters along, and finally departed, foiled and ill-tempered and smiling broadly.

Thirteen

Adelaide Kearney met Hard Luck at the Gold Street door of her flat, handed him a picnic hamper, smiled, and closed the door behind her. Hard Luck scarcely knew what to do; he wasn't used to the smiles of women.

He led her upslope toward the mines on that quiet Sabbath morning in October. She was dressed for anything; a great straw hat protected her face from sun that could still be fierce, while a canvas coat armed her against the sudden chills she might find in the mountains. He approved.

They reached the ridgeline, where the mines, all in a row, stood silent on that day. From the far side of the ridge the country slipped steadily downward into a maze of canyons, and then galloped up again into the forested San Juans.

"I've never been here," she said. "I had no idea what was on the other side."

"The slope's gentler, but there's no water anywhere down there, so the town got built where it is, near the spring," he said.

"It's so beautiful, so empty."

There was no habitation anywhere, nor would there ever be, he supposed. "See those wagon tracks?" he asked, pointing to two-rut trails that laced that desolate country. "Those are made by woodcutter wagons. There's about forty men in town that do nothing but cut and haul firewood. A mining town has a lot of stoves and a few mine boilers."

"I guess I hadn't thought of it that closely," she said. "That's what I want you to teach me; everything about this land and the rock under us."

He nodded. He would be a teacher to this woman on this quiet day, with only a few zephyrs to toy with her hair and his. He often came up here to the ridge, where he could see a vast distance to either valley, the tumbled one she had never seen, or the familiar one viewed by everyone in Yancey City.

"This was once a seabed," he said, "and that's why there's this thick layer of limestone that's been thrust up this high. And the silver and other minerals gradually percolated into that limestone and ended up here. There are fossils of sea creatures high up on Table Mountain."

"A seabed?" Her voice was disbelieving.

"Over time, more time than we can imagine, this land was lifted. We're the tiniest moment in time, when we're talking about the earth."

"It is sort of frightening, isn't it, Will?" she asked.

"No, it's beautiful and miraculous," he said, wanting her to see what he saw. "It's also a mystery, why some places rise, old seabeds for instance, and others fall, and giant faults pull the earth apart. On the other side, in the valley below town, that's really a fault, and the valley is there because giant forces pulled the rock apart."

"How do you know that, Will?"

He shrugged. "The way the strata differ."

They walked along the ridge, past the Poco Loco and Minerva Mines, and then to the Liverpool, the Consolidated, and the Silver Queen.

"See that? These last two mines run their tailings

down the other side, away from Yancey City, but the rest dump their tailings down our side, and it's going to cause trouble some day."

"Trouble?"

"All sorts of trouble; rain and snow will leach the minerals out of that waste rock and poison the land below. Or the rock piles might slide down into town if there's a quake."

"But the town won't be here that long," she said.

"You know more about mining camps than you think," he replied.

"I feel so small up here, just a dot in a country so big it swallows up all of us. What's down in all those canyons?"

"Dry gulches, twisted and hard to get in and out of, dangerous country, impassible except with horse or on foot. And beyond, the great spurs of the mountains, easier country even if higher and wooded."

"Are there minerals there?"

He grinned and shrugged, knowing better than to deny the presence of minerals anywhere in this sort of country. He enjoyed her fascination with the land; it was the first time a woman had ever been interested in anything he had to say. Somehow, miraculously, he had her for company all this Sabbath day.

"I thought to head up the ridge," he said. "See how it climbs? This is a spur of Table Mountain, like a tree root, almost. We might get partway up that mountain and have us our picnic, and from there we can see pretty near a quarter of Colorado, almost."

"What makes a mountain, Will?"

He laughed, and regretted it. "I guess mountains get made so many ways it'd be hard to describe them. What pushed all this limestone up so that a seabed became this ridge at the top of the world was some magma pushing up from down inside the earth, forming a huge dome."

"Like a volcano?"

"Only in the sense that a lot of hot rock was rising up over thousands of years, and then it cooled off and left the limestone lying above it. You'd find fish fossils in it if you started looking. Or maybe trilobites, things like that."

They strolled slowly past the last and uppermost of the mines, and followed a narrow pack trail along the ridge. Yancey City vanished behind them, lost in country that dwarfed it.

"Why are there no springs on that far side?" she asked.

"Probably because the granite underlying this ridge is tilted toward our side, and the limestone strata on top of it are all tilted, so the ground water collects and bursts free there at the hospital. But I don't really know that."

"You're always saying you're not sure, you're guessing, you're theorizing." She was smiling right at him.

"I guess smarter men have firmer opinions than I do," he said. "Some people know everything, but I sure don't."

He discovered that she was staring at him, and wondered what he had said that piqued her. She was about twice as smart as he was.

"A mile or so up the ridge, Table Mountain seemed to rush up to meet its great root, and soon they found themselves in an arid canyon, walking a perilous trail along one side.

"How did this form?" she asked, waving at the walls of limestone.

"Erosion. Water cut this gulch."

"How do you know that?"

He scratched his head wondering how to explain how

he knew. "Well, there are some places where the rock didn't get eroded, some places where it did. The rock's harder in some places, or more impervious to water. See how some strata stick out, and the rock under them's been eroded away. The harder rock capped the softer rock, and you see all those overhanging ledges where water and wind and sun dug out the softer stone. Probably some caves along those walls. Mountain-lion country."

They paused, catching their breaths. They had been climbing steadily. The gulch was utterly silent; not even the wind whispered there. They weren't far from town, but had penetrated a different world.

She stared solemnly at him. "We would never be found here, if they had to search for us."

"I've found arrowheads in here," he replied. "Up at the seep."

She was curious, so he led her another fifty yards up a steep incline to a horseshoe of stratified rock. There at the base a few cattails grew, along with some grasses and sedges. Bees and moths flitted in the sunlight.

"It's so shocking to see green in all this yellow rock!"

"This was a giant spring once," he said.

"How do you know?"

He liked that in her. "See its channel? It cut a ten-foot-wide channel. It took a lot of water a long time to do that. We've been walking along it for quite a while."

"That much water?"

"See for yourself," he said. "See how the channel's worn and smooth? See how the loose stones in it are rounded, like cobbles? Water and motion did that."

"What happened to the spring?"

He shrugged. "Lots of things. Upthrust might have tilted the strata, maybe the aquifer drained out, maybe a slide blocked it. I'm thinking this one got blocked."

He pulled a knife from a waist scabbard and cut away the moist earth where it met the rock. Slowly, a few spoonfuls of water accumulated.

"Oh, you know so much," she said.

He didn't. He was an amateur geologist, but he didn't mind the admiration. He felt her presence beside him, felt the nearness of her young, rounded body, the brush of her hair.

"Where did this water go?" she asked.

"There's a channel running down the gulch, but it turns to one side as it nears the ridge. The water ran not far from town, but long ago, maybe tens of thousands of years ago. There's a gulch near Yancey that carried it off."

"You see so many things, Will. You make me feel blind."

"Want to picnic here?" he asked. "It's a place I come to when I need to."

She smiled. "It does that to you? I think it'll do that for me too!"

Bright-winged birds swooped to examine them.

"Let's move back from the seep," he said. "These creatures all want a drink, and we're keeping them from it."

"That's what I like about you, Will," she said.

She spread a checkered cloth on a level shelf of rock in the fresh bright sunlight, and pulled a loaf of bread and a half a wheel of cheese from the wicker. And two brown bottles of Durango ale.

Smiling, she broke the moist loaf into pieces and handed him one of them.

"I guess this is a little like a communion," she said.

Will thought that was the most beautiful thing any woman had ever said to him.

Fourteen

The evening of October eleventh turned into a nightmare for Sister Carmela. Six miners burst into the hospital, jostling each other, carrying one of their own on a litter. She saw at once that the man was gravely injured; his right arm was twisted and bloodsoaked, the humerus broken.

"There," she said, steering the grime-streaked miners to a table. "Get Dr. Borden."

"Already have; he's coming," one said.

The miner was groaning, gasping with pain, sobbing all at once. She needed Slow Eddie, and sent a miner after him.

"Bone's busted clear through."

"There now, lie still, lie still, help's coming," she crooned, helping the suffering man stretch out. His arm was soaked in red; a crude tourniquet below his shoulder stayed the flow of blood, but this man's face was white, and she didn't doubt he had lost much blood.

"His name's Terrence Manx, British lad," said one.

She was cutting away the bloodsoaked shirt, horrified to see yellow bone poking through flesh. Manx's sobs reduced her to anguish.

"What happened?" she asked, snipping at the shirt, tightening the tourniquet and loosening it, cross and agonized and pitying all at once.

"He's a timber man; putting up a beam when it fell and crushed him. Arm's broken, but he's bloodied up all over."

She nodded. Manx was breathing convulsively, in gasps.

Slow Eddie appeared, drew water, and brought clean cloths to her.

"Tell his family, please," she said, dismissing the miners. "Find a sister, Elizabeth is on duty, I believe, and tell her everything. What happened, when, how, which mine."

"Got none, roomed alone," one said. "It was the Minerva gold works that felled him. That drift's haunted by tommyknockers."

She sighed, still working, stanching what blood she could as it gouted from the pierced flesh. Tommyknockers were the miners' version of gremlins or trolls.

It was barely an hour into the night shift; the accident must have happened just as Manx was beginning.

"Give him some morphia," she said to Eddie.

He looked at her, questioning whether he should.

"He's writhing; we can't do anything unless he's quiet."

"Indeed, the young man was twisting in pain, screaming, the awful gargle of noise echoing out into the ward, through the small building.

But then Dr. Borden rushed in, florid-faced, irritable, unhappy. He slapped his Gladstone onto a chair.

"Would happen now, wouldn't it?" he growled. He swiftly washed his hands in a carbolic solution, and raced to the injured man. It took him only a few seconds to register the compound fracture, the weirdly twisted arm, the writhing man.

"All right, fellow, we'll do what we can."

The man stared up through a haze of tears.

"Morphia," Borden snapped. Slow Eddie raced to a cupboard, removed a brass and glass syringe with a wicked needle, brought it and a vial to the doctor, who drew a measured amount.

"Wipe him there with the carbolic," he snapped, so angrily that Sister Carmela stared. She sponged the dorsal area and he jammed his needle into Manx.

"Any other injuries?" he asked.

"He's bleeding at the knee."

"Anything else broken?"

"We haven't looked."

"Well, why haven't you?"

Slow Eddie sprang to work, cutting away the trousers, revealing a bruised and abraded calf.

"That can wait," Borden growled.

The morphia worked swiftly and the man's anguish seemed to lessen before her eyes.

"May have to amputate. These always turn septic," Borden said to him."

"Oh, God, no," the man mumbled.

"I'll do what I have to do," Borden said. "Bad choices."

Sister Carmela stared at him. She had never seen him so abrasive. She reached over to touch the man's face with her hand.

"Get the carbolic mist going," Borden yelled.

This was a new device developed by Joseph Lister. When pumped steadily, it sprayed droplets of dilute carbolic acid over the wound, reducing the chance of sepsis, fever, death.

Slow Eddie sprang to work once again, set up the device, poured the carbolic into it, and began misting the arm wound.

"Get me some light! Why haven't you gotten me light? How am I supposed to see?" Borden bellowed.

Sister Carmela eyed Eddie, who was pumping the carbolic mist, and then went herself after some coal-oil lamps. She had two with reflectors behind them, which would help. But there wasn't much light in the little hospital, especially for surgery.

She lit them and set them close to the doctor.

"Is that all?" he snapped.

She hurried away, looking for more. Sister Elizabeth was still busy. She found one in the ward and returned with it.

Borden had stretched the demolished arm as far as he could, while Manx drifted into his own world. The doctor tied the arm down with strips of bandaging. Every movement evoked a scream. Borden looked taut and pale.

"Maybe save it," he muttered.

He rummaged through his surgical tools, dropped them into a flask of carbolic, and withdrew some small things, including a roll of gut and some tiny brass screws, all of which he dropped into the solution.

"What are you going to do?" she asked, adjusting the third lamp.

"What do you think I'm going to do?"

Chastened, she retreated into a rote prayer she often uttered when things were very bad.

He washed the wounded arm with a sopping cloth, and then began a surgery, slicing gently through flesh, severing muscle, working furiously to bare the bone to either side of the fracture. He clamped a vessel that was leaking blood, finally reached the bone, and peeled back flesh. The fracture angled across the bone about four inches. Roughly, he tugged and hauled the arm until he lined up the bone. The man groaned; not even the morphia spared him the agony that the doctor was inflicting on him.

Sister Carmela stared at the furious doctor, not fathoming his roughness. Maybe it was sheer pity; maybe Borden was seeing more than he could bear. The young miner was pitiable, might well die of loss of blood, or sepsis, or shock, another life taken, another victim of man's quest for silver and gold.

"Hold his arm just like that," he said to Slow Eddie. Eddie reached over, pinned the arm to the table so that the two bone fragments, now held in place, were lined up along the fracture.

Using a tiny drill and screw driver, Borden screwed pins into each piece of broken bone and then wrapped catgut back and forth and tied it down. He started drilling for the second set of pins when a wild cry escaped him, a long moan, and he sank to the pine floor, groaning, his face purple, his jaws clamping and his body arching.

The grand mal.

Sister Carmela cried out. "Not that! Not now!"

"Eddie! Get a stick!"

Slow Eddy got a stick, knew just what to do, pulled apart Borden's clamping jaws and jammed the stick between his teeth. The doctor had bloodied his tongue.

They watched, horrified, as Borden spasmed, huge rolling waves of muscle contraction that twisted his whole body, minute after minute.

"Mother of God, not this," she murmured, "not this."

But Eddie had returned to the patient, continued spraying carbolic into the wound, mopped the oozing blood.

She felt helpless. Dr. Borden lay on the floor, slowly subsiding; there was a patient needing the doctor's attention, and there would be no attention. She knew about grand mal, knew that it would be hours before Borden was himself again.

At last Borden quieted. He opened his eyes, stared vacantly at her, closed them, said nothing. Epileptics often went blank, suffered temporary amnesia, scarcely knew their world after they came to. There was nothing to do, unless to drag the doctor away.

She turned to the table, wondering what to do, and marveled. Eddie, his hands dripping with the carbolic he had poured over them, was drilling the holes for the pins. Then he screwed the brass pins into bone and laced the gut around them. They stared at each other. He smiled.

"But Eddie," she said.

He ignored her, found severed muscle and sewed it together, pulled the wound tight, nodding to her to help him hold the flesh together, and then with a needle and surgical thread, he stitched the flesh of Manx's arm together, just as he had seen Borden do many times.

She marveled. Maybe it wasn't done right; she didn't know. But he had done what he could. Together they splinted and wrapped the arm in bandaging until it was immobilized from fingers to shoulder.

Borden lay on the floor, staring at them, his ashen face slowly gathering blood and color once again.

Manx's pulse was weak and fast, and she didn't know whether the miner would live. There was nothing more they could do for Manx. She and Slow Eddie helped Borden stand, and settled him in a chair, and washed him. They wiped red foam and saliva from his mouth, saw that his tongue had stopped its bleeding, saw that his eyes were tracking them now, that Borden was aware of where he was, maybe even aware of the surgery he was performing.

"I knew it," Borden mumbled.

She laved his face, and cupped his hand in hers.

"I can feel it sometimes," he said. Tears welled in

his eyes. "I never wanted to be . . ." He paused. "Not when . . ."

"Terrence Manx is all right," she said.

"The surgery . . ."

"Eddie finished it. He was watching you, screwed in the other pins and bound them together, did what you did in reverse, sewed him up, cleaned it all with carbolic. I was so afraid. I never knew that slow man could do anything like that, and I almost forbade him, but God spared me my conceit, and that almost speechless man did what needed to be done. But the miner will recover. Together, all three of us, we've given help to those in need in this wilderness."

Borden lifted his hands to his face to hide what lay there from her. She and Sister Elizabeth covered him with a lap robe, and then they moved Manx to the ward.

She would not cry, not tonight when she was so needed.

Fifteen

The Sunday picnic elated Will Yancey. Adelaide had been a delightful companion, curious about the natural world, minerals, how mountains were formed, and finally about Will himself. He had told her, shyly, about his lonely, bookish, odd life wandering wildernesses.

Now he brooded. It was as if he had peered through a window into a sunny life he could never enjoy. Hard Luck Yancey would always be out in the dark street, catching glimpses through lit windows of better lives than his own.

He didn't know what to do, or whether to hang on in Yancey City and hope for a break. As much as he had enjoyed Adelaide's company, that picnic had wrought pain in him too. He was almost a vagrant, with no future there, dead broke, harassed by powerful men who considered him a menace and who didn't want to be reminded of their own rapacity by his very presence. The mine, the town, the land office that had been wrenched from his grasp still had an odd hold on him, as if they might come back to him if he lingered there.

Will Yancey lay in his bunk behind the hospital, knowing he couldn't stay long; the bunk was intended for orderlies, for the help the sisters needed at all times, for people like Slow Eddie. But Will had no place to go, and no future, and the charitable sisters had given him a roof over his head—for the moment.

Back in Michigan, where he grew up, most of the people in his small town lived according to unspoken rules. The merchants, the trades people, the bankers, the logging companies, the farmers, the town mayor and aldermen lived in some sort of harmony. And that is how Yancey himself lived and expected others to live.

When he had uncovered a silver bonanza and founded a town, he had tried to treat others as fairly as he could, paying miners well, timbering the mines properly, operating his Yancey Town Lot Company in a way that helped miners settle there, helped the town grow around his mine and the others.

What he hadn't counted on was the sheer rapacity of people out in the Far West, sorts he had never before encountered in settled Michigan, sorts who spent their waking hours figuring ways to euchre him out of his possessions. That was the great puzzle: How did a mild man like himself deal with brutal and rapacious ones who stopped at nothing? He felt he had been born without defenses. Nothing he had learned at his mother's knee had equipped him to deal with the darkness in others.

He had become one of the best prospectors in the West, employing not only the skills he'd mastered in the field, but also what he'd garnered from learned books, his restless mind seeing ore that eluded less lettered prospectors.

And what had been the result? His first bonanza, a gold strike in Nevada, had been outright stolen from him by a gang of armed toughs who drove him off, threatened to kill him, tore out the page in the district record book that held Yancey's claims, and rewrote it to make themselves owners. His second bonanza, a silver and copper strike in Arizona, was stolen by local politicians and corrupt courts, his property taken from him and divvied up by a secret ring, and he'd ended up with nothing but a new name: Hard Luck Yancey. Only it had not been hard luck that had brought him to grief.

And his third bonanza, here in Yancey, Colorado, was ripped from him by ruthless Eastern men colluding with shysters and bought judges. He wondered what was wrong with himself: Maybe he didn't belong in the Far West, among all these brigands hunting down wealth and caring little about victims. Maybe he was too trusting, too principled, for the frontier, and it troubled him. All he knew for certain was that the mining camps were populated by men and women so sharp and reckless and determined that there was no safety of property; everything of value was something to be stolen or swindled or bullied from the softer, the weaker, the more ethical or honorable. People like himself.

So Hard Luck Yancey brooded about his naïveté, his innate belief that most people were upright. It didn't help much that he could look himself in the mirror each morning and know that he had not cheated others out of their livelihood or their property or their health. He was broke, an outcast, and a sense of his own decency didn't put food in his mouth or a roof over him or give him means to live comfortably. And in truth, he wasn't so sure how decent he was; he only knew he lived among harder, meaner, more rapacious men. Maybe that was his destiny.

He itched to take back his property, but what chance did a lone man have against a powerful syndicate that had lawyers, courts, cash, and influence at its disposal? No chance at all. But Yancey was a stubborn sort, and tired of being euchred by calculating and hard-souled scoundrels. Maybe he would just stay around, if only to remind Alfie Noble and his cohorts that there was someone in town who refused to knuckle under.

He was tired of running; tired of having his considerable skill at locating minerals turned into someone else's fortune. He was the ghost at their tables, the brooding presence in their counting rooms. And maybe if he stuck there in the town named for him he would find his chance. Maybe he could even take Adelaide on a Sunday picnic now and then . . . if she stayed. She had confessed to him that the town was just a roosting place for her; her heart was on the Isle of Capri, her soul was in the Sandwich Islands; her body was destined for Tahiti, her education equipped her for the cafes of Paris. But Yancey City was a roosting place for everyone. No one in the whole rookery intended to stay there long, on that barren windswept ridge where nothing grew and there was no level land.

He had been dead broke before, and he was dead broke now, and unsure where his next meal would come from. He headed for the hospital, found Sister Drill Sergeant, and made his case.

"Sister, you need to know what's in that gold seam," he said.

She started to protest, but he had anticipated all that. "I can work quietly, using my pick and shovel. That surface rock's weathered and crumbling, and won't firm up until I'm a foot in. I'll be able to tell you a lot more about what's here on your property."

"No explosives! This is a hospital."

"No explosives. I'll just take a wheelbarrow down there and dig with a pick and crowbar, out of sight. You won't even know I'm down there. I thought to send things out for assay. Silverton, not here, because the syndicate owns the assayer here and it'd know the result sooner than you would. But we can express the samples on the stage, and get an answer in a day or two."

She didn't hesitate. "If you can do it quietly, go ahead, Mr. Yancey. Mr. Noble says it's just a pocket, and not worth fussing about. But I do need to know."

"Could you feed me for that?"

"Mr. Yancey, we can always find a way to feed you, of all people. Consider yourself employed."

He nodded. "Maybe I can do you some good," he said.

He gathered his tools and spent a quiet morning below the hospital meadow, out of sight of anyone, chipping and prying the rotted granite away, and prying out the quartz seam of ore. Some places were dry, others under water. The seam ran broadly beside the spring runoff, but Yancey managed to stay dry as he worked in a pleasant October sunlight. Farther in, where sunlight and rain and oxygen and wind had not crumbled the ore, he would make little progress against the granite with only a pick.

He examined the ore as it fell, found it laden with the telluride gold, silvery speckles visible in the quartz, sometimes as wires or nubs, and knew it would assay very high. It was hard to fathom the direction the seam ran or how the creek erosion had tapped into it, but he could at least say it was wide, and would require not only a drift but laterals.

By sundown he had bored into the seam at half-a-dozen points, and at each one had taken a sample for assay. He didn't know what to do with the ore, two wheelbarrow loads of it, heaped on a small flat well out of sight.

At the hospital he found that the sisters were at evening prayer, and Sister Carmela unavailable until morning, so he took a small pasteboard box that had once held medical supplies, loaded in his samples, addressed it to the Silverton assayer, Bates and Son, and waited for the morrow.

There was a cold meal awaiting him in his room. The sisters had not forgotten. Slow Eddie had already eaten, and waved Hard Luck toward the food: a boiled potato, thick slabs of bread, and a bowl of savory stew. Hard Luck ate gratefully. It was tough to feed people on an isolated mountaintop, miles from gardens and rails and warehouses. Food in Yancey was scarce and without much variety. There had been annual flour famines when winter snows blocked the ox teams, but in the last year or so those had eased.

"Have a busy day, Eddie?"

Slow Eddie smiled, and Yancey waited for the response to percolate toward the mouth and lips. But then Eddie nodded. "The miner with the broken arm . . . he's hurting, and feverish, Manx is his name . . . and we had to keep watch. Maybe he'll live now."

"You saved his life."

Eddie blinked, stared out the tiny window, searching for words. "I just watched the doctor . . . and did it all in reverse. I watched Dr. Borden. Think what it means to him . . . to have the falling disease."

"You have a good mind. I couldn't have done that."

Eddie shook his head, and nothing issued from him for a long time. "All gone," he said.

"No, Eddie. Something's got your tongue tied up, but that's all. Maybe we could be mining partners someday. Maybe even right now. I've got some mining to do."

He stared, hunting for the words that failed to rise up in him, until Yancey thought there would be no reply. But when it did come, it had a finality to it. "Sisters . . . need me," he said.

"Yes, they do," Yancey replied.

Eddie formed his lips and waited for words, and Yancey waited patiently. The words would come. They always did.

"I have an affliction," Slow Eddie said. "Can't mine anymore. I'm strong, though . . . I thought my life is over. But maybe God had other designs for me. The sisters needed someone . . . needed someone slow and strong to lift patients, and clean up, and carry things, like me. . . . So they put me here, and feed me . . . and I help."

Slow Eddie peered at Yancey. "You got an affliction too, Hard Luck," he said. "The sisters . . . need someone like you too. It is good to be needed."

Sixteen

Rufus Borden, M.D., slumped in his rocking chair, chasing away the cobwebs in his mind. He scarcely knew where he was. It had always been like that after the grand mal. But he had always found himself restored in time, no worse for wear. Someone had brought him to his flat. Someone had finished the surgery on that miner, Manx, with the compound fracture of the humerus. They told him Slow Eddie had done it, put in the remaining pins, wound catgut over them to pull bone together, sewn up the incision and the wound, wrapped the arm to immobilize it, and carried Manx to the ward.

Slow Eddie.

He had taken over in spite of Sister Carmela's protests. He had completed a difficult surgery. He had scrubbed with carbolic and plunged in, somehow knowing what to do.

Slow Eddie . . .

Maybe Manx would recover.

Borden waited quietly for his senses to return, staring into the young night. The thing he had always dreaded, an attack during surgery or a delicate procedure, had finally happened. This was the very thing that had kept him out of medical colleges, that had frustrated him, thwarted him, and almost defeated him but for his sheer determination to be a physician. He had been warned not to practice, not to risk the lives of patients. He had absorbed those warnings solemnly, wanting only to heal others and not endanger them.

He had thought maybe in medicine he might find a cure, or at least an alleviation, of his frightful disease, this visitation that had become his curse, the wrath of God upon him. He found no cures. And regularly, through his training at the only medical college he could get into, the Philadelphia College of Medical Practice, he had suffered the attacks, and found his fellow students taking notes. By the time they graduated they were all experts on the grand mal.

His accursed disease followed him afterward, and he could not practice except in places where he was the sole physician and patients had no choice. That was how he drifted toward the frontier, where mushrooming new mining camps were starved for doctors. That was what brought him to Yancey, where no physician in his right mind would want to practice. The sisters knew of him, and asked him to come, and promised him a hospital and an income, and he came.

He stood at last, feeling himself again, and peered out the window where lights tumbled down the slope below. The strangest thing of all was that he, Rufus Borden, a starchy New Englander, liked Yancey City. In fact, he delighted in the place. He knew he was the only soul in town who actually wanted to stay there, in that rookery up on stilts just under a barren ridge, at the butt end of the world. It amused him, this ridiculous burg, and he had come to a vast affection for the miners—men of many tongues and nations, for the bawds, for the merchants, and especially for the hardy sisters who, by sheer will and courage, offered comfort and hope and the sweetness of the Lord to those in their care.

He hoped Yancey would last forever, perched there

like an impending avalanche, waiting for the day when the mines shut down and the whole town would tumble thousands of feet to oblivion.

The other amazing turn in his life was his discovery that he loved the low and wild places down on Copper Street. He repaired to the saloons of Copper Street most every evening after he had completed his rounds, and there, in the woolliest corner of Yancey City, he played poker with the card sharks, patched up men wounded by lead propelled at high speed, drank a little red-eye to settle his stomach, and usually won unless some tinhorn was euchring everyone at the green baize table. He was tolerably good at cards, but one time he'd had a seizure there, and when he came to, his formidable stack of chips had vanished and the table was empty.

Earlier in his life he'd discovered that the medical texts claimed that the cause of grand mal was self-abuse. In college he had experimented diligently with this, and found it to be untrue, a fiction of moralists. A man who could not marry because of an incurable affliction had hard choices, and Doc Borden made them.

So Doc found a cheery life in the low and wild places of Yancey City, something the sisters were mostly unaware of because they always sent Slow Eddie to summon him when they needed help and Slow Eddie didn't tell them where he fetched Doc from. Doc had no wish to alter his life an iota. He was a fierce and cunning poker player, with a stone face and disciplined hands that revealed nothing. The proprietors, tinhorns, barkeeps, and bawds all welcomed him, not only because he paid, but because he was a handy doctor, dentist, and pharmacist, a sort of house physician, stanching quarts of blood each week. He patched them up for free, out of an odd sympathy with the world's rowdiest people.

Many evenings he repaired to the Bucket of Blood, a wind-rattled dive on stilts, ordered a pint carafe of Old Apple Orchard, suitably ghastly liquor, lit up a yellow stogie, and bought into a game with an assortment of pasty-fleshed and pocked sorts for whom sunlight was alien and dangerous. Other evenings he repaired to the Calabash Club, a better sort of den.

He discovered that the dives were the best and truest source of news; gossip that eluded loftier locales found common currency among the lowlifes. And there he learned that the mines were in parlous condition; the seams of silver carbonate were thinning and showing poor assay values. He began wondering what camp to head for next, and was contemplating a new silver town named Tombstone, where a doc specializing in gunshot wounds might get tolerably rich. But then came the whispered news of a gold strike in the Minerva, down, down, down below the limestone, down through walls of granite. Telluride gold, they said.

And Doc rejoiced. He had a new lease on life.

Now, at his window, he wondered whether to trudge downhill to Copper Street or go to bed. As it turned out, he did neither. A knock drew him to the door, and he found Alfie Noble standing outside. He nodded the mining magnate in.

"You have a moment?"

"I have nothing but moments."

"Doc, are you all right?"

"Sometimes I am," Borden replied. "But it is rare."

"I want to talk about something that requires the utmost delicacy," Noble said, settling in the one other stuffed chair.

"If it's self-abuse, then I'm probably not the man to talk to."

Noble smiled broadly, taking it for Doc's famous sour humor.

"This is about the future of Yancey City," Noble began. "Yes, the fabulous wealth beneath our feet. This place can last for decades, even generations . . . if things go well."

"I'm not sure anyone wants that," Doc said.

"Well, the Rhode Island Syndicate does!" He leaned forward. "We found gold in the Minerva, black gold, telluride gold down in the granite under the limestone. A rich seam, so wide we still haven't found just where it goes, but we're shooting our first crosscuts now."

"I guess Yancey's going to be here a while."

"Nick of time. Silver's pinching out in some of the mines, and values are dropping in all the mines. Confidentially, Doc, we thought maybe the whole operation, and the town too, might last six more months—until we hit bonanza gold."

Borden waited. Alfie Noble was smiling so hard it made Doc's teeth hurt. Noble was always smiling like that when at his most nefarious. Doc figured he shouldn't complain: Noble's dubious mining practices kept Doc in business.

"You want something from me."

"Why, Doc, how did you guess?"

"It's when my teeth hurt that I know," he said.

"We have big plans, Doc, big plans. Black gold requires costly smelting, you know. And this ore's deep down, deep, and it's hard for us to keep ourselves in firewood for the boilers to keep the lift going, bringing up all that ore, and men and machines, and pumping air down there.

"Now, it'd make more sense and be much cheaper to drive a horizontal tunnel into the cliff below town, and join up with the Minerva shaft, and take all the ore out that way, on the level or downhill. Terrific ventilation, air flowing into that tunnel—it's called an adit—and up and out the shaft at the top of the hill all by itself. Double our profit, that way, process low-grade ore easily, well, you're a man of science, and I'm sure you get the idea."

"You need some Wildroot Blood Thinner and Tonic?" Doc asked.

"I'll get to that. In fact, yes, I've been giving Gertrude two tablespoons at bedtime, and she finds it a great comfort, and she even winks at me before putting on her nightcap. And of course it's become the fruit and flower of my daily life."

"Yes, bright as poppies, I'm sure."

"Well, now, back to business."

"I thought the tonic was our business."

"Alfie Noble's smile reached an heroic width.

Noble sighed affectionately. "You sure are an old curmudgeon," he said. "But I wouldn't have any other physician."

Doc grunted. "You should have seen me two hours ago."

"Doc, that tunnel we want to dig, it needs to go on the hospital land, right under the hospital. That's the rub. We want to move the Minerva Mine and our headquarters into the hospital, and start boring that tunnel on the cliff just below, and run it maybe twenty, thirty yards under the hospital."

Borden grunted. This was getting interesting.

"Of course we've offered the Sisters of Charity a generous settlement, a twenty-bed hospital here in town, and five hundred dollars, and we'll even throw in a new convent. But they seem a little reluctant. . . ."

Borden wheezed. "You mean Sister Drill Sergeant said to get yourself lost."

"No, no, nothing like that. She said they'd think about it, consider their mission to be of service to the needful, and so on. That's why we tossed in the five hundred dollars, so that they end up not only with a hospital but with a little cash."

"And what?"

"They're not budging. So I'd like to enlist you, old friend. Coming from you, they'll listen. Give them the word."

"What else have you done?"

"Talked to the vicar in Denver, and he's in no hurry either. But he did promise to come have a look."

"Why is Sister Carmela resisting?"

"Ah, it seems a small pocket of gold ore's been located on their land. Just a pocket, mind you."

"And you want this physician to prescribe a sale."

"Why, Doc, you're the authority. They'll listen to you."

"How'd they find this gold?"

"Yancey. I've done all I could to drive that vagabond out of town, but I know he's still lurking here, causing trouble, bitter because he lost the lawsuit."

"What did Yancey tell them?"

"Now, I don't know, but we've assured the sisters that small pockets of black gold are common and mean little. We'd be glad to have them talk to a geologist."

"So I'm to put a little pressure on them?"

"Just tell them that the future of Yancey City depends on the move. If we shut down because we can't mine the gold profitably, and the silver is playing out, what good does it do them to hang on to worthless land?"

Doc Borden laughed heartily. "Let me get you a bottle of Wildroot Blood and Liver Tonic," he said, "and I believe you owe me for several past visits and medicinals."

"Will you do it?"

"Not until I talk to Yancey."

Noble smiled ferociously. "You'll talk sense to the sisters, won't you?"

"Whatever sense is, I'm for it," Doc said.

An eagle, a half eagle, and a blue bottle changed hands, and Noble vanished into the night.

Seventeen

Rufus Borden found the young miner, Terrence Manx, staring up at the ward ceiling, awake but fevered.

"How's that arm, son?"

"Still there, I guess. I can't move my fingers."

Bad news. Doc Borden took a fountain pen from his pocket and tapped the fingers.

"Feel that?"

"No."

Borden tried some other things, including clasping the man's hand, heat, cold, but without response.

"Will I get my arm back?"

"I don't know yet. We'll see when it's not inflamed."

"What good am I with one dangling arm?"

"Let's wait and see how it heals, Mr. Manx. Maybe the nerve's all right. It won't be good as new, the way the arm was torn, but you'll have an arm and you'll be able to do things with it."

Manx turned away, retreating into silence. He knew what Doc Borden knew; he would not be mucking ore in a mine again. And he might not be doing anything muscular for a living ever again.

The mines mangled men and spit them out, and now Manx was another. But Doc had seen men make new lives out of what was left of them. And he had seen others who didn't try, or want to try, and who sank into bitterness.

Doc himself had passed through that crisis long ago, when he was young and despairing about the curse he was born with, and ready to slide into nothingness. Instead, he took hold of himself, took responsibility for his life, no matter that it would be plagued until death by epilepsy, and made what he could of it even though he was impaired. Now he devoutly hoped that Terrence Manx would find the fortitude to make something of himself, would fight for a good life, no matter what afflicted his heart.

Doc finished his rounds and headed for Sister Carmela's little cubicle to report. She nodded.

"Manx still has a fever that needs watching," he said. "If it goes higher, put on cold compresses, and keep on until it breaks. He's lost feeling in his arm. I was afraid of that, compound fracture like that. We'll see."

"I will pray," she said.

She said that often. The sisters not only served and toiled; they prayed. No one brought into their care was left out of their prayers. Not even Alfie Noble. Maybe especially Noble, he thought.

"I don't think he'll go back to mucking in the mine," he said. "Not with an arm like that. But you never know."

"I don't know what he will do," she said. "I wish we could help. . . ."

She was thinking of Slow Eddie, whose livelihood was now what little the sisters could spare him for his very valuable services at the hospital.

Doc settled into the tiny chair opposite her.

"Visitor last night; came about when I was feeling myself again, except for a headache. Noble."

She stared. "He wanted his narcotics."

"That too. He wanted me to persuade you to move up to town."

"And what did you tell him?"

"I made no promises."

"Pray, what did he tell you?"

"Oh, that he needs to drive a tunnel through your property, that he's made you a fine offer, that there's a bit of gold here, but just a pocket, and he's offered an extra five hundred for that, and if he doesn't get his wishes he might have to shut down the mines and Yancey City would die. That sort of thing."

She smiled. "Did he tell you he went to Denver to talk to our vicar?"

"He mentioned it."

She plucked up a manila folder and extracted some sheets, and handed them to him. They were assay reports, done by a Silverton concern. He studied them, trying to make sense of unfamiliar nomenclature. But the gist was, of four samples of quartz ore, the lowest ran $1500 a ton, and the highest ran three thousand dollars with silver, zinc, and lead byproduct. The ore would require milling, roasting, and smelting, and was rather refractory, but these were considered excellent prospects.

"Will Yancey says that's bonanza ore, Doc. He took those samples from an outcrop on our land, below the hospital, where the spring creek tumbles down the draw. He doesn't think it's a pocket, and if it is, it is a very large one. The quartz seam is six or eight inches thick, but the gold is concentrated in the bottom inch. Here," she said, digging into her desk drawer. She handed him some samples of the ore. It was silvery.

"I thought telluride gold was black, black gold," he said.

"It is when it's exposed to oxygen and weather; it's

silvery in its matrix. I'm learning more about mining than I ever imagined I would."

"And Alfred Noble wants to buy you out."

She nodded. "I made him an offer on the spot: half the profits from the mining and moving the hospital to town, but he pretended not to hear me. He wants everything, and . . . I don't know what to do. Gold isn't why the sisters are here. We're here for Terrence Manx, and those like him, and for Slow Eddie, and for anyone who needs us."

"And what if the money could help you do more?"

She sighed. "That's what troubles all of us. Suddenly we're rich, and suddenly very powerful men want this patch of ground and would drive a hard bargain—"

"Cheat," he said. "Cheat you, cheat your order. Let's say it plain."

"I do hate to use language like that; I'd prefer to think that according to his lights, he's doing the right thing."

Doc laughed derisively. "Well, I've passed along Noble's message," he said. "And I'll add something. He's sour on Hard Luck Yancey, calls him a vagabond, said he'd like to drive him out of town because he's a troublemaker."

"Hard Luck has devoted several days to helping us. He chipped out these assay samples. He dug deep enough to tell me that the ore is not superficial; the seam continued a foot into the stone. And he expects nothing in return; and there is nothing we can give him, except shelter for a little bit." She pointed to an odd canvas sack in a corner. "That's ore; he dug out forty pounds of it, and gave it all to us."

"And what are you going to do, Sister?"

"They don't call me Drill Sergeant for nothing," she said. "The vicar is coming, and we rejoice in that. We see a priest so rarely. He'll talk to people. This land is owned by the Sisters of Charity of Leavenworth. So it's going to be our decision."

"Sister, did Alfred Noble put anything in writing?"

"No. He just said he would turn one of the buildings in town into a twenty-bed hospital, find housing for us, and give us five hundred dollars."

"I don't know that any building's for sale in Yancey City. But I know how he can get one cheap. Just let word out that the silver reserves are dwindling, and there'd be buildings for sale all over town. He told me that, you know. The silver won't last much longer, and unless he can make the gold strike profitable, Yancey will be another ghost town on top of a mountain."

"Doctor, what should I do? If we keep this place, and he shuts down the mines, what good is it? Should the Sisters of Charity throw hundreds of miners out of work, and impoverish them and their families?"

"Sister, it's not you who would close the mines. It's the syndicate, playing its cards to squeeze what it can out of this. Alfred Noble is mining that gold ore right this minute, and it's being brought up the Minerva shaft, and he can continue doing that even if it costs him a little more than tunneling from here. All the rest is maneuvering to squeeze more profit out of the mine."

"Is there something I should be doing?" she asked.

"Yes, get a written offer, with specific proposals about the new hospital and a new convent building for you, including furnishings, clear titles, the costs of moving, the cash involved, dates, method of payment."

"What would you do, Doc?"

"You've already done what I would do: offer him this ten acres for a hospital and half the profits. And then sit tight as a tick."

She laughed, then turned solemn. "Is this serving Christ?" she asked. "Maybe we should just walk away from this property. We are poor by choice, so that we can escape this very thing, this wrangling over property. I sometimes think the best thing we can do is to say, Mr. Noble, if you want it this much, take it, it's all yours. Our reward is the comfort we give to the sick and dying. Our pay is to see a wounded man get up and walk away from our ward. Our pay is to know that what we do unto the least of God's children, we do unto the Lord."

Doc Borden so loved Sister Carmela in that moment he almost clasped his hands over hers. But at the same time, he dreaded the possibility that she and her colleagues might do just as she said, smile, praise God, and turn away from a fortune lying under their ten acres.

"I guess we'll find our answers in the chapel, won't we?" she said. "Would you care to join us?"

Doc had never considered the chapel. "Ah, no, I'm going to play poker this evening."

She stared, a faint smile building around her lips. "Where?"

"Bucket of Blood Saloon."

"Is this becoming your custom?"

"I hold my own against the tinhorns, except when I'm having a fit," he said. "Then they steal everything but my drawers. I'm their house physician." He laughed.

She turned away. "We will find the path, and do what is required of us, and heal whether we are poor or . . . not."

Eighteen

The vicar was coming and Sister Carmela had nothing to show him but some assay reports. She wanted the matter resolved: They would sell or not, move or not, and the vicar would not act without written offers.

She sat down and penned a simple agreement: The Sisters of Charity would sell the hospital property and its mineral rights to the Rhode Island Mining Syndicate in exchange for a twenty-bed hospital of finest quality in Yancey City, an adjacent convent of suitable quality, plus half the proceeds from the sale of all ore taken from the ten acres. She drafted a fair copy, stuffed the document in a portfolio, paused before an image of the Blessed Mother to seek her help, and then marched up the hill.

She had always been like that, pushing, working through snarls, getting things done because someone had to get them done. She didn't regard herself as a woman with any business sense or experience; simply someone who needed to get things done.

She had always thought of herself as a woman without courage; a stocky, timid, gravel-voiced female who preferred to avoid confrontations of all sorts. Now she would face a grandee more powerful than any other in Yancey City, and maybe in Colorado too; a potentate more educated, sophisticated, and better equipped to get his way.

But when she was bound and determined to get something done, as she was now, she got it done and it didn't matter where her courage came from. She thought that maybe the finger of God touched her whenever she was feeling so frightened that she couldn't even think of what to say or do. She was a David, and Alfred Noble was the Goliath.

So steep was the road up to Yancey City that she was panting by the time she reached town, and exhausted by the time she ascended another several hundred feet to the headquarters of the Minerva Mine, now the austere whitewashed board-and-batten offices of the Rhode Island Syndicate.

She entered a barren room redolent of tobacco, and confronted a bald and oily clerk with a sleeve garter.

"Mr. Noble, please. I'm Sister Carmela."

The clerk eyed her as if she were a rhinoceros, vanished into the inner sanctum, and reappeared at once. "Mr. Noble is delighted to see you," he said.

She proceeded into the office, discovered that it was sybaritic compared to anything else in Yancey City, with flocked red wallpaper, brass and teak furnishings, and heavy maroon velvet drapes. Noble was behind his walnut desk, smiling treacherously.

"Sister Carmela, what a surprise!"

"It's Sister Drill Sergeant," she said.

"Yes, an entertaining name. Someday you must tell me how you got it."

"We needed a hospital and we emptied the saloons until we got one," she said. "I got pretty bossy."

He laughed, as if this were the merriest joke ever told.

"Here's an agreement," she said, wanting to hustle this along. "It's exactly the offer I made before; we want a new hospital and half the profits. You can sign right there and keep one copy."

"Ah, ah . . . ." His lips distended until she thought they would squeak over his molars.

"Look it over," she said. "And these assay reports. Hard Luck got them for us. We're sitting on bonanza ore, and we've had four samples assayed, and he dug into that quartz far enough to know this is more than an outcrop. If you want to mine it, you may sign on the line. If not, some other company will be glad to."

Noble snatched the documents, studied the assay results first, and muttered, "Bonanza ore, no doubt about it. One ran three thousand a ton! My lord!" He collected himself swiftly. "Of course, we'd have to have it done again by a competent geologist and our own assayers. You can't always believe assay reports, especially from out of town."

She nodded. She didn't care who did the assays or how many.

"I'm interested, of course," he intoned, "but I can tell you right now, Sister, that we'd never enter into an agreement of this sort."

"All right, then the gold will be mined by another mining company. We will invite bids," she said. "I'll get word out."

"Ah, I trust you will not be hasty."

"The vicar will be here later today, on the stage from Silverton, to counsel us. He will have these assays, and an offer from you or no offer, as you choose. It's up to you."

"Today, you say? A most admirable man, your vicar, Father Longbranch. I was most taken by him in Denver."

"Well?"

"I'll discuss matters with him, unless of course you

accept our counteroffer, a twenty-bed hospital and a convent."

"That's not even in writing, Mr. Noble. So far, there's been no written offer from you or anyone else, just talk. What is the vicar to do, approve of something that isn't even down on paper?"

"We'd rather keep things fluid for the moment," Noble said, drawing out the words. He sighed. "Actually, a hospital in Yancey City is going to cost more than we anticipated, and we cannot include the five hundred dollars that I'd first proposed." Noble beamed and smiled and nodded. "Now, I'll just explain matters to the vicar, man-to-man over a little sip of wine, show him some financials, and I know he'll come to an agreement that we can all live with, and you needn't worry your dear little head over it, Sister."

"Perhaps my dear little head is going to worry anyway," she said.

"I can tell you flatly that we can't agree to split the sale of the ore. Telluric gold is hard to reduce and it has to go by wagon and rail clear to a Denver smelter, and such an arrangement would not be profitable for us. And there's not the slightest evidence that you have gold under your land; only a minor outcrop, what they call a ledge. So you may as well forget that."

"All right, if that's what you want. I imagine you can continue to mine what you found in the Minerva," she said, "and we'll see what we have on our grounds. When we know, we can accept bids. There are mining companies all over Colorado and the West that would offer us very favorable terms to mine that gold. I know of several companies right in the San Juan Mountains."

He sighed. "You're not well versed in mining, Sister. It's an illusory wealth," he said. "Gold's there in the Minerva, all right, but making money with it is a most difficult proposition. We're on the brink of shutting down all the mines and waiting for better times, or maybe a railroad someday. That is, unless I can work out a little agreement with your vicar."

"Maybe you can," she said. "But it's the custom of the Church to let the orders manage their affairs, and he will no doubt do just that. You'll deal with me."

He steepled his hands piously. "I wonder if you've thought about what it means to Yancey City if the mines close. What it means to your mission if there's no one left in this town to nurse and comfort."

There was a threat here she didn't like, and she thought she just might grasp the nettle. "Go ahead," she said. "Shut down the mines. That would be your decision, not ours."

"Surely you don't mean that."

"We would be saddened to leave here. But for each of the several towns where the Sisters of Charity run a hospital, there are ten others that want us to come and nurse their wounded and sick. If we had a thousand more sisters, and thousands more dollars, it would not be enough. There must be a hundred mining camps without a hospital. So we'll go where we are called, and be glad to help the suffering wherever they may be.

"We built this hospital out of nothing but the love and toil of the miners themselves, and we'll build another if we must. Perhaps we'll do nothing but wait for a proper moment. I'm told a railroad would make these mines much more profitable, and make our ore much more valuable. We like to think of things over the long term, Mr. Noble. If the Sisters of Charity can benefit much more from this gold ten years from now, because a railroad has been built and it's worth twice as much, then perhaps we should hold our minerals in trust for future

generations of sisters, something for them to work with
and profit from. We're in no rush at all."

Noble nodded and distended his mouth. "I see. You'd
let several hundred miners lose their jobs so that your
order can profit in the future. Businesses would suffer,
families would go hungry, but you'd sit on your fortune."

That was an ugly accusation issuing from those
stained teeth in that smirky mouth. She smiled back, not
acknowledging a thing.

They sparred another few minutes, and she left a copy
of her agreement for him to examine, and took with her
no proposal at all from him.

She left feeling out of sorts. This was not her calling,
and she thought she hadn't the slightest aptitude for it.
But mostly she was thinking thoughts about Alfred
Noble she would need to expunge from her heart. She
was wrangling about money, about worldly things, discovering in herself all the antagonisms and passions that
she had renounced long ago.

She trudged down the steep slope, finding it harder
on her muscles than climbing. She had entered the
lion's den and emerged unscathed, and now wanted only
to circulate through the ward, visit each patient, see how
Terrence Manx's fever was doing, and convene the sisters to report to them what had transpired this day.

"A letter was awaiting her, the return address in Denver a familiar one. The vicar wrote that he couldn't
come; he had been called East for a conclave. He wrote
that he was leaving the matter of the hospital property
entirely to the order, and that Sister Carmela could handle the matter herself, obtaining such counsel as she
needed to draw up an agreement, and of course appris-
ing the motherhouse at Leavenworth of her decision.

She sank into her seat for a moment. Some of her colleagues would have preferred that authorities above them decide what was best, but now it was entirely in their hands. For better or worse, she and her beloved sisters would decide the fate of the hospital.

Nineteen

The editor of the *Yancey Miner* appeared just when Sister Carmela was serving lunch to the patients.

"You'll have to wait, Clarence," she said.

"It can't wait, Sister."

She refused to abandon her task. Sister Mary was out of sorts, and Slow Eddie was running an errand, and Hard Luck Yancey had vanished, so she was doing the serving herself. She had seven people to care for, including a woman with childbirth fever and a miner temporarily blinded by a rush of acrid gases in the pit.

When she was finished, she nodded to Clarence. "In my office," she said.

"The Rhode Island Syndicate says it's going to shut down the mines; it can't make a profit anymore," he said. "That's big news."

She stared. "What else did Alfred Noble say?"

"He said the company could mine the new gold works profitably by tunneling under the hospital flat, but the Sisters of Charity have so far refused to move. He added that three hundred seventy mining jobs are at stake, plus hundreds more jobs with local businesses. I might add that my own job's at stake; if this town dies, I'm packing up my press and heading downhill."

"What else did he say?"

"That the silver ore's declining in some mines; might

last a few more weeks. That the telluride gold could keep Yancey City going for decades. That all it would take would be horizontal access to the gold through an adit to save lifting and ventilating and transportation costs. With that in place, the gold could be chuted down to the valley floor and hauled to the Denver smelters for a thin profit."

Clarence lifted his hat and settled it. "He says it's up to you whether the town dies or not."

"He said that, did he?"

"Those were his words, not a half hour ago. So what's your response?"

"My response is to advise him to accept our offer."

"What offer?"

"Oh, he didn't tell you? The syndicate would move the hospital, expand it to twenty beds, build us an adjacent convent, and share the profits from the gold lying under this building fifty-fifty with my order."

"What gold? I've heard rumors, but no one has ever confirmed it."

She pulled out the assay reports and handed them to him. Clarence read them and whistled.

"This is bonanza ore," he said. "Three thousand the ton? Do you realize, at eleven dollars the ounce for telluric gold at the smelter, that's a two hundred seventy-odd ounces a ton?"

"That was just one assay; the rest are much lower, Clarence."

"All bonanza ore, though."

"He can keep this town going if he wants," she said. "I'm advised that he could make a large profit on ore of that quality. All he has to do is accept our offer."

"What was his response?"

"He said there's only a pocket here, nothing's proven except a surface outcrop, and they won't pay anything."

"And what's your position?"

"If the syndicate doesn't want to meet our terms, then we'll invite other companies to bid, which, by the way, will keep Yancey City booming right along. Rhode Island Syndicate isn't the only mining company in Colorado. There's Peterson Brothers and Mission Creek Minerals. The town of Yancey won't die; miners will simply work for another company, that's all."

Clarence stared at her. "Where'd you learn all of that?"

"Will Yancey has been my counselor, and there's no one better. He took the samples from the outcrop here and had them assayed for us. In fact, he found the outcrop and pointed it out to us. I'm most grateful for his advice. We're going to do what's best for the order, and what's consistent with our mission of helping here in the West, where the need is so great."

"The way Noble is carrying on, Yancey City is doomed unless you turn this flat over to the syndicate."

"He would love for everyone in town to think that, wouldn't he?" She sighed. "Forgive me for saying it."

"What are you going to do?"

"On Mr. Yancey's advice, we will invite bids from other mining companies if we do not receive a fair offer from the syndicate in the next day or so. He points out to us that the gold outcropped here, he says it apexed here, a word I was not familiar with, and that entitles us to pursue the vein wherever it may go, off our property, and even into existing mining claims up the hill. He said that the apex law is what the syndicate used to force him to surrender the Minerva Mine, so the syndicate understands exactly what's involved."

She enjoyed that, and watched Clarence scribble furiously in his notebook. Let Alfred Noble read that and fume. God forgive her.

"Did Mr. Noble say anything else I should know about, Clarence?"

"Yes, Sister, he called upon all the town's miners and their families and others interested in a good future, as he put it, to gather here tomorrow night with candles to vigil at the hospital, so that the Sisters of Charity can see that the sentiment of the whole town of Yancey is in favor of jobs and security and steady paychecks."

Sister Carmela stood, hands on hips, agog at such things. "And we're to blame, I take it?"

The editor nodded.

She laughed, that gravelly voice resonating through the hospital. But then she turned serious.

"Please quote me properly," she said. "The sisters here live in poverty. Our mission is to serve God and our brothers and sisters in the Lord by helping with the suffering and the afflicted. That is what we do, why we are here, why each day we devote ourselves to the tenderest and best care we can offer you and others.

"Our Good Lord has bestowed a great gift upon us, and it is our intent to put this gift of God into the hands of our order, not for ourselves, but to enable us to serve more of those who need help, need hospitals, need medicine, need succoring of all sorts. I'd move the hospital in an instant if that was what is required of us. But a gift from God must not be taken lightly, so we will wait until a mining company makes us an offer that will help the needy and the suffering."

She waited for him to write it, but he didn't.

"I hope you'll print our response," she said.

"Sorry, Sister, I can't print anything that's been said here this afternoon. You understand."

"No, I'm afraid I don't understand."

"I'm in business," he said. "That's all you need to know. I'm in business."

She watched a weak smile build on his face, which vanished under her stare.

"Very well," she said. "We will be here today, tomorrow, the next day, and the next, nursing the sick. This is what we were called to do, and this is what we will do, in all quietness. We will be here when someone takes ill, when a miner is hit by falling rock, when a child is trampled by a horse, when a girl has measles or smallpox, when a boy breaks his arm, and when the very old need a place to die in peace. We will be here."

The editor nodded abruptly and wheeled away.

"Thank you for coming to see me, Clarence," she said to his departing back.

She sat in her swivel chair, looking about her, wondering how sturdy the walls were, how strong was the roof, how tamper-proof was the deed to the land that she had received long ago.

She had no time to worry about it. She was shorthanded this day, and would do what needed doing herself.

That afternoon she helped Rufus Borden change dressings on three patients, including Terrence Manx, whose arm was slowly improving, though still angry and swollen. The young man had not recovered any feeling in his hand or arm, and stared listlessly into space.

She went through the shopping list: It was Slow Eddie's daily task to pick up what groceries and meats were needed from town. She reviewed the monthly statements for Vasnick and Son Butchers, from Grubbs Grocery and Dry Goods, from the several woodcutters who brought in the cordwood, and paid them, drawing drafts on the bank. She reviewed the fees paid by the patients; two dollars a day if they could afford it, less if they could not. Some in town owed the hospital a great deal, but would never pay. But there were others, blessed be their sensitivity, who added a little to their bills, a way of thanking the sisters. There was never enough in the account, yet always enough to get by. She could pay no one. Slow Eddie received shelter, a bed, food, and gratitude. The sisters worked for whatever the Lord provided.

Later, after the sisters had retired, Sister Drill Sergeant made her way through darkness to the tiny chapel in a corner of the hospital building, and there knelt before the altar.

"You are always with me," she said. "You are with me now. I am in need of your direction, for I am but a poorly educated woman given responsibilities. I do not know what do do. I would gladly abandon this gift, this gold, and move up the hill to a larger hospital, if that is your wish. We do not want to cause suffering, or put a single person out of a job, or cause the collapse of this fragile mining town. All those men who run the mines are wise and strong, and I am a small sister who has given her life to you. I know that you bless the weak, and those like us who seek to work your will in the world. So I plead with you for good counsel, that we sisters may be perfectly obedient to your will, and that we may be free of the worldly things that lead mortals astray. And I pray as well for the miners, and Mr. Noble and his colleagues who want this land. So, hear my prayer, Loving Father. You are always with us, and you will be our strength, for we have none."

Twenty

Adelaide waited impatiently for Yancey to show up at the Clover Club, but he didn't, and the days slipped by without a glimpse of him. She knew he had no money, having been thrown out of work, and he couldn't afford her meals, so he didn't come. At least she hoped it was that, and nothing worse. She gladly would have fed him, but knew that a free meal would embarrass him.

When he didn't appear for the better part of the week, she took matters into her own hands and sent a message to the hospital: Would Yancey like to go for another picnic hike on Sunday, and read some poetry?

He materialized in the Clover Club on Friday, softly agreed to meet her there Sunday at noon, and just as softly vanished from a place where he could not afford to be. Adelaide was delighted. She had finally found a friend. She would bring some of his own poetry books in her wicker picnic basket, and have him read to her. Among his books there was a collection called *Sonnets From the Portuguese* by Elizabeth Barrett Browning, and she wished to hear them read.

He met her on a chilly morning, dressed warmly against the wind, and they again hiked along the ridge, and into the canyon of Table Mountain until they got to the horseshoe of limestone and the dry spring. It had its own magical warmth, well out of the wind, and they settled in the wan sunlight to take the air and read some poems.

She had packed another half wheel of cheese and some fresh bread, and even brought a red checkered tablecloth, but food would come later. This was a Sabbath place, quiet and intimate and somehow evoking a reverence for all the natural world, and it touched something in her heart.

"I brought Elizabeth Barrett Browning and Dante Gabriel Rossetti," she said.

"Then we will sing to the mountains," he said.

He had such a wondrous way of saying things, she thought. It was odd; his shyness, his love of poetry, and his intense knowledge of geology somehow all melded together, so that his presence in this natural chapel in the mountainside made the place seem sacred.

"How did your week go?" she asked. "I missed you."

"I helped the sisters. They need to know what's there in that outcrop, and what value it has, so I took samples, dug into the outcrop to see what's there. I've gone three feet in, at one place, all without explosives because of the hospital, and the gold-quartz seam is holding steady, no change." He shrugged. "That's it. All I do is get some facts for Sister Carmela, so she can deal with the syndicate."

"Noble's hinting that the mines might close. That scares me, Will. When Kelly died, he left me a club that had not yet opened and nothing more. If the town dies, so do my fortunes."

She was hoping he would say that Yancey City would live on, and life would remain the same for a while, and miners would still come through her doors and buy lunches and dinners and beer and play billiards, and she could put enough by to escape.

Instead, he frowned. "I wish I could give you answers.

But mining companies are in it for one thing: to get what they can. It could be that they'll close the mines and wait."

"Wait?"

"We're far from everything, especially railroads."

"You'll have to explain that to me."

"Every pound of silver carbonate ore that was mined here for years was either stockpiled or carried by wagon or packsaddle, by animal power, down that long and dangerous road to the valley, and hauled to the Denver and Rio Grande Railroad. They took only the highest-grade ore and stockpiled the rest. Those huge mounds of rubble, those aren't tailings, those are lower-grade ore waiting for better times.

"Well, the same with the gold. They would have to send several wagons of ore down that slope each day, paying plenty to the teamsters, and maybe they don't want to. Maybe they want to wait for a railroad and just shut down the mines for a few years. Or take a little high-grade ore out, and then close down."

She thought of her club, and the ruddy faces of the weary men who filled it after each shift, and how they could all vanish at the stroke of the syndicate's pen. And how her own meager income might vanish too.

"Please don't tell me that," she whispered.

"I think they'll try to take the high-grade ore out fast, make themselves a profit fast, then shut down and wait for the railroad. That's why they want the hospital so badly. It's not just the ore under it, it's the tunnel that would save them a fortune. From there they could even chute the ore down to the valley."

"I guess the Clover Club will survive a while," she said.

"I wish I could agree with you."

That didn't sound good. "Why?"

"Water."

"What about water?"

"If anything disturbs that spring, the whole town could vanish overnight."

"What would disturb it?"

"Tunneling through that granite only a few yards from the spring. The limestone that carries that water to that spring lies on a hard granite shelf which is impervious, which means the water doesn't work down through it. But if the blasting were to open up fissures in the rock . . ." He shrugged.

"Will Yancey, are you telling me that the town might die?"

"A geologist sees through different eyes," he said. "Now, look at this dead spring right here. You can see the watercourse draining from this horseshoe of limestone, a big stream, lots of water long ago, and yet there's nothing now. What happened? I don't know. But look at that fault."

He got up and pointed to a place where the strata didn't match. "It dropped three feet here. See this reddish line? Now it's three feet higher here than there, the same line down there."

She nodded.

"There's lots of reasons the spring quit, but the one that intrigues me is that there was a quake or a collapse here that plugged it, and made this fault."

He led her to the seep. "There's a tiny bit still working through, so I think maybe there's plenty of water dammed up somewhere back in the mountain. I don't think the aquifer ran dry."

"If something happened to the hospital spring, could this be developed?" she asked.

He grinned at her. "I've just filed a Homestead Act claim on one hundred sixty acres here."

She was puzzled.

"Not a mining claim?"

"No, just a homestead claim, and since it's unsurveyed, it's a preemption claim."

"I wouldn't know about that," she said. "You prospectors have as many angles as the syndicate does."

"There's all sorts of wealth in the earth," he said.

"Well, mine is poetry," she said, wanting to reach familiar ground. "I will read you a verse from Rossetti."

She pulled Will Yancey's own poetry book from her basket and found a poem that had struck her one evening.

> *The sunrise blooms and withers on the hill*
> *Like any hillflower; and the noblest troth*
> *Dies here to dust. Yet shall Heaven's promise clothe*
> *Even yet those lovers who have cherished still*
> *This test for love:—in every kiss sealed fast*
> *To feel the first kiss and forbode the last.*

He turned suddenly shy, and she smiled at him. "Does poetry not touch you?" she asked.

"Too much, I fear."

"Yes, that's why it's so sweet. A poem touches where no prose could possibly touch me."

The October sun plummeted swiftly, throwing the canyon into deep shadow which cast a chill over the bower. It reminded her of another verse:

> *"And now that I have climbed and won this height,*
> *I must tread downward through the sloping shade*
> *"And travel the bewildered tracks till night,*
> *Yet for this hour I still may here be stayed*
> *And see the gold air and the silver fade*
> *And the last bird fly into the last light.*

She discovered him smiling at her.

Later, she packed the tablecloth and the remains of the bread and cheese, and they started down Table Mountain in the settling light, crossed the ridge, passed by the gaunt headframes of the mines, and descended into the city.

She had found a friend. A shy friend who needed coaxing, but a friend who opened doors of knowledge and understanding for her, and whose tastes were somehow close to her own. She wondered at his shyness; it was less plain when he was with males, but with her he seemed self-conscious, as if he feared she might not approve of him. He certainly was a strange-looking man, but she didn't mind that at all, not in a man with such a vision of the good earth, of the stone they stood upon, of the way poetry illumined places of geography and heart. She felt protected by him too. He could supply answers to the mysteries of mining, give her some sort of grasp on the future, warn her against tribulations.

They descended from Mineral Street to Silver to Gold, and were close to the Clover Club when the town constable, Abner Cruikshank, yelled.

"Hey, Yancey, hold up," he said, hurrying through the twilight.

"What is it?" Will asked.

"Yeah, well, I'm taking you in for vagrancy. Some complaints about you, unemployed and wandering around and all, so come along."

"I have a home. I work at the hospital."

"Well, that don't matter. Come along or I'll make you come along."

"Will!" Adelaide cried. "Will!"

Twenty-one

Abner Cruikshank was one of those short and porky cops who was twice as dangerous as the tall variety because people tended to dismiss him. He wielded a swift and cruel billy club and knew how to hammer with it.

"I'm employed and have an address. Does that satisfy you?" Yancey said.

"Come with me," Cruikshank said.

"What for?"

"He's no vagrant! What are you doing?" Adelaide asked.

"You stay out of it or I'll take you too."

"Then take me! See what the town thinks of that!"

Cruikshank whacked her hard across the head. She gasped, slumped backward, and held her head.

"That'll be something to tell the newspaper about," Yancey said.

The crack of the billy club across his shoulder shot pain through him. The club jabbed, pushing Yancey back. "Yeah, well, come along now."

"Who complained?" Yancey asked.

"You'll find out."

"This charge is a joke."

Yancey took another hit across the skull. His ears rang. He felt a knot rise above his ear.

"You leave him alone," Adelaide snapped. "If you

take him in I'm going to talk. Everyone in town is going to hear about this."

"Then I'll take you too," Cruikshank said softly.

"Go ahead. It's the only way you'll shut me up," she retorted. "Just wait until my club opens and I'm not there. Just wait. You'd just better lock me up too, because if you don't I'm going to talk to the sheriff and the governor and every paper in the state."

Cruikshank turned to her, jabbed her with his billy, shoved her away. "You'll go away and you'll clam up or you'll feel the pain."

Yancey knew what that was about. Cruikshank had some "special deputies," actually Rhode Island Syndicate toughs, he employed whenever someone needed a little pounding on. Such people usually ended up in the hospital or limping out of town. It was a handy squad to keep the lid on the dives on Copper Street, and it was the Rhode Island Syndicate's private army.

"Then I'll feel the pain," she snapped. "And so will my customers."

Cruikshank suddenly turned very silent, stared at her, and waved his billy back and forth. She stepped back, defeated for the moment.

Yancey was amazed at her courage. Even more amazed by her passionate response to all this. He knew what this was about. The mining syndicate was tired of him and wanted him out of town. He was helping Sister Carmela assess the gold vein under the sisters' land, and that was enough to stir up Alfie Noble. The syndicate could not swallow the hospital grounds with Yancey around.

"All right, I'm your guest," Yancey said.

"What you're going to do, Yancey, is get out of town."

"No, I'll just stay and you can lock me up. I'll stay,

even if your food is lousy. If I'm a vagrant, then I'll just settle in for a spell."

For a response Cruikshank jabbed the billy into Yancey's stomach just under the rib cage, which whipped the air out of his lungs and stopped his breathing for a moment. "Get moving. I'm taking you in, and we'll persuade you to leave the hard way if you won't get out on your own."

The special deputies would do the persuading, and make sport of Will Yancey. He would be lucky to escape without serious injury. Still, he was stubborn.

"What's the deal?" he asked.

"You're going to collect your gear and get out right now. Either that or you'll be persuaded to get out."

"And what are the charges did you say?"

"This ain't going on the books, Yancey. This is my little party. Get rid of the riffraff in town, that's what I do."

"Riffraff!" cried Adelaide. "Copper Street's full of riffraff, real vagrants, half of them crooked, and you don't pick on them."

The constable waved his billy in her direction. "Git," he said.

"What happens if I stay around?" Yancey said.

"Don't ask."

"How far do I have to go from here?"

"Don't ask."

Yancey smiled suddenly. "You tell Alfie Noble that Yancey's on his way. But I'll be out there. I'll be around, waiting."

"Don't go, Will!" she said.

"I warned you," Cruikshank said. "The Clover Club's gonna have an accident, like maybe everything in it gets busted."

She turned quiet.

"How much time do I have, Cruikshank?"

"None. From here you'll walk to the hospital, get your stuff, and keep going downhill, and if I see you around here, or even hear of you around, you'll end up in the hospital for good."

The billy club wavered menacingly.

"All right, fatman, I'm on my way. Adelaide, I'll be in touch."

The constable let it ride. He watched Yancey retreat downslope. Adelaide held her head. Hard Luck thought he saw tears in her eyes, though the darkness veiled her. Neither she nor the constable moved, and finally they vanished into the darkness.

Yancey's shoulder and upper arm ached. That copper was a master of the billy club, and could knock a man flat before he knew he was in a fight.

He thought maybe he should have barreled into the porker, knocked him flat, but he hadn't and it was too late anyway. If he had, he would have been a hunted man anywhere around Yancey City.

Such was the law in a town that probably wouldn't survive another two years.

He knew one thing: He had unfinished business in Yancey City, and he wasn't going very far. When he reached the hospital he realized that it had shut down for the night. The sisters had retired. But a light was on in the orderly quarters where he and Slow Eddie lived.

He found Slow Eddie there, reading by the light of a coal-oil lamp. Yancey collected his gear: one bag stuffed with clothing, another heavy one loaded with prospecting gear. He would carry his bedroll over his shoulders, a bag in each hand.

Slow Eddie watched him and finally summoned words.

"You going away?"

"Cruikshank decided I'm a vagrant and booted me out of town."

"You let him?"

Yancey sighed and pointed to the lump on his head and his sore shoulder. "I guess I'm no hero, Eddie."

"Bastard," he said. "Anything I can do?"

"Rustle up some chow?"

Eddie jumped up at once, vanished into the darkened hospital, while Yancey rolled up his blankets and packed his gear. He had enough for a pack mule, but he would have to haul it on his back. And it wasn't going to be downhill either.

Slow Eddie returned with a loaded gunnysack.

"Beans, flour, like that."

"I owe the sisters."

"Nah, you helped them."

"Tell them I got booted out, vagrant, can't stay, all that. They'll figure out why. They've treated enough of Cruikshank's victims."

Slow Eddie nodded. His quick gestures almost made up for the slowness of his words sometimes.

"Tell them I'm not going far. Tell them that I'll try to stay in touch. My friend Adelaide Kearny, Clover Club, will be the way to reach me."

Slow Eddie nodded.

"Tell Sister Carmela I'm still going to help her. She can count on me."

Slow Eddie stored that away and nodded.

Yancey picked up his bags and staggered under them. He was carrying his household, such as it was.

"Adios for now, Eddie," he said.

Eddie reached out, gently clasped Yancey's shoulder, and then closed the door behind Yancey.

Darkness engulfed Yancey, but at least the heavens were starlit. He did not head downslope, but labored up the hairpin road to town. The weight was so heavy he had to pause every hundred yards. He thought of caching part of it, but decided to wrestle the whole outfit up to where he was heading. Near town he left the road, worked overland along the rough slope, always toward the looming bulk of Table Mountain.

When he was below the uppermost mine, he struggled straight up the grade, not quitting until he stood on the ridge near the dark mine. He let his heart slow and his arms rest for a few minutes, and then shouldered his load and hiked up the ridge, veered into the familiar canyon of Table Mountain, and continued until he could walk no more.

He rested again in the icy air, then hefted his bags and struggled up to the horseshoe and the dry spring, rested again, struggled up a narrow path around the dry spring, so steep he could lift only one bag at a time and had to portage his load up there, but once he was up there he hiked another fifty yards and paused in the dark, orienting himself.

There it was: an ancient cliff dwelling, built by prehistoric peoples. He had seen it several times and believed that it was abandoned when the spring just below it quit running. It was cemented under an overhang, barely visible now. Small steps notched out of rock took him up to the place. He knew it well, knew every room, had wondered at the purposes of some, especially round ones with benches around them. Now that he was moving in, he might find time to discover the uses of each room.

He headed toward a room he had stayed in long before, when he was prospecting. It would be chilly, but not icy as it was outside, warmed by the earth's own heat. He entered it, felt his way around in the virtual darkness, felt its forbidding silence, felt the ghosts of some long-lost tribe watching him, found the corner where he had stayed, and settled his packs on the rock floor. He went to the small window, peered out upon the starlit canyon, seeing little. Just below was the dry spring. The place was somber, forbidding, and melancholic.

But this was as good a home as any.

Twenty-two

The hand-delivered summons arrived early in the morning. It took the form of a letter, on the engraved letterhead of the Rhode Island Mining Syndicate, and was signed by Alfred Noble. It asked Sister Carmela to be at the superintendent's office of the Minerva Mine at two o'clock to discuss matters of vital interest and benefit to the community.

She sent Slow Eddie up there with a note saying she would attend.

She left on a blustery fall day, a black shawl wrapped about her, and toiled up the long grade, passing the endless procession of casklike wagons that supplied Yancey City with spring water. By the time she reached the city, her heart was hammering, so she paused for a moment. She still had as much of a climb to reach the mines on the ridge.

"Lord, I'm glad you make me work hard at the hospital, or they'd have to carry me up there," she said aloud.

Strengthened, she toiled up slanted streets and then up a wasteland of tailings and loose rock, arriving at last at the ridge, where several buildings stood. The whitewashed one was the superintendent's offices. She paused to get her breath and admire the stunning view down upon Yancey City, the hospital below, the valley that swept into mist many miles away, and the looming mountains behind the ridge, peaks she had never studied.

She would probably be late, but had hurried as fast as she could. She had left the hospital in the care of Sister Elizabeth, who would have her hands full because of three new patients, all miners whose lungs had started to fail from underground gases.

She entered the spartan anteroom lorded over by an oily clerk.

"Ah, they're expecting you," he said, and ushered her through a gate and across a plank floor to the office at the rear. And there she discovered a dozen gentlemen arrayed around the handsome room with flocked red wallpaper, shining desks and tables, and a pressed-tin ceiling. The sheer number of these men startled her, but she swiftly picked out Alfred Noble and Gustav Moran, the only two she knew.

She smiled.

"Ah, Sister Carmela, let me introduce you," said Alfred Moran. "This is quite an occasion, a moment to celebrate, and I'm sure you'll wish to know who all these gents are."

"Yes, surely," she said. "I'm Sister Carmela."

The air was close, with all those males filling the office, and she wished someone would crack a window. They all wore dark suits and cravats and starched white collars, and many had gold watch fobs across their fronts, pinstripes in their suits, and shiny black shoes that gleamed sunlight off them.

"You know our vice president in charge of production, Gustav Moran," Noble said.

She knew Moran, all right, and nodded.

"Now, over here is Joseph Wolf, one of our major stockholders. Next to him is Judge Elmer Bark, a Rhode Island chancery magistrate, also a major investor in our syndicate. And next to him is our corporate counsel, Elliott Leffingwell, and our associate corporate counsel, Bob Twill, and next to him is our Denver legal associate, an expert on Colorado mining law, I might add, Gaspar de Filo; while the man next to him is our recording clerk, Peter Nimrod, and our corporate secretary, Oscar De Bono, and next to him is our chief corporate accountant, Jarvis Anhauser, and his assistant, Jake Pick, and over there is our stenographer, Lambert Will. Did I miss anyone?"

"You missed me," said a bald man.

"Oh, yes, our corporate geologist and assayer, Vincent Garamond."

She nodded.

"Now, please be seated, Sister. We have good news to impart to you. It is our deepest desire to supply jobs for the mining men in this fine city, and we are pleased to report that we will be able to continue to employ miners at the same rate as before, in spite of declining silver reserves. Thanks to the new gold discovery here in the Minerva, we can assure not only the miners, but the businessmen in town, our suppliers of cordwood, the transportation companies and their teamsters, and many others that the future of Yancey City has never been brighter." He smiled. "And that means your little hospital can continue to serve our people for many years to come."

There certainly were a lot of white shirts and cravats in the room, she thought. Like priests. She felt uncomfortable under the steady gaze of a dozen men.

"Now, it's been our dream of supplying Yancey City with a fine twenty-bed hospital and appropriate quarters for your lovely, self-sacrificing, and hard-working colleagues, but the news of the gold strike resulted in skyrocketing real-estate prices in Yancey City, and indeed, there were no suitable properties on the market. So there is little prospect of moving the hospital into an existing building.

"Our thoughts immediately turned to the marvelous way the original hospital was built, with the loving labor supplied by the miners themselves, who did everything from scratch. That is a legend in Yancey City, Sister, and won you a name that is fondly remembered by all in town." He turned to the Easterners among the gentlemen. "Sister Carmela organized the whole process, having extracted the miners from their saloons, and put them to work in squads, each assigned to do something, such as laying the foundation or sawing wood. She was a marvel, and the miners called her, with great love, of course, Sister Drill Sergeant!"

There was suitably soft laughter rippling through the assembled gents.

"Well, you won't have to do that again," Noble said, "although we hope you'll enlist the miners to build the new hospital and your quarters, just as in days of yore."

"I don't think we'll move, Mr. Noble."

"Ah, you haven't heard it all, not yet," he said hastily. "What we propose is that our town lot company will give your order two city lots and three hundred dollars. Three hundred dollars will buy much of what is needed. And our fine miners, who benefit so much from your loving charity, will gladly contribute the rest of the material and labor. Indeed, we will encourage them to do so. The result will be that a fine new hospital will rise right in Yancey City, along with your, what do you call it? A nunnery? Yes, well, your quarters next door, and you'll proudly move in before snow flies."

Sister Carmela pondered that. "There must be more to your proposal, Mr. Noble."

"No, basically, that's it."

"We have ten acres, some of it level, and two fine buildings, Mr. Noble."

"Ah, actually, Sister, you don't. You see, we've been researching the titles and conveyances, and there seem to be several grave problems. . . ."

"You are saying?"

"Ah, well, I'll let Mr. Leffingwell explain."

The corporate counsel smiled at the sister, genuine warmth and affection brimming from his kindly face. "Oh, you know how it is, Sister. Illiterate, uneducated men on the frontier make mistakes and get the laws all wrong. In this case, the company was founded by a certain Will Yancey, I believe—"

"Yes, where is he?" she asked.

Leffingwell stared at Noble, who responded. "We haven't the faintest idea."

"At any rate, Mr. Yancey, the original developer, proceeded to lay out a town site without adequate legal counsel. I won't trouble your head with all the details, but suffice it to say that we've had to redo the titles and conveyances of the town lots. As for the ten acres he conveyed to you, these weren't even in the boundaries of the town lot company, though we have made haste to annex the property, and now own it."

"Own it."

"Yes, I won't trouble your dear head with all of that, but we rescued land that would otherwise have been up for grabs and might even have reverted to the federal government, and so the ten acres, including the flat area, are safe."

"And the Sisters of Charity?"

"Ah, you're squatting on our property. Not intentionally, of course, but by the fruits of carelessness, of ignorance, such as this early miner, Yancey, is guilty of. He wasn't giving you his town lot company land, but unclaimed federal land, I'm afraid. We've claimed it, and the mineral under it, if there is any, of course."

"There's mineral," she said.

Noble intervened. "Well, Sister, that's highly questionable. Let me have our assayer and geologist explain matters for you, just to put your mind at ease. We wouldn't want you to feel that the syndicate is taking anything of value from your esteemed order."

He beckoned Vincent Garamond, who wiped his bald head, wringing oil from his scalp.

"Ah, are you by chance familiar with minerals and geology, Sister?" he asked.

"No, sir."

"Well, let me explain that surface manifestations of mineral are usually richer than ore that has not been exposed to oxygen and sunlight, water, air, wind. What happens is that the gangue, or matrix, weathers or oxidizes away, leaving the mineral in greater concentration than before, so anyone assaying surface ore would likely find higher values, higher percentages of valuable metals, then deeper within. Now, I did some tests and assays on that pocket below the hospital, working back a foot at a time—someone had been there ahead of me, it seemed—and sure enough, the values declined steadily, and within a few feet, by my best projections, they would be minimal, so you see, there's nothing there of consequence. You really weren't sitting on a bonanza there. I'm explaining this so that you and your sisters won't feel that you lost anything at all."

She saw the way this was going. "So, the gold isn't ours, the land isn't ours, there really isn't any gold anyway, and you won't build a new hospital for us."

"Oh," said Noble, "it really is much better than that. Soon you'll be snug in a new building closer to the families you are serving."

"What happens if we choose to stay, sir?"

"Well, you can't stay. We're requiring that you move at once."

"At once?"

"To temporary quarters, of course. We're starting to bore that tunnel tomorrow. We'll be unloading machinery for our new stamp mill, which will be built on the flat. When we're operating, the stamps will create quite a roar, and you wouldn't want the patients to be disturbed, would you?"

Twenty-three

Sister Carmela quieted herself as best she could. She stood there, in that gaudy office, surrounded by men in cravats and white collars, a priestly class of the business world.

They were politely waiting for her response to their polite banditry. Mr. Noble was smiling politely, bland goodwill oozing from his pursed lips. But she really had no answer, not a thought in her head.

"I'm a very simple woman, devoted to a humble mission, helping the needy," she said. "I have little education, none like yours anyway. There are many offices I have memorized, and I know the ordinances of the Church, and many things given me by our order. I know a little about medicine and nursing, much of it taught by our Dr. Borden, so that my sisters and I can be helpful to the sick and wounded and very old and very young. But I don't know much else.

"I hope I understand this correctly. You are saying that because of some obscure flaw, the Sisters of Charity don't really own the ten acres deeded to them by the Yancey Town Lot Company, and the land belongs to you.

"You're saying, I believe, that the minerals not only belong to you, but are a mere pocket, with declining richness as one goes into the rock, and of little value. You're saying that these minerals don't matter; what you really want is to build a horizontal tunnel to your mineshaft, and this will keep miners employed, and the sisters are keeping you from doing this.

"You're saying, I take it, that there is no suitable building in town for the hospital and a convent for us, but you will donate two lots and three hundred dollars of supplies so that we can start a new building . . . with more volunteer labor.

"And you're saying we must move at once, that we are evicted from land you claim, that you intend to start blasting. And that we will need to find temporary quarters, is that it?"

She beheld a dozen bland faces, various pairs of eyes focusing on her, some through spectacles.

"Oh, Sister, it's not so difficult as all that. We'll help you find a place, and even move you and the patients, and with all the care that we can manage," said Mr. Noble.

She stared at him. "I have no one at my side to advise me, so I cannot dispute your case," she said. "Perhaps all that you say is correct, and we have no right to the property. But we can do this much: The Lord looks after us. Would each of you affirm before God that what you tell me is correct and complete in every detail?"

Noble was smiling again. "Why, I'll speak for us all, Sister, and say that as far as we can ascertain, the facts are as we've presented them to you."

"I would like each of you to swear to it, you know, so help me, God. If you swear to it, then I'll see what to do next."

"Why, my dear Sister," said Alfred Noble, "I will personally affirm before all of Creation, all the hosts of Heaven, that we have presented you with the very best information we can summon!"

The lawyer, Leffingwell, cleared his throat noisily.

"Sister, we won't engage in that sort of oathing," he

said. "This is simply a business matter, not a divine tribunal. And you may be assured that we are acting upon our honor and integrity, and that we have looked carefully after your interests and those of the community, and have decided after much consultation what course to follow for the good of the entire community as well as our company, always with your best interests in mind."

"Well," she said, "if I do not have your affirmation sworn before God that everything you have told me is true, then we are done here."

"Done?"

"We will stay right where we are," she said. "And God will provide."

She turned to leave. Time stretched slowly. She took a step, then another and another, toward the fresh air and the sun and the breeze and the view of distant snowclad peaks.

"Sister! We're taking over the flat tomorrow," Leffingwell said. "It's a pity, we know, but necessary for the good of all. Count on us to help you move."

She ignored him and closed the door behind her, closed the door on that row of cravats and black suits that reminded her of a row of undertakers.

Only when she breathed the fresh November air did she tremble a little. She did not know what she would do. The most important thing was to guard the patients, keep them from harm. She didn't know how she would do that, or do anything that might be required of her now.

She toiled down the slope, passing the water wagons, feeling her legs tremble under her, her mind an empty vessel waiting to be filled. When she reached the hospital compound, she did not go to her office, but to the small chapel, and knelt at the rail, and thanked God for the chance to be of service to the wounded and the sick, and prayed that He would let her continue to do so, she and the sisters.

She could hardly bear to tell them.

The sisters were busy at their duties. Dr. Borden was examining a miner who had suffered a skull fracture from falling rock. She decided, swiftly, to let the day pass. There would be time enough to reveal their dilemma after evening prayer. But if she could catch the busy doctor, for a moment, she would inform him. He was an educated man, a man who would know about real estate and deeds and mineral rights and all of that. And a man who might have some idea what to do.

She caught him after he had finished his morning rounds. The man with the skull fracture and concussion lay groaning in his cot. She beckoned him to her cubicle.

"We are being evicted," she said.

"What? What?"

She described the morning's meeting to Dr. Borden.

"They can't do this. You have rights. You've possessed that property for years. Possession is nine tenths of the law."

"They're doing it."

"Get a lawyer. Start a suit. Get an injunction. We can't let them do this. I have two patients who can't be moved. It'd kill them. I just can't believe they'd do this."

"I'm not going to move the hospital," she said. "God will provide."

"If you're not going to move, then I'm not going to move," he said.

She loved the quiet passion of his voice, this man who had become a doctor against all odds, and practiced medicine where no other doctor would go.

"I propose to do nothing at all," she said. "That is all I can think of. Nothing. We'll go about our business of healing."

He paced about the cubicle so fiercely she feared he might have another fit, but it did not happen. "I will go talk to them. If you could stand alone before a group like that, then I can do so too, and take some courage from you."

"I'll tell the sisters after evening prayer," she said.

"How will they respond?"

"They are women of great courage and faith."

"Would you want me to come and address them?"

"We have given ourselves over to a higher authority, and we will accept our fate."

"You're surrendering then?"

The question troubled her. "No, we will await what comes," she said.

He stared into the afternoon light. "I'm not so trustful. Put me down as a weaker person than you. I will see about a refuge. Whatever else, we cannot simply abandon our work, our patients, our purposes."

"Where would we go, Doctor?"

He shook his head. "I'll make some inquiries. Have you talked to the press? To miners? To merchants?"

"No, I received the news from the syndicate early this afternoon, and I have spoken to no one but you."

"There's going to be outrage! This is a scandal!"

She wasn't sure there would be any outrage at all, not with the promise of new jobs, security, a future for Yancey City, full pay envelopes, good times, advertising for the weekly, sales for the merchants, contracts for the various suppliers, business for teamsters and the stage company, sales for the hay and feed merchants.

That evening, in a peaceful twilit quiet, she told the sisters about the trip up to the ridge that morning. About discovering that the land under them wasn't theirs. That the minerals weren't theirs. That the hospital was in the way. That they would be required to leave. That there was no suitable place to move. That they would receive two town lots and a few dollars, if that. And she told them of her decision simply to stay and wait for events to shape their lives; that they all would continue to nurse and heal and help the ill for as long as they could, against whatever opposed them, and with the devotion and love and faith that had always been theirs.

She had expected a great turmoil, emotion, shock, tears, anger, despair, sorrow. Instead her dark news was greeted with silence. No one had anything to say, not even Sister Elizabeth, who always had things to say, words in overflowing abundance.

"Have you nothing to say to me? Do I hear no advice?"

One by one, the sisters clasped her hands until they formed a circle bound by held hands, and they prayed.

At dawn she watched a meadowlark circle the verdant green oasis where the hospital had always stood. She saw the sun paint distant slopes with gold. She saw the mist in the valley far below, and the sliver of moon fade into blue sky. She saw all of creation before her, as she did every morning, and she rejoiced in it.

That morning the hospital continued as it always had, one of the sisters always on duty, Slow Eddie performing the needed chores, the patients fed and comforted, Dr. Borden making his rounds, and nothing happened until mid-afternoon, when a nearby explosion sent shocks through the very rock under them, and a cloud of smoke and debris shot down the slope below them.

Twenty-four

Hard Luck Yancey awakened to the warmth of a new-born sun. The cliff dwelling proved to be a safe and comfortable haven, as if those ancients who had built it sometime in the misty past knew more about natural heating and ventilation than did modern men. He was safe, for the moment, and only a mile from the heart of town.

He devoured some of what Slow Eddie had provided, and headed for the seep, carrying his prospecting tools. He studied the damp sand, dug a small pocket into it, and watched it fill. He dipped a tin cup into the water and tasted it. He filled the cup again, fearing that what he would do would foul that tiny supply.

He studied the rock, seeking the source of that tiny dribble of water, which probably amounted to a quart an hour, and concluded that it came directly out of that massive fault he had discovered earlier, when Adelaide was with him.

Water was wealth, and he would dig for this liquid gold with the same canny sense of geology that had served him so well when he hunted for minerals. He had no blasting powder now, and wouldn't use any because he wanted his effort to open up the spring to be totally private. This spring had once run heavily, carving a pool and a channel in native stone. He thought it might run again, given a little encouragement. And if it ran again, he might recover all that the syndicate had stolen from him, if things went as he foresaw them.

He was a patient man, and began patient digging, prying rock from the fault line using a pick and hammer. He rejoiced as each small piece of limestone broke loose, and he carved a tiny hollow into the base of the horseshoe where the spring once ran mightily. The clicks and taps of his hammer were lost in a chill clear day. He bloodied his knuckles tearing out rock, and smashed a finger when the hammer glanced off his rock chisel. But he persisted, bloody-handed, breaking off chunks of anonymous gray limestone.

There was nothing else; quietness, sky arching above, an occasional cawing crow, sunlight briefly heating his small world, only to vanish into shadow and chill. He was familiar with this sort of life, having spent lonely months and years all alone, digging at obscure ledges, scores of miles from any other mortal. It was not his favorite way to live, but he was comfortable with it. He was no recluse, but anyone prospecting for minerals alone was bound to have only the company of his thoughts.

He paused to wash his skinned knuckles and eat a little more of Slow Eddie's provender, and knew he would need to slip into town and get help in a day or so. That was all right; he knew how to dodge Cruikshank. And maybe he could get a few things from Adelaide, including some of his own books. Sometimes he hiked down to the base of the defile, where he could look out upon the ridge and see the distant headframes of the mines. It all belonged to the syndicate now, including his own Minerva, the best discovery he had ever made, one that would have kept him comfortable the rest of his life.

Some people got wealth by means of sharp lawyers and compliant judges. He preferred to get wealth the real way, by developing the things found in the good earth into something of value. In all his life he had never been tempted to start a lawsuit, though he had grievances enough. Maybe that was why they called him Hard Luck; he let things be taken from him. That was the way he was, and he didn't know how to change himself. Maybe somehow he would develop some wealth that wouldn't be stolen from him by greedy opportunists. He had an ability more valuable than theirs: He saw riches where they saw only rock.

By afternoon he had cut a small hollow in the stratified limestone along the fault, but it yielded no more water; nothing but the almost invisible flow of droplets that moistened the sand. He wondered whether he would ever dig his way through to the aquifer, at least with hand tools. Maybe it was a hundred feet back; maybe five hundred.

He settled into his cliff dwelling that evening, turning the barren stone room into a habitation. In time, with the onslaught of winter, he could shutter the windows, build fires in a well-designed firepit that took the smoke off, add mats to carpet the cold rock floor. With a few supplies, he could winter there.

All the next day he chipped away at the fault line, gained a foot, but he did not unloose any more water. By evening he was out of food. Dark came early to that high country. He slipped on an old black sweater, which with his work-stained trousers would render him nearly invisible in town, if he stayed away from lamplit windows.

He wasn't sure what he would tell Adelaide; only that he needed help with some supplies and would trade some of his books for them. He waited until full dark and then hiked warily down the long ridge, past the silent looming frames at the mine heads, past dark shacks, past the whitewashed offices of the syndicate. Then he cut straight down a slope, avoiding the well-worn pathway miners used to climb from town to the works.

He reached Silver Street, where he might enter Adelaide's club, but he continued down to Gold Street, because she usually turned over the club to her barman in the evenings. He moved like a wraith, staying in deep shadow, dodging windows. He saw occasional pedestrians but no one saw him, and when at last he reached the door of her flat, he knocked softly.

There was no response. He tried again.

"Yancey," she said on the other side of the door.

"Yes, how did you know?"

"I just knew. Just a moment."

He watched the light vanish from the window, and then the door opened and she waved him into the dark room.

"Oh, Will, I knew you would come."

"I'd like to trade a few things," he said.

"Oh, don't talk like that."

She motioned him through the dark room toward a lit one, the kitchen, and motioned him to a seat. The ceiling creaked with the weight of many feet on the floor above, and it gave him an odd feeling.

"Are you hungry?" she asked.

"No, but I will be soon unless I can trade."

She ignored that and bustled around. "Here's some elk stew left over from yesterday. A lady gets to eat her leftovers when the club closes."

"I'll give you poetry books," he said proudly.

She laughed, and for a moment he thought she was mocking him, until he heard the kindness in it.

"Where are you?" she asked.

"Above the dry spring. There's a cliff house up there,

almost invisible. I was going to show it to you . . . if you want to come there."

"I would love to see it," she said. "They fascinate me, the ones who built those places long before the world was known to us. Are you warm and dry?"

"It's under a south-facing overhang that catches winter sun and heats the rock, but the overhang keeps it in shade during the summer when the sun is high. It's a work of genius."

"And they left when the water stopped?"

"I think so."

He found himself wolfing down the savory stew. Even lukewarm, it exuded meaty aromas. He caught her watching him as he ate.

"What happened to you?" she asked when finally he pushed the bowl away.

"Cruikshank told me to get out and never return, and if I didn't, the 'special deputies' would deal with me, which was his way of saying I'd be pounded on."

"Or killed. A good kick to the head," she said somberly.

"That too."

"But you came here. And you're staying."

"I see a future here," he said. "I collected my gear; Slow Eddie raided the hospital kitchen, and I lugged about eighty pounds of stuff up to my hideaway."

"And?"

He smiled slowly. "I'm mining water."

"Any high-grade ore yet?"

"Not a drop."

"And what will you do with this bonanza?"

"That depends on how scarce water becomes in town. Maybe nothing."

She seemed puzzled. For the moment he would not explain. She would become alarmed about her business, about the town, if he told her what he thought might happen to the spring.

"Adelaide, what's happened here?"

She pulled the bowl away and dropped it into her dry sink. "It's so terrible I can hardly tell you. And I don't really know. But the syndicate's started a tunnel down below the hospital. Every few hours there's another blast shooting rock down that slope. It rattles the hospital and everyone in it."

"Are the sisters moving?"

She laughed briefly. "Where? There's no place in town. There's lots of rumors, but nobody knows what's happened or how the syndicate got the rights to tunnel down there, or what."

"The sisters are letting them do it?"

"I wish I knew, Will. Everyone says it's good for the town. The mines will be more productive. There was a lot of talk about the silver ore running out, but now everything's perked up. My business is better than it's ever been. Miners were saving a few dimes to move if they lost their jobs."

Some dark anger bloomed in him. "Could you find out more for me, Adelaide? Talk to Slow Eddie?"

"It's not easy to talk to Slow Eddie," she said.

"Ask him to send me a note? He'll nod yes or no."

She nodded. "What are you going to do up there, Will? Especially with winter coming on?"

"Wait out the syndicate. I might even get my mine back."

That puzzled her, and he really didn't want to venture too far into the future.

Another explosion from well below town rattled her dishes and echoed into the night.

"They're working three shifts down there. I hear they want the tunnel to join the Minerva shaft by Christmas.

They've gone twenty feet already. There's timbering crews and they're starting to lay down rails, and there's men sorting out ore down there and carrying it off in ore bags. And the hospital ground is full of stuff, you know, mining stuff, rails and cross-ties and boxes of blasting sticks."

"That adit will run only a few dozen feet below the hospital," he said. "I can't imagine the sisters are letting this happen because they want to."

"I could talk to Dr. Borden," she said.

"Please do. But he might not say much, at least not now."

Somehow the sisters had been browbeaten into this, he thought. And the syndicate wasn't even helping them move. An old black rage bloomed in him, filled his face.

She leaned across the kitchen table and placed her hand over his. "I know," she said.

"Adelaide? Would you trade some food and things for books?"

"No," she said.

"But books are all I have."

"No," she said. "You have me."

Twenty-five

The explosion rumbled up out of the very stone and rocked the hospital on its foundations. The rumble lingered, and then fell away. A glass jar pitched off a shelf and smashed, spilling a tincture of mercury. Over in the ward, several patients moaned.

Rufus Borden suppressed a blistering diatribe not intended for sisters' ears, and set aside his scalpel. These eruptions came unannounced, and as the tunnel bored straight toward the hospital, they increased dramatically, from subdued thumps at first to violent quakes that seemed to lift the building several inches, and the rock beneath it, and shiver every timber.

He had been cleaning out a dangerous abscess near a miner's groin, one close to the femoral artery. He paused, bringing himself under discipline.

Sister Elizabeth mopped up the tincture and swept aside the glass. Slow Eddie operated the carbolic-mist machine. Trembling, Borden cleaned out the abscess and sterilized the raw red flesh before suturing the incision. No one had said anything. During the first explosions, days earlier, everyone had gabbled and babbled on, and now people just winced and continued doing whatever they were doing. But the blasts were becoming intolerable. He didn't know how far down they were; it felt like ten feet, but he guessed forty or fifty. Close enough.

"All right, Eddie, take him back," he said.

Eddie wheeled the patient back to the ward.

It wasn't just the blasts: The syndicate had unloaded mountains of mining gear on the hospital grounds, great timbers, cross-ties, spikes, rails, ore cars, feed for mine mules, cases of blasting caps and boxes of DuPont's Hercules dynamite, firewood for a small boiler and pump that would push fresh air into the bore. Roughly dressed men talked and shouted just outside the windows. Not even morning and evening prayer were sacred to them.

The sisters, following Sister Carmela's lead, said nothing, gritted their teeth, continued to nurse and heal and pray, and didn't give an inch. But the hospital was becoming untenable and the patients were suffering. Some awaited the next blast so anxiously that Borden feared for their healing. Those blasts often erupted in the small hours of the night, when men slept the hardest and needed peace the most.

Each day, some clerk from the syndicate had arrived, sought out Sister Carmela, and notified her that she was trespassing; that the syndicate would help with the move to undisclosed quarters only if it began at once, with no further resistance and obstruction of the law and property rights.

"And each day Sister Drill Sergeant had stared back at the pocked youth, withering him with a wordless silence until he fled. But it was plain the situation could not last more than a day or two more.

Dr. Borden scrubbed his hands, noting the tremble, and donned his suit coat and overcoat and homburg. For days he had quietly queried the town's businessmen about emergency quarters for the hospital, and had met walls of resistance.

"Oh, a most worthy cause, Doctor, most worthy, but land's at a premium just now, the gold strike, you know, and there's not a room or a building to be had."

He had heard a dozen variations of that sort of talk, and finally knew that the flint-hearted merchants had more care about gold than about the desperate and sick, themselves excepted of course. Let one of them be felled by anything and he would demand the best that medicine could provide.

Borden lived in a small flat, and thought to turn it over to the sisters as a last resort. It didn't matter to him where he hung his hat. But the place could hold six patients at the most, and the sisters would all be crowded into a single rear room. It was foolish even to think of it.

The muted booms of the explosives drifted up to the city on the ridge and stirred men's imaginations. Most applauded. Gold! More gold!

A Biblical story came to mind: what Jesus did with the money changers in the temple. Borden doubted that the story was authentic; for that matter, he doubted that anything in the Bible was authentic, but the money changers of Yancey City certainly were real, and they were invading the only temple that Borden knew, which was the hospital. It would do, it would do. He would deliver a Biblical lesson, and hope it would accomplish its purpose.

He stopped at the harness shop and bought a bullwhip, cracked it menacingly while the proprietor watched with morbid fascination, paid his three dollars, and marched up the hard slope to the Minerva Mine, on the rocky heights above. He entered that plain outer office, where he had occasionally visited before, mostly to remonstrate against the careless protection of human bodies in the bowels of the mines.

The coiled and braided bullwhip felt splendid in his strong hands, its weighted tassel dangling daintily at the end of the long snake of leather.

"I'm going to see Alfred Noble," he said. "Be sure to plug your ears with both fingers."

"But Doctor—"

"I will see him," Borden said, letting himself through the gate, and marching steadily toward the inner sanctum. He felt an old, familiar irritation in him, and only hoped that he could finish the task first, before the fit took him.

"Borden! What are you doing here?" Noble said, rising swiftly, his smile growing glandular.

"I'm here to teach you what words won't teach, and only corporal punishment teaches, you bounder."

"Ah, Doctor, ah . . ."

Noble spotted the bullwhip, and was edging toward a brass bell on his desk.

"I'll teach you," Borden said. "I'll teach you what thirty lashes can teach."

He uncoiled the bullwhip and snapped it. It snaked across the room, an oddly cruel force in that haven of red-flocked wallpaper and polished walnut furniture.

He jerked the bullwhip back and swung it easily, and it found its target with a whack.

"Ow!" Noble danced and staggered. The whip had cut through his shirt and lacerated his left arm.

Whack! It sounded like a gunshot to Borden, a fine sharp whack that cut across Noble's spasming back, tearing his waistcoat and striking soft white flesh.

Whack!

"Stop that!" Noble howled.

The clerk materialized, and Borden aimed one blow

in his direction to hold him back, but his target was not the clerk, it was the author of the hell that had descended on Yancey City and its injured and sick.

Whack!

Noble screamed.

The fit dropped him. He felt the grand mal strike, felt his grip loosen, and felt himself vanishing from the world.

He knew nothing for some while. When he awakened he stared stupidly about. Men were pinning him to the floor, and he didn't know what that was about. He had bitten his tongue, and it bled, the salty blood leaking from his mouth, his boiled white shirt soaked with it. He couldn't think. They lifted him up, and he recognized fat Cruikshank, the town constable, and some of his toughs, mine toughs, holding him.

He felt wobbly.

"Now you've done it, Borden," the constable said. "Now you're sure as hell going to get it."

Borden didn't know what all that was about until he glimpsed Noble, red oozing from several lacerations on his arm and back, and then he remembered, or thought he did, or was it all fantasy?

They dragged him off; he couldn't put one foot in front of another, but they dragged him, his legs caving under him, down the rocky grade, through town, past Silver Street, Gold, Lead, Tin, and finally Copper Street, where the constabulary and small hoosegow stood, close to the tenderloin.

They threw him into a stinking pen. Borden wiped his bloody mouth.

"You're in for a week, for certain, Borden, whipping a man like that, aggravated assault, disturbing the peace—oh, wait until the J.P. gets you in front of him."

Borden still wasn't oriented, but he was remembering the whip.

"I think he received his lesson," he said.

"What's a sawbones like you doing, hurting a man?" Cruikshank asked.

"It's called education," Borden said. "Some men require stripes."

Three hours later that toad of a J.P., Marcus Bullwinkle, fined Borden a hundred dollars and gave him a week in the pokey.

"Who's going to take care of the sick?" Borden asked.

"You should have thought of that before attacking an innocent man."

Borden started to laugh, and began bellowing so loudly that Bullwinkle fined him another fifty for contempt of court.

They kept him in that stinkhole overnight, but let him go in the morning. Not even the toadies of the syndicate wanted to keep the town's only doctor locked up for a week. It was a long and foul night, shared with half-a-dozen unwashed louts. But Borden was entirely unrepentant, believing as he did that corporal punishment had its uses, especially among those who least expected it and considered themselves above all the laws of the universe.

They let him out before breakfast so they wouldn't have to buy him one, and he found himself on the quiet street, the least respectable in Yancey City, where saloons and whorehouses never closed. It was a soft cold dawn. Wearily he toiled upslope to his flat, let himself in, bathed, changed to another suit, rested in the gentle silence for an hour, and then headed for the hospital where he would minister as best he could to those who needed him. He felt oddly elated; Alfred

Noble would never forget yesterday's whipping, and maybe it would produce some glimmering of good in the man's greedy mind.

Twenty-six

Alfred Noble alternated between rage and sulk. Whipped by his own physician. He would sue the man for every penny he had. He would turn loose his mine-security goons on the doctor. But then he thought better of all that. If he sued, word would leak from one end of Colorado to the other. And if his security men worked over the doctor, there would be little medicine in Yancey City.

The lash across his arm had lacerated flesh and spilled blood copiously, ruining his shirt and long underwear. The lash across his back had been softened by his waistcoat, but had raised a cruel red welt that ran a foot and a half across his back, and made sitting and sleeping miserable.

He lifted the Wildroot Tonic and drained the blue bottle dry, but was swiftly solaced. That would be another problem. He would have to find another physician; the sole one in Yancey City was no longer available to him. He jammed the cork back onto the tonic bottle and pitched it out, worrying about what he could use for a substitute until a fresh supply could be brought in.

Then, calmed for the day, he eased gently back into his swivel chair, waited for the jolt of pain to subside, and began his day's task, which was to find ways and means of evicting the sisters at once. The matter could wait no longer. He needed the flat and its steady water supply for a mill. He needed to sort out the country rock, and then break down the quartz and extract the telluride gold. This could be carried economically down the endless grade on mules to Silverton and the railroad. Later, the low-grade could be chuted to the valley floor and hauled away.

The matter wouldn't wait. A fortune hung in the balance. Machinery and a boiler were on their way. He would boot out the nuns; the only question agitating him now was how. It would take some finesse. In two days the adit would run directly under the hospital, and with every blast the building would rock on its foundations. Maybe that would be all that was needed: just wait. But whenever he thought of Sister Drill Sergeant, he knew it would require more than underground blasts to loosen her grip on the place.

For Alfred Noble, there were only winners and losers, and the only virtue he recognized was prudence. Winners understood the world. The whole world was a great smorgasbord, ready to be plucked up by whoever could pluck up what he wanted and keep it. The losers never got to the table, most likely because they had been inculcated with civic virtue, not religion, which put restraints on their conduct and compelled them to stop short of victory. But Noble was not inhibited by any such thing, and regarded those who drew lines as fools.

He could find not the slightest virtue or value in caring for losers, such as the sick and injured. It was beyond him just why some women became nuns and gave themselves to caring for the humble, the poor, the sick, the elderly, the downhearted, the demented, the tragedy-ridden. Life was hard, and the great virtue of struggle was that the weaker ones fell and the strong survived, to the benefit of the human race.

Sister Drill Sergeant was bizarre really, devoting a lifetime to a hopeless enterprise. What did it get her? Nothing. What did the human race get from it? The preservation of the weak and disabled. Ideally, there should be no hospital at all in a mining camp; almost all mine injuries were the result of a man's own foolish conduct, and fools ought not to be rescued from their folly. A man who knew there was no hospital within fifty miles was a lot more prudent than one who knew that he'd be nursed back to health. It was all so plain to Alfred Noble that it amused him how blind the world was to the simple realities of life.

It was time for a last visit to the hospital. But this time he would take two mine guards with him, just to avoid the sort of trouble he had suffered from Borden. He sent for his biggest toughs, one of them six and a half feet and three hundred pounds, and he started downslope on foot to get his daily exercise. Yochim Mueller, the biggest of the syndicate's security guards, was so ugly he shattered mirrors, and so big he cast a shadow halfway across town in the middle of summer. He also stank; he exuded some weird animal musk that choked the freshness out of any room. He would do fine. The other guard, skinny and vulpine, reminded Noble of an osprey.

The threesome descended through Yancey City like an avalanche, and arrived at the flat twenty minutes later, just in time for another blast in the granite underfoot to rattle the timbers of the hospital. When they stepped inside, they found dust and smoke whirling in the air, though nothing else seemed amiss.

They found Sister Drill Sergeant picking up a folder that had flown off her desk. When she straightened, her gaze swept past Noble to the two security men behind him, and then she stood resolutely.

"Sister, we won't permit this trespassing anymore. You'll have to move now."

"And where is the twenty-bed hospital and convent and where is the help you offered?"

"We found nothing suitable. Yancey City's a boomtown with this gold strike. We're going to put a mill here, starting now. Everything's been ordered. Boiler's arrived in Silverton and is being hauled here. These gents will carry your patients out if they can't walk. And your sisters can gather their things and leave."

She drew herself up. "That which ye do unto the least of my little ones, ye do also unto me," she said.

"You've had ample time to make arrangements. You've defied us. So the consequences are yours alone. Remember this and count it as a lesson: You've had days and days to make arrangements. You were notified that you did not possess this property and were offered help, which you did not accept. Now you want more time, I suppose. The plight of your patients is totally on your head, not ours. Were you in town, drumming up support? No, you assumed, I suppose, that we would back down. We can't and won't. If these patients now suffer, you have made it so."

"Very well, move us," she said, sitting down.

"You can walk."

"No, we will not. I have instructed the sisters not to participate. Which patient will you move first? Beth Adamack, who suffers from childbirth fever, and her infant? Joseph Cripps, whose heart is failing him?"

Noble nodded toward the guards. They headed for the ward, and found seven patients plus Slow Eddie, who was collecting chamber pots.

"Eddie, carry that fellow out. We're evicting you," Noble said.

Eddie stared at the mountainous men behind Noble,

and sat down on an empty bed. His lips began to move, and in time he spoke. "No, you carry me out. I won't participate."

Noble hadn't counted on that; hadn't counted on dragging the sisters out, and he didn't like it. The eviction would reverberate through Yancey City, and then across Colorado, and maybe across the country, and his investors would find themselves embarrassed and maybe worse, enraged.

It was maddening.

But Noble was a prudent man; it was out of prudence that he had fashioned several fortunes. He smiled suddenly, beaming with glandular joy.

"Well, Eddie, we'll help you do it tomorrow; bring up some wagons and get you folks out. You can pack up this evening, and we'll do the hauling, courtesy of the Rhode Island Syndicate."

Slow Eddie stared.

Noble retreated from the ward, under the steady gaze of several patients, whose stares seemed to lock on him.

He found Sister Carmela rooted to her chair. "Sister, on second thought, we'll help you move tomorrow. You can tell the nuns to pack their kits, and we'll bring some wagons and men down the hill to take you all up to town."

"Where?" she asked.

He headed into a cold afternoon. This was not the first tactical retreat of his life, and he would take it in stride. So the mill was delayed a day or so; it would hurt the profit only a little.

By the time he had labored back up to his office on the ridge, he knew he had to move the sisters and their patients somewhere; not just out the door. He stepped into his Minerva Mine supervisor building, and thought perhaps he could move the sisters into it; he intended to take over the hospital anyway, and operate the company from there.

The office building had but two rooms, an outer room where the accountant, paymaster, shift foremen, and two factotums had desks, and his own elaborate office. About six beds could be stuffed into the outer room; the sisters could all be jammed into his office and enjoy his flocked red wallpaper.

But he dismissed the idea. The building was valuable company property, close to the mine head, and could be put to better uses.

He summoned Moran, and then he closed his office door behind him.

"How are we going to get those sisters out of there?" he asked.

"Arrest them for trespassing, turn them over to Cruikshank, and he'll put them in the hoosegow for a night or two and then take them to the J.P."

The idea amused Noble. "What about the patients?"

"That's easy. Haul them to their residences and leave them there. Their wives can take care of them."

"Gus, you've solved my problem for me." He gazed fondly at the man who had even less compunction than he did. "What'll the sisters do after the J.P. fines them?"

"Go away obviously."

"No more hospital?"

Moran shrugged. "Town still has a doctor, and he makes house calls."

"Gus, you've just saved the syndicate two town lots and three hundred dollars. And we can move into the hospital whenever we want."

"That's what I'm here for," Moran said.

Twenty-seven

Rufus Borden listened to Sister Carmela's somber report: Tomorrow they would be physically thrown out, and they had no place to go. Noble was blaming it all on the sisters, who refused to budge when they should have been seeking new quarters and taking advantage of the syndicate's offer of two lots and three hundred dollars. Somehow, the blame had shifted; now it was all the failure of the Sisters of Charity to act that had brought them to this pass.

"They will have to carry us out," she said.

He grunted. That was not going to help the patients, two of whom were gravely ill. And now they were down to hours. In the morning, the syndicate's bullyboys would carry them out and deposit them on the grounds.

"I will talk to some people," he said. "I don't know what can be done."

He stood, plucked up his Gladstone, and was about to leave when Sister Carmela pressed her hands over his. They stood there wordlessly, she in prayer and he in tenderness. When the moment had passed, he gazed into her face, and discovered bonfires burning in her eyes, and her whole face lit to luminosity by something bright and sweet within.

"Let me see," he said.

He lumbered up the steep road in November darkness, his coat collar high against the sharp cold. He had asked a few merchants about space, even temporary space, and received only a shake of the head: Yancey City was booming; there was no space, especially no space that could be given, rather than rented. The hotel wanted no part of sick and injured patients in its rooms.

At Copper Street, the lowest and meanest of the town's arteries, he headed for one of his favorite haunts, the Calabash Club, operated by Blarney O'Rourke of County Mayo. It was the haunt of serious poker players, of which Doc Borden was counted among the town's finest. It was a tad less gamy than most of the dives along Copper Street, though it did have a faro layout leased by a tinhorn named Bowers. It served generous helpings of corned beef and cabbage, and employed no women as barmaids or serving girls. There were lithographs of Irish castles on its walls.

O'Rourke was busy pouring Denver red-eye behind the bar, and there were a dozen males waiting their turn. It was O'Rourke's gift to conduct intense conversations while his hands flew from bottle to glass to dipper. Each drink landed before its purchaser even while the conversation never faltered.

Doc Borden settled his Gladstone on the bar and waited, but not for long. A double shot of Bushmill's materialized, a sign of O'Rourke's favor. He did not serve his Irish whiskey to everyone.

"Tomorrow the bullyboys close the hospital," Borden said.

"Close it, you say, close it?"

"Right out the door, patients and all."

"It makes a man want to start a revolution, and light a stick or two and toss it at the syndicate."

"Ah, I believe that's why you left Ireland?"

"Brits, syndicate, what difference does it make, eh?

Blow 'em all up, I say." O'Rourke filled three glasses and shoved them down the counter. Each glass skidded to a stop before a customer, and not a drop spilled.

"I need less revolution from you and more help."

"The best thing, Doc, is to call the Fenians and ask for help. I know a man who'd send Noble to his reward. I know a gent or two who'd blow the top off this ridge. Help, you say?"

"Help for the injured, the sick. The ones about to get tossed out."

"The sick, you say?"

O'Rourke poured a shot and downed it neatly. Except to redden a little around the gills, he managed the feat without a twitch or a hiccup. "I think maybe I'll blow the syndicate off the map," he said. "What help?"

"I would settle for the upstairs."

"No, not the upstairs! Put the holy sisters in that profane place?"

Doc nodded, and sipped his Bushmill's.

"Put the bloody hospital upstairs?"

Doc smiled.

"No, it'd cost me too much. I get four bits a flop, and I'm full every night. Do you know what that comes to, that tidy little take each night? Sixteen dollars, clear profit. And eight of it goes to the Fenians each day, every day."

O'Rourke's second story was a flophouse, with thirty-two louse-ridden pads in a dormitory, and barely six inches between each thin pad. The upstairs stank of male odors, vomit, urine, and unknown vile smells. Doc had been there many times, patching up stab wounds, checking stopped pulses, evaluating strange fevers. It was a favorite of Copper Street drunks, vagrants, homeless men, and miners escaping their wives. It was also a haven for pickpockets, thugs, footpads, and twisted hobos.

"I canna do it, Doc. I canna put the holy sisters up there, and the bloody patients."

"Thanks, Blarney, I'll tell them, and we'll be here in a couple of hours."

"I canna do it, Doc."

"You'll need to evict a few bums."

"That and burn the pads and scour the floors. How am I going to do that, tell me?"

"The sisters are very good at that."

"And where will the holy sisters stay, Doc?"

Borden sighed. "I will put them in my flat, I guess, and I will find other digs."

"No, no you won't, laddie. Your flat's unholy, with all those medical books in it. I'd not want a sister looking at those books. I'll tell you what you'll do. You'll bring the sisters to my apartment at the back, and I'll find me a place. There's room enough."

"I knew I could count on you, Blarney."

"And what if a bloody hospital bugger dies up there? Then it's bad luck upon this club."

"How many men bought a flop and never woke up? How many?"

"Two or three now."

"Well, then."

"It's bad luck you're bringing me, Doc."

"Are the sisters' prayers and thanksgivings bad luck?"

O'Rourke stared sadly. "It is bad luck on the Calabash Club to have all that praying directly over the faro table and right over the poker table, and on top of this very bar."

The hospital would hie itself to Copper Street.

Doc smiled, downed his Bushmill's, smacked Blarney O'Rourke on his meaty shoulder, and braved the night.

He made a stop at the livery barn, and then hiked down the slope, wary of footpads.

He found the sisters vigiling in the chapel, and was welcomed there by Sister Carmela.

"We have a place," he said to those stern and troubled faces before him, soft in the light of a single candle.

"Oh, Doctor, how can that be?"

"It is not what one might hope for . . . it's upstairs, and over a saloon."

"Is it quiet for our patients?"

"Not always. There is a pianist some evenings."

"Well, they might enjoy the music. Is it an apartment, this place?"

"It . . . was a boarding place for transient men. With an outside stair. You won't need to go through the saloon."

"Oh . . . not very safe."

"I think it will be safer than anywhere else, Sister. Safer than here."

"Is there space enough?"

"For the ward, yes; every bed. The owner, Mr. O'Rourke, has an apartment behind, and it is yours."

"But what of him?"

"I don't know. He has a small office in his saloon."

"Well, praise God!"

"And praise Blarney O'Rourke too," said Doc. "He fears all that praying above his club will ruin it, but he will do it."

He thought they would laugh, but they didn't.

"What must we do?"

"Move. On my way here, I stopped at the livery barn and talked to the hostler. In an hour or so, every wagon he has will arrive. It's hard to corral teamsters at this hour. They're drinking up the day's profits." He didn't add that he had promised the hostler a hundred dollars, and the move would leave him in debt.

"Is it cold, this place?" asked Sister Elizabeth.

"No, it's closer to hell than here," Doc replied.

She laughed.

Sister Carmela stood. "Are we agreed?" she asked.

No sister responded. None could or would assent.

"Then I will agree for all of us," she said. "If Doctor says it will be all right, then it will be all right."

"I'll go talk to Slow Eddie," Doc said.

The women needed time to digest all of this. He slipped out of the chapel, peered into the peaceful ward, where pain and hope had permeated the very plank walls, and regretted that he would soon be rousing these four desperate patients and hauling them into a sharp night to a miserable smelly upstairs dormitory on the seediest street in Yancey City.

He headed into the night, rounded the building until he found the little shelter built for the orderly, knocked, and soon was informing him. Eddie nodded.

Another blast rumbled through the night, jarring the hospital, rattling anything on a shelf. The tunnel was directly below the hospital now, and the blasts were disturbing patients. The syndicate would have its gold.

"Will help now," Eddie said, crawling out of his bunk. "After that, what?"

"The sisters will need you there. Maybe you'll need to stay in the new ward for a while."

Slow Eddie digested that, smiled, tried to form words. "Maybe," he said. "Maybe I should go away."

"Eddie!"

But Eddie had turned his back to Doc, who took the hint and slipped out into the cold mean night.

So it had come to this, he thought. A night flight into a stinking flophouse, and all because of gold.

Twenty-eight

In spite of Sister Drill Sergeant's formidable powers, the move did not go well. It took two hours for the stable man to line up some teamsters and wagons and harness drays. It took four hours for Blarney O'Rourke to evict the last of his flophouse habitues, pull his bug-ridden pads out, swamp the floor, and lime a foul privy on the slope behind.

But finally, the first wagon toiled up the slope carrying empty iron-framed beds, bedclothes, and medical supplies, loaded in the light of a single lantern. Another carried the sisters and their few possessions. Then Slow Eddie and the teamsters tenderly loaded two patients into one wagon, and two into another.

Dr. Borden didn't like it a bit. Joseph Cripps was failing; his heart was barely pumping blood. He looked ghastly in the deep shadows.

"Keep him warm, Eddie; take him upstairs first and settle him ahead of the rest. Then Mrs. Adamack and her infant."

Sister Drill Sergeant watched over the loading of that wagon, tucking the blankets tight around Cripps, who gasped for air. She wondered whether he even understood what was happening. He seemed to, but had not spoken. Not long before a bitter cold dawn, the wagons rumbled off the flat and up the winding road to town, and suddenly she was alone.

She watched as the wagons vanished into the darkness. There was no moon to gild the path to town with silver. She slipped into the dark and silent hospital, knowing her way around by instinct even without light except the faintest glow from starlit skies. There would be more things to take up to Copper Street in the morning, but that could wait.

She stood in the empty ward, which had sheltered desperate and sick men and women until only an hour before, never once empty since it had been built, for there had always been people in dire need harbored there. She smelled carbolic acid, and pus-soaked bandages, and always the odd odor of fear and desperation. But she also smelled the hundreds of bouquets of wildflowers that had sweetened that healing place during the summers.

She remembered the ones who had been brought there, ones with frightful wounds who had died soon afterward; ones who lingered; ones who endured pain and horror and left crippled or maimed or mindless. She remembered those who left on a crutch. She remembered those whose bodies, wrapped in winding sheets, had been taken away to be buried in the little cemetery a mile beyond the ridge, where there was a patch of earth and a modest slope.

She remembered the screams, the sobbing, the groans, the whispered prayers, the jokes, the coughing and choking and sneezing and gasping for air. She remembered the sudden confessions of shy men, as if she, a sister, were a confessor instead of a woman married in a certain way to Christ.

She remembered wiping their sweaty brows with a cool cloth, and sometimes holding their hands. Many were alone; she and the sisters suddenly became their mothers and sisters and daughters, the family who saw them through until they were healed enough to leave.

She remembered the ones who couldn't pay, the ones who did pay, the ones who struggled to pay, a bit at a time, and kept at it, two bits a week, or a dollar a month, until they had settled their accounts. She remembered the vagrants who didn't pay, and the affluent who said they would and didn't.

She thought of the newborn. Not many; ten or twelve in all. Dr. Borden had delivered far more in their cottages. She thought of the stillborn, small lifeless things that made her grieve; of the sickly ones, sucking desperately for life; of the robust, bawling, angry, smiling ones brimming with life. And of exhausted mothers, torn and bloodstained mothers, some of them filled with boundless joy; others too worn to care.

But most of all she remembered the healing and the release from pain. She remembered those on death's door who gained color, whose pulse grew strong, whose eyes brightened, who took their first steps, who walked out of her hospital all by themselves. She remembered those in screaming pain, sobbing, unable to endure the torments inflicted on their heads or limbs or chest or lungs or neck; how the morphia had freed them; how the laudanum, the Dover's powder, and yes, the touch of loving hands, had somehow transformed torture into peace and rest and sleep.

Some had headed straight to the chapel upon being discharged, there to rejoice and give thanks. Others acknowledged no God, but every one of them had been remembered in the sisters' petitions at the altar rail each day. Rarely had a priest shown up in Yancey, but those had been special occasions, and the sisters rejoiced when they could hear the familiar Latin of the Mass in their own chapel.

Now she walked the lonely and hushed rooms and halls, feeling a terrible loss, feeling the stories of lives that had embedded themselves into the very walls. She grieved for the hospital as much as she had grieved for her mother. It was already dead; the living, breathing hospital was even then winding its way around the hairpin curves to Yancey City.

She reached her little cubicle, where she had administered the hospital, ordered supplies, wrestled with funds, received news, shared hope and defeat with Dr. Borden, listened to the tearful, dreamed of adding beds, healing better, bringing the Lord to hardened hearts. She touched the wall of the building, felt its solemnness and something new: It was an alien wall now, and would serve Mammon in the morning, gold and wealth and all those things she knew so little of.

She thought she saw a faint streak of light across the southeastern heaven, and knew it was time. She stood, reluctantly, and walked toward the door, her footsteps hollow in the forlorn building. An icy cold shot wakefulness through her. She stepped into a predawn quiet. Her sweet meadows were littered with construction debris, iron and wood, and she was glad the light was still so vague she wouldn't have to look upon the barbarous tangle.

She wrapped her black shawl tightly about her and labored up the steep and alien slope. Man had not been put on earth to live in places like Yancey City, without a level square foot of land, and not a tree, and not a flower. She turned for a last look at the hospital and the flat; a place that, those men told her, had never been theirs; never had been owned by the sisters. A place where they were not wanted now. It had been a sweet green notch in the great slope, but now it was nothing at all; a bench to park heavy things.

When she reached Copper Street, out of breath, she found the town stirring. A mining camp never slept. A muffled boom echoed softly, disturbing some crows into flight, and she knew another shot had been loosed under the hospital. Copper Street stretched westward toward Table Mountain, and was lined with saloons and pawnshops, some on stilts, some dug into the hillside, like all the other structures in town. She had never been in this quarter, and understood at once the sort of life that was squandered there. She saw consumptive men, miners in their jumpers, carrying a lunch bucket, and a weary woman wearing rouge and something gauzy meandering along the street.

The Calabash Club announced itself with a gourd-like sign hanging over the narrow street, and beside it was an open door and a staircase rising bleakly upward. The smell of urine and rotgut and vomit caught her nostrils.

Here was the place where the Sisters of Charity of Leavenworth would minister once again to the sick and broken and suffering. She thought to thank Mr. O'Rourke, but thought she would first ascend those grim steps and discover what sort of place lay upstairs. She stepped upward on creaking grimy stairs, one step at a time, feeling the loss of a whole night's sleep. The whole building seemed transient, carelessly erected and ready for the least excuse to tumble down. She feared fire; how would she help patients trapped upstairs if this steep stairwell were ablaze?

Well, there were things to thank God for, and one of them was this very haven. She reached the top of the stairs and turned into an odorous dormitory, discovering there her beloved sisters, the beds arranged in two rows, Slow Eddie making order out of a chaos of supplies, and three patients.

Sister Elizabeth was weeping.

"Where's Mr. Cripps, Sister?"

"He's dead."

"What happened?"

Sister Elizabeth gathered herself. "He died in the wagon. He bolted up, and fell back, and was gone."

"Oh, oh, oh. And Doctor looked at him?"

"Doctor wasn't here. Not until later."

"Has anyone told his family?"

"Doctor called the funeral man and they took him away, and he said he would go to the family. There's a brother, also a miner, that's all."

Sister Carmela thought momentarily of accusing Alfred Noble and his syndicate of this, but knew she never would. They would say it was really her fault for resisting the move and would wash their hands like Pontius Pilate.

She sat heavily on an empty bed and peered about. A single lamp threw yellow light over the place. It seemed to be all right, except for the foul smell, one she had never experienced and found repulsive. There was a closet with a privy in it, which took waste somewhere. Its odor befouled the room. She would ask that something be done.

She rose, moved from patient to patient, lingering longest at the iron cot of the new mother and her infant, fevered, hot-fleshed, and afraid.

"Sister Elizabeth, she needs to have her fever brought down at once," she said.

"Where is there cold water?"

"Eddie, where is water?"

He stared wordlessly, and finally descended to the street. It took a long while, she thought, for him to return. But he carried a bucket brimming with water, and at once two sisters began to sponge the fevered woman.

"Thank you, Eddie. We will need fresh water."

He struggled with words. "Hard to find water," he said.

"Is there a place for you to stay? And what will we do about food?"

He shook his head; the words didn't come. She realized he was very tired; more tired than she had seen him since his injury.

"We will solve these things," she said. "For now, this dawn, let us give thanks."

Twenty-nine

Adelaide hurried through the supper hour and turned the Clover Club over to her barman, Glenn. She had an urgent task before her. Down in her apartment she packed her wicker hamper with beans and cheese and flour for Hard Luck, wrapped a cloak about her, and stepped into a pitch-black November night. The icy air caught her hair. She pulled the hood of her cloak about her and headed upslope, barely seeing where she was going. Ahead, on the ridge, the dim lights of the mine boiler rooms glowed.

She had never been alone on the ridge at night. All the mines were running; their second shifts were underground ripping silver carbonate out of the rock, although a few top men were handling the ore cars as the cages brought them to "grass," as the miners called the surface. That part of the trek wasn't difficult, though a cruel wind toyed with her cloak and eddied cold air about her legs. It was the rest of the trip that scared her.

In a few minutes she was past the last of the mines and into a world of looming darkness, so dark she could not see where she stepped. And yet she had to go, had to reach Yancey with the news. The ridge didn't scare her, but the gulch did. There, the trail crawled along a vast slope, and a false step could send her tumbling hundreds, maybe thousands, of feet. But Yancey had to know, and she had to tell him, and if she walked slowly, testing each step, she would arrive at Yancey's cliff house.

She found courage as she negotiated the trail, and also that keen night vision that comes after all the lights of civilization fade away and there is only starlight to guide a person. The stars above glittered brilliantly in the wintry night. On one side was solid rock, radiating the last of the day's warmth; on the other was the abyss.

She took heart. The trail wasn't long, only a mile or so, and she could even recognize some of the landmarks along the way, especially the side canyons where the trail suddenly dipped, leveled, and climbed steeply. Still, if she fell and hurt herself, she might never be discovered. No one had seen her leave, or walk the ridge, or enter this wild. But her news could not wait.

So she walked slowly, carefully, and no mishap befell her, and in a while she recognized the dry flowage, and then the horseshoe of rock that formed the hollow where the dry spring had once flowed.

"Yancey?" she called. "Yancey?"

She heard nothing but the strange whisper of wild animals in the night. She waited some more, and then he materialized, an obscure presence.

"Adelaide?"

"Oh! Yancey, I didn't know. . . ."

"You're here. At night, on a weekday, when you should be working. Are you all right?"

"I guess so. That cliff . . ."

"What is it, Adelaide?"

She wondered why she had come; why the news that seemed so important to her in Yancey City seemed unimportant here. She peered at him shyly, barely making out the thin odd-looking man beside her.

"I brought you some stuff."

She thrust the wicker basket toward him, and he took it.

"You did? I guess you did. Thank you. I was going to go down to town later this evening and ask you for some."

The silence was awkward, and she felt foolish. "I shouldn't have come," she said.

"I'm glad you came. Would you like to come up to the cliff house?"

She had been there only once, by daylight. "Oh, yes, I was hoping you would invite me."

"I guess I'd better lead you," he said. "These steps up this rock are steep."

She found his waiting hand, and felt his clasp, and liked the firm grip that seemed to end the vertigo that was affecting her. "Adelaide, you're here. I just can't believe it," he said, leading her slowly, one step at a time, up the tiny trail that would top the horseshoe of rock and lead up to the cliff house tucked under the huge overhang.

She felt his hand steer her, guide her, lift her, invite her, warm her, caress her own, and then the hand tugged her over a lip of stone and onto a gentler slope. She clung to that hand, which succored her and filled her with gladness. Then, in starlight, the masonry walls of the cliff house loomed, the home of ancient ones before her. She gladly let him steer her this and that way, around looming walls, up orderly stairs, and onto a flat interior space, and finally into a room vaguely lit by the night. It was warmer there.

She paused, wanting to hug him, resisting an impulse that rose unbidden. They were friends, no more. He had never kissed her, nor would she have let him. Decorum had always ruled, comforting her and making her feel safe. But now it was she, not he, who wanted to cast it aside.

Still, his hand had not released hers, and as soon as he set down the wicker basket his other hand found hers. "I am very glad you came," he said. "I can build up the fire a little, so we can see."

She didn't want to let go of his hands.

"Just a little," she said. "Just a couple of twigs."

"Sit here," he said, and she settled on something that seemed like a buffalo robe or a bear skin. It was warm. She pulled apart her cloak and drew back its hood.

She watched him feed kindling into the coals, watched a tiny flame flicker to life, and then a bright yellow blaze rise from the fire. Some mysterious ventilation drew off the smoke. The flame reflected warmly on solid walls. Suddenly she felt that this was home; his home, but hers also.

The wavering light revealed him; his slender frame, his high forehead, his steady gaze, his reticence. He wasn't used to women visitors in the night and was being very cautious, as if she were something terribly fragile that could break like a crystal goblet.

"Are you thirsty?"

"No, Will, I had supper."

He settled beside her on the robe; it was indeed a buffalo robe he had gotten somewhere. She wondered whether he slept on it.

"You are very sweet," he said.

She wasn't expecting that. She didn't even know why she had come, why she had braved the black night and a dangerous path to this lonely place. She pulled her cloak off, and felt his gaze upon her.

"The sisters left," she said. "The hospital . . ."

"Gone?"

"Not gone. They're in that awful place above the Calabash Club on Copper Street."

"What happened?"

"No one knows, but everyone knows they were driven out. The syndicate claimed the flat and said the sisters didn't own it, and the hospital had to leave. Sister Drill Sergeant refused. They stayed until they were forced to leave." Her voice hardened. "A patient died; a man with a bad heart died when they were carrying him. It's all over town. But nobody's saying much."

He sighed. "Gold does that," he said.

"Gold?"

"That was no pocket, but the same seam that the syndicate hit when they pushed down their shaft in the Minerva Mine. There's a bonanza under the hospital, and now they'll take it all and leave the sisters with nothing."

"Will, how do you know these things?"

"I looked at the ore from the Minerva and the ore at the outcrop below the hospital under a magnifying glass, and did some tests on it."

"They stole the sisters' land and gold, Will."

He nodded. "And my mine too."

"No one can get it back. They've driven you out, and the sisters, and meanwhile they're saying it's all for the good; it means jobs, booming business, plenty for everyone, a town that'll last for generations, peace on earth, goodwill to men."

"Is anyone troubled by this except you?"

"Will, did you hear about Dr. Borden? He walked into Noble's office with a bullwhip and told Noble that nothing but some stripes would cure him! Then he had one of his grand mal attacks and they put him in jail."

Will smiled. It was the first time he smiled. He

reached over to a stack of dried wood and tossed another into the dying flame.

"Are the sisters all right?"

"I guess so. I just get gossip at the club. They're in Blarney O'Rourke's apartment behind his club."

"Is Slow Eddie all right?"

"I don't know, Will. They're up there in that awful room doing what they can, giving love and comfort as best they can. Will, I—I can't bear it, I can't stand this. This whole town, it's becoming a sinkhole, an evil thing, run by evil men, and I shudder to think of what is coming next."

"I'm glad you told me," he said. "Where is the tunnel now?"

"Under the hospital. Every blast shakes the building."

"Fifty yards more," he said.

"To what?"

"To the place where it will be closest to the spring. Then we'll see."

"Tell me, Will."

"If they are careless in their greed, they'll disturb the only water that the town has, and then what?"

"Careless?"

"They're blasting through a layer of impervious granite that forms the floor of a water table. If they open fissures in it, the spring that drains all the limestone strata above it might quit; the underground water might just drop into the fissures in the granite."

"Surely that won't happen, Will . . . would it?"

"I hope not," he said. "Within a few hours or days, there would be nothing left of Yancey City."

Thirty

Hard Luck stared at this woman who had braved a precipitous trail on an inky night to tell him that the syndicate had run the nuns off, and he knew there was something more in it. Why had she struggled through an icy night to tell him that?

"Are you cold?" he asked.

"Yes."

He added piñon pine wood he had gathered to the tiny fire, and she edged closer to it, to the edge of the buffalo robe. She was only inches from him, this generous soul whose love of poetry matched his own. He wanted to reach out to her.

She gazed into the flame, and then gazed at him, and into the flame again.

"Will? I'm afraid."

"I am too," he said.

"Something bad is happening to the town. Everything was all right until the syndicate pushed the sisters out of their land. Everything changed today. I can feel it. The syndicate, it just says it's all for the good; jobs and business and all that. But Will, it's not like that anymore. Everyone's afraid. If the syndicate can push the nuns from land they owned, and steal the gold from under them, then it can do anything, it can run anyone out, it can destroy anyone. It even destroyed a hospital."

"Yes, it has that power," he said.

"Should I leave, Will? I can't sell for much, not for enough to start over, but I'm thinking that something very bad is happening and maybe . . ." Her voice trailed off. "Maybe it's time."

"I have no answer for you, Adelaide. I think maybe it's time to go, all right. I think any time now, they'll destroy the spring. Nearest water is miles away at the bottom of the valley, and no one can afford to haul it that distance. If they do wreck the spring, your place wouldn't be worth a plugged nickel. The town would die. On the other hand, maybe I'm just imagining things. Borrowing trouble."

"Will, you just made up my mind for me."

He was stricken. "Adelaide, I'm just speculating. I don't know. I'd hate to—"

"It's not the spring; it's the place, the city. It's gone bad. Those men, Alfred Noble, how could they do that? What will stop them? They didn't stop until they had stolen all you possessed, didn't stop until they'd driven you out. They never stop, they take whatever they want."

He was filled with such tenderness he couldn't find words to express it. There she was, lovely, vulnerable, widowed, struggling on her own, turning away many men because . . . they didn't like poetry, or whatever was her true reason. She was a mystery to him. There she was, her fate hitched to a town run by a ruthless company, a gang that owned the constable and the justice of the peace, owned the land company, owned or controlled every business, and virtually owned the residents.

She had come a long way through a bitter night to find a safe haven in this ancient dwelling, and he wished he could provide that for her. The ancients too had depended on a spring that failed, and when it failed they had abandoned everything here, so painstakingly built, so comfortable.

"I haven't found any water here," he said. "Except for the seep. It's enough to fill my cup when I need it. I've dug four feet in without using a stick of powder, just with a hammer and pick and pry bar. I just want water. It's the ultimate wealth, you know. It's more valuable than gold. If I find water, I might be able to get back what was stolen from me, what was stolen from the sisters. Then I could help you."

"You're helping me now." She smiled so warmly at him, he thought she was thinking of someone else.

"I'll help you any way I can. You know that. I'll help you pack and move if you want me to."

She smiled fleetingly. "Will, you've helped me all along. You helped me most reading poetry."

That puzzled him.

"I am alone, and what people who are alone need is a kindred spirit," she said.

He wondered who was helping whom. Each time she came, each time he saw her, he was encouraged to go on, keep struggling, keep believing that things would turn out well if he persevered. It wasn't romance; he understood that. But she was the friend he had always wanted, and how could a solitary prospector ask for anything more from life?

"You're the one who's helping me," he said.

He discovered such tenderness in her face, as the firelight washed over it and wavered lightly on her flesh, that he was moved. She reached across the small space between them and took his hand into hers and caught his hand between both of hers, and held his hand in her lap.

"What will happen to us?" she asked.

"I don't know," he said.

There she was, holding his hand in her lap, and that was all he could think about, all that was in his heart. He leaned toward her expectantly; she fixed him in her gaze. He kissed her. She responded, kissing him back. He felt her lips on his, felt the tug of her arms, felt something sweet and ancient flood through him. He lifted her to her feet and drew her into the circle of his arms, there in the gentle yellow light, there in the home of ancients, and he hugged her, not at all tentatively but with a great burst of love, and she wrapped her arms about him and held him wondrously close, and his heart raced.

"Adelaide . . ."

"That's the sweetest poetry of all," she whispered.

He felt her suppleness, felt her melting into him, forming herself to him even as he felt a great rush of something so sweet that he could not fathom its beauty.

The firelight flickered, lighting her brown hair. He ran his hands through it, feeling its thickness in his fingers. He felt the strong stirring of her heart against his own heart, the pressure of her breasts.

Her fingers limned the lines of his face, the very face he had thought so odd and plain, finding his cheekbones and forehead and the muscles of his neck.

They stood there, poised upon a precipice, and then she slowly pulled away, smiling.

"I'm not afraid anymore," she said.

He felt his own heart slow. Slowly, so slowly, he let go. She squeezed his hands in hers.

"Adelaide . . . I'll walk you home if you'd like."

"I'd like that very much, Will."

"I know the path, and I can get past the constable all right."

"If you would take me to the mines, I would be all right."

"I want to take you home. I need to know you're safe."

She smiled at him. The little fire had died, and only the embers revealed her soft smile.

"I didn't help much," he said. "You wanted to know what to do. I have no answer."

She brushed a finger to his lips, as if to still such thoughts, and drew her cloak around her. She looked lovely, wrapped tightly in that flowing cloak, its hood rising behind her undone hair.

He found his old jumper, left over from mining days, slipped it on, and they pierced into a brittle night.

"Oh!" she exclaimed, amazed at the icy air that eddied down from Table Mountain some mysterious distance above. He led her down the steep slope, his feet floating on air. It was so strange, how his body floated, how strong and alive he felt, as he helped her. He held her as she took each step, notched in stone, until they reached the horseshoe of the dry spring and the way leveled out. There he found her hand, or intuitively they found each other's hands, and walked slowly through darkness, lit now by a sliver of moon. When they reached the place where the trail curved along a precipice, he placed her in front, and held her as she stepped gingerly, both of them aware of the long plunge at their right, into a misty abyss silvered by the palest of light. After they reached the ridge they walked side by side, their hands clasped tight.

At the first of the mines she turned to him: "I can find my way now. Thank you, Will."

"I'll take you home."

"But the constable . . ."

"He's easy to dodge."

She seemed glad of the company, and they slipped past the mines, past men unloading ore cars by the light of dim lamps, and finally cut down the ridge on an obscure trail to Silver Street, and then Gold. They saw no one in the misty cold night.

"I'm all right now, Will, thank you," she said.

"I want to take you to your door, Adelaide."

She peered at him in the night, happy with his gallantry, and they slipped quietly down the street, staying in shadow, until they reached the door of her apartment under the Clover Club. There in the dark they waited quietly for a man to pass, and then she turned to him.

"You are a poet," she said.

He did not fathom her words.

They stood at the fateful door, not wanting to part. She had wrapped her cloak tight against the chill. She reached upward and kissed him gently, and then urgently, and he responded like a budding flower to the brightness of the sun.

"Adelaide—"

"I'll see you soon," she said. "Thank you. I'm not afraid any more. This evening was . . . a miracle."

He was tongue-tied, and all he could do was squeeze her hand.

She opened her door and with a small nod slipped into the darkness within, and loneliness and longing engulfed him. And puzzlement too. How could any woman care for a penniless and homeless man?

She liked him as he was, and not as what he thought he had to be. His whole world had turned upside down. He didn't have to get rich to win a woman. It didn't really matter to a woman he loved and who loved him.

Thirty-one

A former flophouse on Copper Street was no place for a hospital, and no place for sisters, but it was the only place. And in its way, it was an oddly sweet place, offering healing and hope in the heart of a street of vices. Sister Carmela wrestled with unexpected troubles, such as the vagrants and drunks who ascended the stair only to find they weren't welcome. Sometimes Slow Eddie had to force them out; once Dr. Borden roared them off. Swiftly the city found out where the hospital had gone, and found its way to the door.

The sisters' quarters in Blarney O'Rourke's cramped apartment at the rear of the Calabash Club were next to impossible; there was room for only two cots, and some of the sisters had only a small pad on the plank floor to sleep on.

The only thing that had worked well was food service. O'Rourke had seen to meals, and sent them up three times daily, a gift from his saloon. She wondered how that kind man could bear the burden, but he just shrugged off her worries.

But what she lacked most, and felt the want of most severely, was a chapel, for there was nowhere the sisters could retire to renew their faith. Copper Street itself was a problem. Next to the Calabash were half-a-dozen saloons, a dance hall, a variety theater, and other places whose purposes she scarcely dared to inquire about. Rising out of the night at all hours were shouts, the music of a battered piano, an occasional bark of a revolver, and drifting conversations as men passed on the streets below.

She didn't have time to yearn for better quarters; no sooner had they had settled and won some sort of order from the chaos than Yancey City was besieged by waves of sickness brought on by the autumnal change in climate. Sweaty miners, fresh from the warm pits, plunged into the whipping winter winds blowing off the ridge, and found themselves fevered with pneumonia. The syndicate provided no changing rooms at the mines. Her temporary hospital was soon overflowing. Every bed was filled with a sick bachelor miner who had no one to care for him in his humble shanty or flat. Most had double pneumonia. Two were probably not going to survive the cruel fever, the rattling, congested lungs, the loss of air.

The sisters, none of whom was well herself, toiled on, lowering fevers with constant sponging, spooning broth into their sick patients, helping the sick up the long dark stairway to the gloomy ward above O'Rourke's saloon. Sister Mary, the oldest, seemed particularly weary, and Isabella was suffering her usual mild fever. But they never faltered. They comforted the sick, changed dressings, administered pills and potions, cooled the feverish, washed bedclothes, held the hands of the frightened, and always found time for morning prayer, evening prayer, and their own holy offices.

Another problem was finding a place for Slow Eddie. He was never more needed, yet there was no nest for him. He had taken to sleeping on a pad in a corner of that ward, trying to rest among the coughs and wheezes of the sick, trying to stay healthy in a place that threatened health, trying to help when he was weary.

She would have to report to the motherhouse; this could not continue, nor would these quarters win the approval of her superiors. She feared the hospital would be closed and the sisters required to abandon Yancey City just when they were needed more than ever before.

Sometimes she thought of the snug little hospital down on the meadow, so quiet and serene and restful that it seemed to heal patients all by itself, and then she was filled with a yearning and sorrow beyond anything she had known. But the hospital was gone forever. It had been occupied the very next day by the syndicate, which had transferred its offices there. And the meadow, once full of birdsong, was a jumble of mining and milling machinery now, and shouting gangs of men erecting a mill and a mine head.

But there was no time to brood, nor did it accomplish anything. Yancey City had fallen into sickness, and for every patient cramming that upstairs room there were twenty lying abed in the cabins and flats and boarding-houses around town. She barely saw Dr. Borden, who rushed from one critical case to another, in and out of the Calabash Club twice a day, looking more and more ragged. Sheer exhaustion had weakened him, and she heard he was suffering more grand mal seizures now, sometimes every second or third day, all over town, and these had convulsed him more terribly than before. And yet in his steady, disheveled, patient way he ministered to a multitude.

Then Sister Mary's heart failed her.

Isabella burst into the ward, where Carmela was applying cold compresses to a fevered miner.

"Come! Come!" she cried.

Carmela wrung the compress, let it soak in more cold water, and placed it gently over the miner's chest. "I'll be back in a moment," she said to the fevered man.

She found Sister Mary lying on a cot in the apartment, her face blue and still, her mouth an open circle.

"Oh, no," Carmela cried, kneeling beside the stricken woman, who opened her eyes briefly, recognized Carmela, closed them, sighed, and fell limp.

Carmela knew at once the sister had died. Her old body had not been able to bear the strain. She leaned over Sister Mary, made the sign of the cross above her, and gently closed her open eyes, which saw nothing at all now. Carmela felt the rising of grief within her, no matter that this lovely old nun had gone to be with her Lord. With the Lord Mary might be, but Carmela knew only loss, desolation at this moment of parting.

"Isabella, we must have Dr. Borden come," she said. "Could you find him, or send Eddie?"

"Is she gone?"

"She is with God."

"Oh, Sister . . ." Isabella, the youngest and newest of them, knelt beside the warm body, clad in winter-black, and prayed. Carmela joined her, then remembered that a critically ill miner needed cold compresses, that the demands of a hospital never slowed, never ceased, never spared her a moment for sorrow. She had a life to preserve if she could. Wearily she stood, held Isabella's shoulders as she prayed, and then clambered slowly back to the noisome ward where a dozen others fought to live and some would lose that struggle.

She pushed back a bitter thought, that this death could be laid to the syndicate, and dismissed it as unworthy. There would be no blame in the death of a gray old sister, no, not Noble, no, not the Rhode Island Syndicate. No . . . But she knew in her bones that if they had been able to stay in that sweet sanctuary on the spring meadow, as they had planned, Sister Mary would have been with them for years to come.

Somehow, all the necessary things got done, largely through the swift sure hand of Blarney O'Rourke. Dr. Borden listened with his listening horn and found no sign of life. The undertaker gently carried Sister Mary away. A wire was sent to Leavenworth, and another to her family in Wilmington, Delaware. Another summoned a priest from Denver.

The sisters, in their checked gingham aprons, worked numbly; one cannot abandon the sick and wounded and desperate, so they continued with their chores and their ministry, and even through the pall of their own sorrow, they healed and comforted and prayed. All of Yancey City, it seemed, heard the news and offered help, and in time, as town women flooded in to help, the sisters could leave the ward to them and draw into their small haven and comfort one another.

And in Sister Mary's death came an awakening in town; one by one, miners, their families, merchants, teamsters, woodcutters, water carriers, children, offered to help build a real hospital, one they hoped would memorialize the fallen sister, one that would pluck the suffering sisters from Copper Street and give them a proper convent and a proper hospital.

Sister Carmela received all these things with gratitude, and sent the donations to the bank. Maybe Yancey City would have a real hospital again; maybe all this had fallen to them because of Sister Mary's death.

Sister Mary was buried two days later. A priest, Monsignor O'Byrne, did manage to come clear from Denver, and sing a solemn requiem Mass in O'Rourke's

Calabash Club, where Sister Mary lay on a wreath-be-decked poker table.

Then the cortege wound its slow and solemn way up Copper Street to Gold, to Silver, to Mineral, and then to the ridge, and over to the Yancey Cemetery in the sloping barrens beyond, the only land anywhere nearby where there was soil enough to bury the dead. The whole city followed behind the caisson that carried the plain pine box and the shawl-wrapped sisters walking behind it; the grieving, the curious, the grateful. The cortege headed toward the Minerva Mine, past huge piles of rubble, and then over the windy top, past the stark cruciform gallows frames that rose from that ridgetop Golgotha into the gray November heavens, and down a rutted trail to a stark place where a thin hole had been carved in the clay.

"And there they said good-bye to one of their own.

Even Alfie Noble was there, clad in black, smiling kindly.

When the burying was done, and Father O'Byrne had scattered a handful of dust over the grave, Noble slipped up to Sister Carmela and handed her an envelope.

"The syndicate wants you to have this, as a memorial," he said. "It's a deed for two lots, with thanks from the Town Lot Company and the syndicate."

Sister Carmela nodded. She wanted very much to be grateful.

Noble smiled widely, and retreated into the crowd that was slowly filtering back to Yancey City.

There was no time to grieve. Back at the Calabash Club, the sisters thanked the volunteers who had vigiled with the sick during the funeral, and there too was Dr. Borden, watching over a dying boy who had caught catarrh three days earlier after his shift in the Poco Loco, and then contracted pneumonia; and Slow Eddie, changing the bed linens of the dead.

Everything was as it was before, except that the sisters had two lots on the extreme upper end of town, farther from the life-giving spring than anywhere else in the city. And they were one fewer.

Thirty-two

Alfred Noble, the Friend of the Working Man, moved his office into the chapel of the hospital, finding the arrangement quite marvelous. He placed his polished cherrywood desk right where the altar had been, but left the altar rail in place; a natural, subtle barrier that kept fools at bay. Let the them kneel. From his new aerie he could gaze out upon the vast valley below him, and the distant mountains lost in haze. Of course that view would soon be marred by the new stamp mill that was rising right at the new mine head, but one couldn't have everything.

He turned the old ward into an office for the accountants and buyers and supervisors, and gave Gus Moran the old cubicle occupied by Sister Carmela. Let poor old Gus toil in a windowless warren. It amused Noble. This was the place to be: level ground, the only level spot in dozens of square miles, and right atop the richest strike Colorado had seen in years.

He summoned Gus, who appeared at once. Like most everyone entering his new office, Gus didn't quite know what to do with the altar rail. Some of the clerks even genuflected. But Moran negotiated the rail and pulled up beside Noble.

"It's a grand view, isn't it, Gus?" Noble said, waving

a languid hand. "One can see almost to Silverton, give or take a dozen ridges."

"I wish I had a view," Gus responded, which was the effect that Noble desired from his observation.

Noble smiled broadly. "We'll saw a window in your fine office someday, Gus, if you'll pay for the glass."

"You summoned me?"

"A report; it's time for the weekly report."

Moran had a folder in his hand, and proceeded to open it and examine its contents.

"The adit is a hundred twenty-seven yards in, as of yesterday, and the ore values are constant, according to daily assays. But the seam has thickened and is now two feet, with a two-inch high-grade stratum at its base. Width as yet unknown, but we cannot say until we do some crosscuts. Ore at the mine head should yield about a hundred twenty ounces to the ton, and the values remain constant.

"The drift from the Minerva shaft is proceeding more slowly because of ventilation and lift problems, but next week, probably Tuesday, there should be a junction between the drift and the bore under here, at a point about fifty yards north of here. This bore's advancing three yards a day, with three shifts; the one from the Minerva's advancing two yards a day. But Tuesday, maybe Wednesday, we'll blast through. After that, it's gravy. All the gold ore will exit the mine from here. When we complete laterals between the Minerva and the silver works on the ridge, we can bring the silver carbonate ore out of here also.

"We should save five thousand a month just in lift costs, and can abandon four of the five shafts on the ridge, using them solely for ventilation. And we can shut down the ventilation systems because the new bore will ventilate every mine on the ridge when the laterals are done. We can run water from the spring right to the boiler here, by gravity feed, instead of using all those water wagons to haul it up to the ridge. We can discharge twelve boiler men in the process. The only water going uphill after we're set up will be for domestic use in town."

Noble smiled broadly, and poured himself some Wildroot Tonic, which he now had shipped in from Silverton on the stagecoach. Wildroot always put him in a jolly mood.

"Now, Gus, let's look at the hard part, transportation."

Moran handed Noble a letter. "This arrived an hour ago," he said.

Noble scanned it swiftly. It was from the Department of Engineering of the Denver and Rio Grande Railroad. It said that a spur twenty-three miles from Silverton would be too costly to consider unless the telluride gold strike proved to be much larger than presently indicated. There would be three trestles and five tunnels, one of them 170 feet, and four bridges, for an average cost of $79,000 a mile. However, if the gold strike should embrace two or three mines and show evidence of lasting five years or more, the line might be built provided that the Rhode Island Syndicate put up half the cost.

"This is not good, Gus. It's the transportation that's killing us. We could double our profit if we had a spur in here. Have you looked at narrow gauge?"

"I have. We can build a narrow-gauge spur ourselves for four hundred seventy-nine thousand, plus rolling stock, three engines, and other equipment, for two hundred twenty thousand."

Noble sank back in his swivel chair, frustrated. The telluride gold ore, sorted, crushed, and hauled by mule in canvas sacks to Silverton and then to the Denver smelters, was earning only a thirty percent annual profit on invest-

ment; with a railroad the profit could run sixty-five percent. The silver ore, sorted and shipped by wagon down
the long grade also to Silverton, where it was milled, was
no longer profitable, but would be very profitable with a
railroad. And with rails, reserves would quadruple because of the vast amount of low-grade ore still in the
mines, but unusable under current circumstances.

"I've finished pricing an ore chute," Moran said. "It'd
cost seven thousand to build a chute from the mine head
here down to the valley floor. There's some gulches to
span, and it wouldn't be cheap. As long as we're milling
up here, it pays to use mules and oxen. A railroad would
change everything. All we'd need to do is chute the ore
right down that grade and into hopper cars."

Noble didn't like it. "We're in a pickle, Gus," he said,
pursing his lips into a wide smile. "Do we want to wait
for a railroad and a sixty-five-percent profit for investors, or do we want to mine at a humdrum profit?
Our investors want a lot more than thirty percent, and
there'll be a committee out here looking us over if we
let them down."

Moran shrugged. "Me, I'd ship out enough ore for a
few weeks to keep everyone happy, finish the new bore
and connect it, do some crosscuts and complete the
basic exploration so we know what's underground, and
then shut down."

"I was thinking along the same lines."

"Shut her right down. Let 'em all go. Keep a guard or
two around to protect property. Then just sit on it.
Maybe, if you want to gamble, do more exploring on the
other side of the shaft. That gold seam heads straight
through the ridge and under that plateau, and we need
to know what's happening in that direction. Then wait
for the railroad to get hungry."

"They're going to hate us, Gus."

"Listen, Alfie, there's only profit and loss, making money or losing it. We ain't a charity. We ain't in the business of supporting a bunch of stiffs; they're meat, they're muscle, and they can go somewhere else and sell their muscles. This town ain't worth a crap anyway, perched on the ridge, built of green lumber, cheap as could be, because everyone knows no one's going to stay around here."

Noble stretched. "Sometimes I wonder if we owe them a little stability."

"What for? Every ton of ore we take out of there and sell at a loss means we're subsidizing those stiffs, paying them more'n they're worth."

Noble smiled. "Gus, you're my conscience!"

"Then I deserve a raise."

"By God, so you do," Noble said. "What I'm going to do is issue you some stock in the syndicate. Ten shares, a bonus. We might shut down, but when we open up in a few years, you'll turn that into a bonanza."

Moran shuffled his papers. "I still got stuff to talk about."

"Yes, the land office. Here's what I want you to do, Gus. Tell our sales clerks to put every remaining lot on sale for half price. We've got a hundred eighty-three lots left, and I want them cut from two hundred to one hundred, and if that doesn't move them, cut them to seventy-five or fifty. With a little luck we can sell off every lot before we shut down Yancey City. Tell them I want the whole platted townsite sold out in six weeks, and don't tell them why. That should net a few thousand. Tell 'em we'll deduct the payments from the pay envelopes. It's a little gravy for our shareholders."

"You think of everything, Alfie."

"That's what I'm paid a small fortune to do."

A sharp thump rattled the old hospital, followed by a

shiver and a roar that seemed to rise from the bedrock. It took a moment to subside. This blast seemed different, almost eerie, as if the earth had been offended by it. But Noble loved each boom; and sometimes he lifted his Wildroot Tonic and swilled a little just to celebrate another three feet of granite and quartz lying in rubble down there.

"Not as bad now," Noble said. "They're thirty yards beyond the hospital and getting farther away with each shot. In a day or so they'll be past the flat entirely. When we first moved in, I thought they'd blow the building down." He smiled toothily. "It was built to last, this place. The miners didn't throw it up; they built it right."

Noble straightened up. "Now, Gus, everything that we've discussed is between us. I don't want one word to leak. If it does, I'll know who to blame. We're going to go for the high-grade for the next few weeks, and we're going to explore with crosscuts, and then we're going to shut down and wait for rails. It may take a year or two, but we'll wait. Our investors will be told they'll get two thirds to three quarters back on their investment each year, after we resume, and we'll have less labor trouble and overhead. But this depends on silence."

"You've got it," Moran said.

There was some stirring in the outer office, some shouting, and Noble wondered what it was all about. He rose, stretched grandly, nodded Moran off, watched him negotiate the altar rail, and then headed for the bullpen.

He found some of the water men, the fellows who loaded springwater into the great casks on wagon wheels that paraded up to Yancey City all day, every day, to feed the mine boilers and supply water for every residence and business in town.

"Something's happened to the spring!" one yelled.

Thirty-three

Alfie Noble stared aghast at the spring. No water issued forth, not a drop. The red granite over which it had tumbled glistened moistly. The small pool at the base, carved out over aeons by falling water, glimmered in the sunlight. A crowd had collected around the stricken spring, staring silently at it. Beside it, half-a-dozen water wagons waited in a line, their drivers standing helplessly before the spring and the pipe driven into it that had filled the wagons, one after another, for all the years that the mines had operated.

That iron pipe had dripped its last drop. No overflow from the small granite pool tumbled downslope toward the valley. Where thirty gallons a minute of sweet cold water had tumbled from the base of the gray limestone, now there was nothing. Where an entire city and its mines had drawn water, now there was no water to draw. Some of those wagons trundled water up to the mine heads, where the water was poured into the boilers that ran the steam engines that powered the lifts and the pumps that ran fresh air into the pits. The rest of the water found its way into every household, every business, every saloon and restaurant, every laundry, every bathhouse and tonsorial parlor. It had been piped into the old hospital, where it supplied water to the officers of the Rhode Island Syndicate, and would have supplied water to the mill.

Gus Moran, who knew more about practical mining and geology, joined Noble.

"That last blast in the bore settled something in there where the spring is. We can blow it open," he said.

"That's it! Blow it open!" Noble said.

Moran sent a clerk on the double for a face crew from the bore to blow the spring.

"Tell 'em to bring powder and drills," Moran yelled.

The clerk scrambled back toward the hospital, and down the grade to the adit.

"Where's the closest water?" Noble asked.

"Sourdough Springs, down in the valley almost five miles, and about three thousand feet lower. It's a long way down a mountainside, Alfie, no place for wagons to pass."

"We'll blow this open, but meanwhile we'll need a little water for a few hours," Noble said. He approached one of the men driving a company water wagon for the mines. "You. Get the company men together and fill up at Sourdough Springs. Moran'll give you directions."

"At the bottom of the valley?" the man asked. "These here two nags can't haul that much water uphill like that. Too much grade."

"How much will they haul?"

"Maybe a quarter of a load. If it gets too heavy, I may have to drain some of that. You need six horses to haul a load like that up here, and they're gonna need water themselves."

"Then bring all you can."

"That's a ten-mile round trip. It's three in the afternoon."

"Do it!"

The teamster shrugged. He walked over to the rest of

the company water men. "Boss wants water from Sourdough Springs."

They stared at Noble as if he were daft.

Noble walked over to them. "We'll get this running again, blow it loose. Now we need some emergency water. If the boilers quit, men'll be trapped in the pits, the lifts won't work, no way up."

"So how are we going to load water down there? Does Sourdough Springs have a pipe like this?" the teamster asked, pointing to the iron pipe that projected from the wall of rock.

"Take buckets," Moran said.

"You know how long it takes to fill up one of these water wagons with buckets?"

"Don't tell me what you can't do; show me what you can do."

"Where are we gonna get a dozen buckets?"

Noble whirled, located another clerk. "Get every bucket in the hardware store."

The clerk trotted off.

The crowd kept growing. Word had reached town, and now scores of people were trotting down the hairpin curves to see for themselves. Some carried buckets, intending to fill them up at the pool.

A teamster watered his horses at the pool and started his private water wagon down the long grade to the valley.

"You'll make money!" Noble said, smiling broadly.

"That's what I figure. I've got a long trip and it better pay out," the man said. "Ought to fetch me a dollar a gallon." Other independent teamsters, the ones who supplied housewives with water, followed suit. By the time their teams had watered, the little pool was half empty, and well fouled.

In all, five wagons rattled down the endless grade that would take them to Sourdough Springs.

"If we can't blow this open, then what?" Moran asked.

Noble did not want to think about that, so he smiled broadly at the crowd, which was hanging on to every word. "It'll be fine; we'll have water as soon as we rattle this rock a bit," he said.

Off-shift miners, a few women, a handful of businessmen, all stared. Some were saloonkeepers, whose need for water was urgent. One enterprising youth appeared with a bucket, scooped water from the dwindling pool, and started uphill.

The enormous effect of all this was only just permeating through Alfred Noble. This was doom. Without water, the mines would close. The town would shut down. Within forty-eight hours an entire city would depart. And mostly on foot, because there would be no water for livestock. Within seventy-two hours there would not even be water to keep a few guards around the mines. Within three or four days there would not be a soul in Yancey City, nor could the mines yield their treasure, nor would the Rhode Island Syndicate earn a dime, nor would anyone get paid. Noble was so shocked that he could scarcely fathom this disaster.

"Where else is there water, Gus?"

"We've looked. We've been to the top of Table Mountain. There ain't any, dry washes, maybe they run when there's some snowmelt. You have to go clear over to the San Juans for steady water; lots of it there. Maybe eight or nine miles. Dam a creek up high somewhere and pipe it over here, gravity feed."

Noble sighed. It would take most of a year to build a flume or pipe system from that distance to Yancey. Eventually someone would figure out how to do it, and what the cost would be. But if this spring didn't open up, the mines of Yancey City would shut down.

And that was obvious to every soul standing there helplessly, seeing the lifeblood of a city vanish.

"I'm thirsty!" yelled a jug-eared boy.

"Gimme some beer," yelled a miner. "Who needs water?"

The crowd swiftly increased, as scores, then even hundreds, of people surged down the hairpin curves from the city, and arrayed themselves silently before the dead spring.

At last the face crew from the bore appeared, lugging heavy equipment. One young man toted a red powder box. These were burly singlejackers who could drive a drill a foot into granite in minutes.

"All right, clear away, this is dangerous, stand back," Gus Moran yelled, but the crowd didn't move.

The crew eyed the dead spring as if it were a failed god, something to propitiate to bless them again.

"Blow it open. Pull out that iron pipe and lay a charge in there," Moran said. "Biggest damned charge you've ever shot."

It took a while to find some ladders, but eventually the face crew yanked the six-inch diameter iron pipe out of the cliff and began stuffing waxy red sticks of dynamite into the wet hole. They kept peering at Noble and Moran with doubtful expressions, wondering whether this was the right thing to do.

"Faster! We haven't a drop of water for a whole city!" Moran yelled. "It's all up to you."

The face crew gingerly stuffed sticks into the hole.

One of them cut open a stick and gently slid a copper-clad fulminate cap into the gelatinous dynamite, attached a few feet of Bickford fuse, wired it all together, and slowly slid the detonator deep into the hole until only the fuse dangled from the dead spring.

"What do you think happened?" Noble asked Moran.

"A blast from the bore shook up that limestone and it sealed up the spring."

"Then it'll open up when we blow it?"

Moran paused ominously. "Let's hope so. The other possibility is too grim to think about."

"What's that?"

"Well, this spring is right where the limestone rests on the granite. The limestone is stratified and carries water through it from up on Table Mountain, but the granite underneath is hard and not fractured and impervious, like a watertight floor. Or was until now. If a blast from the tunnel opened a crack in it, and there's someplace down in there for the water to go, then the spring is draining straight down into granite somewhere back inside the mountain, halfway down to hell, and we'll never see it."

That shot a chill through Noble.

The face crew swiftly loaded the spring, and began yelling to the crowd to stand back.

"Not far enough. We've got forty-eight sticks in there! You, sirs, get back all the way to the old hospital and inside. Stay away from windows," said the shift foreman, who had emerged from the bore.

Noble didn't need persuading.

"All right, but get those spectators out, up the hill, back to town."

It took another half hour just to clear the crowd. Noble and Moran and the clerks watched from below the hospital, where some milling machinery promised protection.

The clocks had all stopped, or so it seemed. A city's

life hung in balance. Mining supervisors cleared every man out of the bore that ran under the flat.

"Cross your fingers, Noble," said Moran, "because if this don't work, you and me are unemployed."

"We'll find water."

Moran laughed shortly.

The crowd had turned quiet. Not a sound filtered through the air. Everyone was at least a hundred yards from the spring, and most people were much farther. Many held their hands over their ears.

"We ready?" yelled the boss of the face crew.

The foreman studied the surrounding cliffside, the crowds at a safe distance, and nodded. "It'll blow toward the hospital, not up behind the spring. You gents stand behind the hospital until it's over. And watch out for falling rock."

Noble and Moran and the clerks retreated further, until the hospital stood between them and the spring.

The crew lit the fuse and ran sideways along the escarpment.

The blast shook the earth under their feet, deafened everyone, and the shock threw one clerk to the ground. The crack and boom blew out the side of the mountain, thundered across the hazy valley, and echoed darkly in the distance. Rock hailed down, driving Noble and Moran inside, where they heard it clatter on the roof. Acrid fumes bellied out from the blast, choking them. In one moment, a thunderous boom rolled through Yancey City.

When the dust settled, Noble and Moran and the rest trotted toward the cliff where the spring had run. Now there was a great cavity dished into the gray cliff, and rubble strewn everywhere, filling the little pool. Gray and red rock littered the whole area. But not a drop of water flowed.

"My God," Noble said, staring in awe at the ruin of a choice corner of the world.

"Maybe it's going to boil up," Moran said.

But no water dribbled forth. What had been a magnificent spring was now an ugly cavity. Where trees and brush had found precious water, now not a splinter of wood remained.

A crowd collected around the ruin of the spring, more and more people flooding down from Yancey City, all intent on seeing with their own eyes the doom of the mining district.

No one spoke. It was weirdly quiet. But every soul knew that all was lost, that the lucky would have horse and wagon to haul away their goods, but that most would plod down the mountain on foot, carrying only what they could load on their backs, and that they would be half famished for water by the time they reached Sourdough Springs only a few miles away.

Yancey City had died.

Thirty-four

It took only moments for Alfred Noble, superintendent of the Rhode Island Syndicate mining properties, to see the immediate future. Before his eyes, residents of Yancey City were racing upslope to capture whatever potable liquid they could get their hands on, and then load up whatever they could carry.

No water.

The saloons would be stripped of beer in a few minutes. Restaurants and cafes would find themselves robbed of every drop of water in their tanks. When the first water wagons arrived from Sourdough Springs that evening, there would be a frenzy, fistfights, and half the water would be spilled. And the water haulers probably wouldn't get paid.

His gaze caught the plumes of smoke rising along the ridge. The mines would need to shut down at once, while their boilers still had steam enough to lift the men out of the pits.

"Gus! Send men to all the mines and tell them to get the miners out. Five bells!"

But Moran had already begun that process, and among those scrambling upslope were company clerks, some with sleeve garters, braving the November cold.

"There's hell to pay," Moran said.

But Alfie Noble was in command, smooth and unflappable and thinking ahead. "Gus, there's not much time. I don't know how long a town this size can last without water. I don't even know how much water's in my own home; how much Gertrude has. We've got to make some decisions fast. What are we taking and what are we leaving? And how can we protect what we're leaving?"

Noble prided himself on his swift and rational decision-making, and now his mind was racing ahead of the tribulation, thinking of how best to cope.

"How the hell should I know?" Moran responded, suddenly petulant.

Noble took it for a sign of what was to come. Even his right-hand man was panicking. Within minutes, Noble would no longer be able to command anyone; his orders wouldn't count. He thought of sending the next ore wagon he saw to his house so he could load up Gertrude and as much as they could carry down the slope. But that depended on whether the teamster would be obedient. He knew at once that nothing he could do or say would affect men trying to save their own hides. Or protect their families. Or commandeer a company wagon to haul their worldly goods to safety. Force was required.

How much time was there really? He saw no panic, no mob gathering, no looting. For a moment all was well. But only for a moment. Once the reality settled in, once those wives in their cottages, and businessmen in their stores, and saloon men behind their bars, got wind of it, the false calm would vanish.

Even then there would be lunatic holdouts, people who were certain the water would flow, that some divine intervention would restore order, supply water, and the town would proceed just as it had. There would always be fools like that, whistling through the graveyard of their dreams.

Then there would be another sort, loosed by crisis: looters, armed men, bullies and thugs, snatching water, snatching valuables, a swift and sinister pillage of the whole city. These would be the ones who would commandeer the last horses and wagons at gunpoint, and these would be the ones riding off with the wealth of the dying city in their wagon beds.

"Gus, round up these company men. And head up to the ridge. I want you to get ahold of every security man we have, and Cruikshank too if you can find him. Load the high-grade ore into any ore wagon you can find. If the miners won't do it, some shotguns should persuade them. We're going to get every ore wagon that has a team attached to it, and we're going to load the high-grade ore, up at the Minerva and down here, and we're going to send them to Silverton. And the guards are going to shoot anyone who interferes or tries to grab a wagon."

"Good. We can move ten tons of ore out of here with a little luck," Moran said.

He began collaring company men, starting with the face crew that had just accomplished the enormous blast that dished the spring. His discipline held: The crew trotted toward the ridge, where a large pile of gold ore rested beside the Minerva.

"And don't pocket any of that ore, or you'll be in trouble," Moran yelled.

"You'd better go up there and grab the security guards," Noble said. "I want shotguns showing."

Moran nodded. "Anything else?"

"Yeah, take by force whatever water you can find, and store it at the Minerva, in our old offices."

"There ain't gonna be much. This town was always on the edge, with nothing but water wagons."

"There's going to be some half-full water wagons in residential neighborhoods. Get that water, by force. If a water man resists, shoot him."

Moran smiled.

Noble watched his dutiful second stride off to set their schemes in motion. Moran had owned one of the mines, the Poco Loco, until he swapped it for a share in the syndicate.

Noble retreated to the old hospital, and found glass everywhere and no one in the building. The blast had blown out every window. It no longer mattered. He passed the altar rail, and dug around in his desk for his blue tonic bottle, and loosed a terrific jolt of it down his parched throat. In moments he was feeling just fine. He headed for the water pitcher, and found it full of cool springwater, as always. He poured a tumbler of it, and then another, and then he carefully hid the remaining water in his desk drawer, an ace in the hole. No one, absolutely no one, poked around in the desk of Alfred Noble.

He headed outside again, past the heaped-up heavy equipment that would have gone into the mill. Now he would have to sell it, but that could wait. Equipment like that didn't walk off. The road to the spring was alive; people moving in both directions, some to gawk at the dry cleft in the rock, others to spread the word in town and start packing.

The road leading way down to the valley floor, and to Silverton, had no traffic at all; no one was leaving. Not yet anyway. Tomorrow, unless the water started flowing, it would be jammed. He paused at the dry spring, and found it mute and gloomy. The merry waters no longer splashed.

Later, he would send in salvage crews to strip everything valuable from the dying town; not just company property but the tons of furniture and clothing and even heirlooms left behind. The syndicate would retrieve the company property; he would keep the rest as a bonus.

An unnatural thirst built in him, and he ascribed it to his imagination. A city without water! Not a drop anywhere! It made his tongue twitch. He smiled his way uphill, smiled past the hordes, the miners in their jumpers, the shrill children, the frowning businessmen all trotting down to the dead spring.

He arrived at last at his own blessed house on Silver Street, and Gertie met him in the sunny parlor.

"What was that awful roar, Alfred?" she asked.

"Never mind that; the spring died. We're leaving tomorrow. I'll have a wagon for us."

"Leaving?"

"No water. Not a drop."

"But Alfred . . . ," she said, waving at an entire household. "I can't pack. . . ."

"We'll get it later. There won't be anyone here to take it."

That wasn't true, but it would calm her.

"But Alfred," she said, and began to dissolve in tears. "But Alfred . . ."

"There, there now. You've never liked this place. It's a mean place. Now we'll go."

"But I love this house. It's all I have, this house, with its view. It's all I possess."

She dabbed at her eyes with a fresh cotton handkerchief. She wore lilac cologne well, and this day the lilac filled the parlor and permeated her voluminous ivory dress.

"Gertie, listen to me! It's God's will that this town be shut down. The saloons! The low houses and evil places.

This is God's will, shutting off water to these lowlifes here who disturb the moral harmony of Yancey City and despoil our safety and peace. Think of it as God's revenge on the criminals who were lining Copper Street."

Noble saw her calm at once, absorbed in this new theological equation.

He patted her veined hand. "There now. You pack a little bag, the things you'll need, and before you know it, we'll catch a train at Silverton and go back to Rhode Island."

"Oh, Alfie," she said, squeezing his hand.

He extracted his paw from her clutch, headed for the kitchen, downed a full glass of cool clear springwater from a pitcher there, and headed into the sullen streets of Yancey City. He needed to go up to the ridge to make sure his instructions were being followed.

He found quietness in the street; no exodus. People were waiting to see whether the company would miraculously discover water and save the day.

There, he at once ran into the last person he wanted to see, Rufus Borden, whose massive frame loomed over him. Borden's glare blistered into him.

"Noble!"

The power of that voice arrested the superintendent in his tracks. "Yes?"

"So it came to pass. Exactly as Hard Luck Yancey said it would." Borden's thick hand caught Noble's suit jacket.

"Hard Luck? The prophet?"

"He warned of it," Borden said. "Any student of geology might have predicted it. He told the sisters to beware of it. I want a big and empty wagon sent to the hospital, and whatever water you can scrounge. We're going to move the hospital again."

"That's not possible."

"I have six patients who shouldn't be moved. But we'll have to move them. I have four Sisters of Charity in my charge. I am going to move them to Silverton as gently as I can in one of your ore wagons. And you'll supply a team, enough water, and a good teamster."

"Unhand me," Noble said.

"We'll go together to the ridge and you'll get me an ore wagon."

Noble laughed. "Sorry, Doc. They're going to be used to clean up the gold."

Thirty-five

The winds of trouble blew into the Clover Club soon after that disturbing boom downslope that had rattled Adelaide's building and set her to wondering.

Several miners burst in, laid coin on the bar, and bought beer. Most of her beer she dispensed from casks, using a faucet in the bunghole. But she kept a few corked bottles on hand, and these were snapped up.

"What is it?" she asked.

"The spring quit," one replied.

"The spring?"

"Company fired a round underground there, and it dried up. So they tried to loosen it up with that blast you heard, and it didn't do nothing. There's not a drop for miles around."

"But this town! How will it live?"

The miner laughed and turned his thumb down.

Dizzily she sold out her beer and what little she had of brewed coffee and a pitcher of lemonade. Men crowded in wanting liquids, and with every passing second they grew meaner and more desperate.

Finally a gang of them hoisted one of her beer kegs to its shoulders and started off.

"Wait! Pay me!" she cried, but they didn't slow down.

Within minutes there wasn't a drop of potable liquid

in the Clover Club, but that didn't stop miners from swarming in, ransacking the place, and scowling at her.

Then one young man she had never seen before pleaded with her. "I got a sick wife in bed and a nursing baby and I got to have water," he said. "Water wagon didn't come, isn't coming, and I want water."

"I don't have any."

"Yes, you do," he said, heading for the apartment door, that sacrosanct door leading downstairs, never violated by any of these big rough customers all the while she ran the club.

"No!" she cried.

But he yanked the door open and plunged downstairs, followed by half-a-dozen others. She felt violated. She didn't follow them down, but waited bitterly. She always had water in her reservoir there, for bathing, for tea, for herself. Now it was gone.

She watched them haul it off in buckets and jars. Some nodded curtly, others looked embarrassed, one sneered at her. But they took it all.

"You can walk to Sourdough Springs," one said. "My baby can't and there's no wagons anywheres."

She nodded. He needed water worse than she did.

So they expected her to walk away from all this, walk away from her business, walk away from her sole livelihood, walk out of Yancey City. So Will was right. He had explained what might happen, making the geology easy for her to grasp, and now it had happened.

More and more swarmed in, angry at her for not having water to give them. Some didn't stop at water either, and hauled away her luncheon stew, a good moist soup that would fend off thirst.

She watched them passively now; shouting at them achieved nothing. They rampaged down Silver Street, plundering water and other things, trying every mercantile door, breaking down any that were locked. The miners angered her, but she knew these desperate men weren't really at fault. It was the syndicate's greed that lay behind this. The company had not prepared for a water crisis and had ignored the danger to the big spring.

Then a young woman carrying a child arrived.

"I need water for him," she said, nodding toward the baby.

"I don't have any. Not a drop."

"I need it so bad. The men took it all. They won't give me any. The water wagon didn't come. My man's in the hospital."

Adelaide watched the tears well in the girl's eyes, and felt utterly helpless.

"I wish I could help you. All I know is that there's water down in the valley, five miles away."

The young woman nodded, eyed Adelaide bitterly, and walked away.

Charley Barraclough wandered in. He was one of her best customers, a miner who ate most of his meals at the Clover Club, and often played chess at one of the tables. He looked around at the stripped bar, the overturned chairs, the grimy floor.

"Cleaned you out, eh?"

"Everything, Charley."

"Syndicate got the water."

"What do you mean?"

"There were half-a-dozen water wagons delivering around town when the spring quit, most half full. But the first thing the syndicate did was put its armed thugs on those wagons, confiscated the water. It's being used to water their drays, so they can haul the best ore out of here before it all dries up."

"But people need it!"

"The syndicate's not in the business of helping people. There's not a drop left. Every joint on Copper Street's been cleaned out of anything people can guzzle."

"What about the hospital?"

"What about 'em? They're as dry as everyone else."

"What's going to happen, Charley?"

"Already happening. People are bailing out. Regular parade down that long road to the valley, people on foot because there's nothing to haul 'em, and people with drays and mules have gotten them out. No water for 'em anymore."

"What about you?"

"I've got a gallon or two in me cottage; I'll stick around for a day and see. And what about you, Adelaide?"

"I have no plans."

"You dry?"

She hesitated. "I'll be all right," she said.

"You run dry, you come see me."

She watched him wandering into the gloomy street.

Adelaide knew where to get enough water to keep body and soul together. She wondered if Will Yancey had dug down far enough to start that spring up on the flank of Table Mountain flowing even a little. She knew she could get a cup of water there; the seep would fill a cup in a minute or so, and that was how he survived, one cup at a time. She ached to go there, but held off. She needed to guard her place. But then she wondered what she was guarding; it was already a doomed shell, a dead business, transformed into worthlessness by a single blast in a mine tunnel.

The crowds of males hunting water vanished. The town had been pillaged, and suddenly she was alone again. She listened to the silence. A great hush had set-

tled over Yancey City, as its mortal wound began draining its life away from it. But there were plenty of people
about, people hanging on, waiting for a miracle, waiting for potable water to well up. One of the mines, she
couldn't remember which, had a water problem, and
had pumped from one of its drifts, but that water was
loaded with arsenic and heavy metals and salts, and was
good for nothing. They didn't even use it in their boiler.

Will needed to be told. He would need food too. And
she would have a drink of water there. She filled a basket with whatever she could find, some cheese and
bread mostly, wrapped her cloak about her, and hiked
slowly up the grade to the ridge, where armed guards
protected ore wagons and watched over the captured
water wagons, even as company crews shoveled ore into
the heavy freight wagons.

She ignored them, walked quietly through a bitter
evening until she left the stricken city behind her. In the
twilight the city looked dead; she saw few lamps. She
could not see the string of refugees traipsing out of the
city, in the evening haze, but she knew they were there,
bearing what little they could carry, their tragedy enormous and mute and ugly. She sensed their heartache, the
cruelty of their fate. They would start over somewhere,
those who survived. Some would probably sicken, suc-
cumb, surrender life because it had become too hard
and mean.

She hoped she could find the courage to continue. If
she did, it would be because of Will Yancey. He had
been knocked down over and over, picked himself up,
and kept on trying. She admired that in him.

He was penniless, but now so was she. That didn't
matter. What counted was his enduring courage . . . and
the tenderness she saw in his eyes whenever they were
together. There was something sweet in him, something

so loving and gentle that she felt aglow just to be with him. She knew she loved him, and feared that he wouldn't notice, or think her unworthy of him.

Enough light remained to help her across that place where the trail edged an abyss, and then she found safer ground and struggled up toward the horseshoe where the seep lay. It seemed a great distance from town because the slopes were so steep, but she knew it was only a mile.

He stood there at the seep, and the sight of him in the dusk gladdened her.

"Will," she cried.

He turned, discovering her climbing up the dry watercourse to the seep.

"Adelaide!" he said, springing down the grade to her. He did not pause before her, but swept her into his arms, and she nestled there, gladdened by the embrace of this solitary man, the safe haven she found there after scores, maybe hundreds, of men had pillaged her home and her business.

"I was expecting you," he said softly as he clasped her to him.

"You were?"

"Ever since that blast this morning. Yes, I heard it and felt it. It boomed up the canyon and shook the rock under me. I knew what it was."

"The spring?"

"Yes, the spring. They were trying to open it up, weren't they? Probably stuffed a case of dynamite into that hole."

"Yes," she said.

"And did they open it? Did water start?"

"No," she said. "Oh, Will, you have no idea what's happened. People are crazy for water! My club . . ."

"Not a drop left, I suppose."

"If it weren't for you, I'd be thirsting by now."

He laughed softly. "Come, I have something to show you," he said.

She followed him through the deepening night to the little hollow worn in the rock by the long-dead spring, and discovered that it was half full of water.

Thirty-six

She stared, astonished, at the black pool of water rippling softly in moonlight. "Will! You did it!" she exclaimed.

"It's a lot of water," he said. "I pulled out another piece of limestone, a big chunk I had been prying for an hour, big as I could lift, and it flowed out. Just like that. I had to dig about three feet down and four feet back, and lift it out piece by piece."

"That explosion. Do you think . . . ?"

"Might have. But probably not. I just kept digging out rock until the water flowed. A blast over a mile away didn't do that, but I sure felt it. I pretty near thought I'd never see water here, that it was blocked hundreds of feet into that mountain. But I kept on prying out limestone, kind of stubborn, maybe crazy too, thinking it's got to be in there somewhere and I was going to get it one way or another and make this old spring flow.

"And here it is. Good water too. It's filling this old pool and then it'll run down that flowage in the gulch about half a mile west of town. But that's weeks away. For a while it'll just soak in around here. This isn't going to start running down there, not after centuries of drying out."

"How much is it, Will?"

"Not as big as the spring at the hospital, but big

enough. Maybe ten or twenty gallons a minute, maybe half what was pouring out of the old spring at the flat. But the town wasn't using all of that. Most of that ran past the hospital and vanished on that slope. This could keep the whole town going, piped down there, gravity feed, stored in a tank on the ridge and then run into homes or public faucets."

She knelt and cupped her hands in the water, and tasted it.

"Oh, Will, this is divine, so sweet. You don't know how much this means. . . ."

"Maybe it's divine at that," he said. "It came just when people needed it, as if I was simply the instrument of something larger." He studied her, so sweet and lovely with her cloak wrapped tightly about her. "I guess you have some stories to tell me about all that."

She rose and took his hand. "The whole town's falling apart. Yancey City's dead. All I could think of was the wrath of God. The first I knew of it, men were rushing into my club buying every bottle of beer and shouting that the spring died and we'd all die of thirst. Later, they stole the beer kegs, and even went into my apartment and took my water. I've heard terrible stories, Will. The sisters, Will, they're out of water and they don't have a thing for their patients, and no one will give them a drop! And Dr. Borden's trying to get water for them."

"Not even the company? Wouldn't Noble spare a few gallons?"

"The company least of all! It stole all the water in town, everything still in the water wagons making their rounds, not just theirs but the independent operators', and now they're under guard up on the ridge. That's the first thing Alfie Noble did—sent his armed guards into the streets to take all the water wagons from their owners. I hear they're using the water for their drays and they're hauling out ore."

A disgust so profound that Will Yancey could barely contain it inside of himself flooded through him.

"I have a bucket. Let's go," he said.

"Where?"

"The sisters."

"Oh, Will, yes."

He clambered up to his cliff house while she waited, and returned with a wooden bucket, which he dipped into the dark pool, making silvery ripples on the moon-lit waters.

"Will? What's going to happen to this water?"

"The syndicate will try to take it."

"But it's yours! You can make a fortune selling it!"

"Adelaide, not long ago that's all I thought of, but then you came into my life."

That puzzled her.

"I've been sitting here for three or four hours watching that water flood into this little pool. I rejoiced at first. I struck it rich! It's all mine. I have a bonanza better than gold. I could sell every drop. This water's above town and doesn't need pumping. Just a downhill line into the city. I could sit here and charge for every gallon.

"I could get even with the syndicate for stealing my Minerva Mine. Now I had something they needed. It was better than the water down at the hospital, which had to be carried uphill. And I thought I'd make sure it wasn't stolen from me, just the way they stole everything else from me. This was mine, and I'd make my money one way or another. That's why I claimed this land; it's a homestead claim, one hundred sixty acres, that covers the land and springs and water, and I filed it one day a week or so ago."

"Yes, Will, and now the whole town will come back. Return to their homes, go to work. I can open up again. You've rescued me from bankruptcy. You deserve every cent you can squeeze out of this town."

He turned to look at her, standing there in the white moonlight. "I'm not going to make money with this water. It will be given to the people."

"But Will, you've struggled so long; it was your vision that saw the need and dug for it here."

"Yes, I did," he said. "But I've changed my mind."

"But Will—you've spent years prospecting. Don't you want a better life?"

How could he tell her what couldn't be put into words?

"I guess I'm crazy," he said. "Hard Luck Yancey, throwing away a chance of a lifetime."

She herself was the life he had always wanted. For all these years he had thought he was such an odd and homely duck that only a lot of money would win him a wife, a home, a family. But then she came into his life, and they read poetry, and she was the first woman he had ever known who was interested in the earth, in the rock, in geology and its secrets.

And she was interested in him. He discovered a sweetness in her he never imagined abided in any woman. And then he didn't care about money, or getting even with the syndicate, or holding Alfie Noble over a barrel. There was only Adelaide, who sometimes hugged him, who smiled into his eyes, who welcomed him with her arms. But how could he tell her that? Tell her he once believed he could never win the heart of a woman unless he was rich? The thought embarrassed him.

"Maybe water ought to be free," he said. "Maybe it's

too important to sell or make money on. Maybe it should just be there, like the air we breathe."

He felt her gaze on him there in the silvery light, felt a shy sweet joy in him.

He lifted the full bucket out of the pool and hefted it. "Let's go," he said. "You can tell me the whole story about the water panic. I can pretty much guess what happened."

She did tell him, beginning with the strange boom that echoed through town, the people racing back and forth from the dry spring to town, the wildfire panic, the pillaging of every saloon and restaurant, the appearance of the syndicate's security guards with shotguns, commandeering the remaining water, booting the owners of the wagons away. The procession of people leaving town with nothing but what they could carry, people hiking for Sourdough Springs, and life-giving water. People suddenly bereft of employment, of all their wealth, of a future. She told of people left behind, of the sick waiting for someone to bring them the very liquid of life. Of women and children in tears, and the miner who was ashamed to take water from her apartment but who had a sick wife and nursing baby and was doing what he had to do to give them life, apologizing desperately even as he pillaged her private quarters.

They walked swiftly through bright moonlight, the cold November air stinging their cheeks. He listened to the terrible stories, there were many stories, and he knew what he had to do.

They reached the ridge, and he switched the heavy bucket to his other hand, and they plummeted downslope to Copper Street, which was eerily quiet now. Obviously many people had fled town; others were holed up and clinging to what little water they possessed.

"There'll be footpads out," he said. "Stick to the shadows."

She veered to the dark side of the street, past silent black saloons, somehow malevolent in the night, harboring who knows what?

They reached the Calabash Club safely, and Yancey wondered where Blarney O'Rourke was. Maybe he had fled, like so many others. Above, in what had only recently been a notorious flophouse, a lamp burned dimly.

"Let's go," he said, pushing open the side door. They ascended noisily on wooden stairs, she ahead of him, into a thickening odor that still clung to the place.

They stumbled into that dank, shadowed dormitory, saw patients lying in their cots, smelled suppuration and urine and pain. A coal-oil lamp burned at the street side of the room, before the window. A single sister sat there, head bowed, her fingers finding her beads. It was too dark for him to know which one.

She was so lost in supplication that she didn't raise her head.

He set down the bucket and hunted for a dipper. The patients were watching him.

"Water," said one.

"Yes," he said. "Water."

Sister Carmela lifted her head and stared.

Thirty-seven

Sister Carmela stared at Hard Luck Yancey and the woman beside him, and at the bucket with water in it.

"Will," she said.

"Here's water."

"Oh, Will."

She rose at once and began dippering it into tumblers, which she took to her patients. The fevered woman turned her face away; the miners drank greedily. She refilled the tumblers and helped them all drink again.

"Water," said one. "I never thought about water before."

Satisfied at last, Sister Carmela rejoined Will.

"Drink," he said.

"Oh, no, Will, this is for the patients. We can get along for a while."

"There's lots more. Drink up."

"Lots more?"

"I found plenty of water."

"You truly did?" She didn't resist further, but drank the cool water, letting it slide down her throat. She had been parched from the long hours on the street begging for water. All the sisters had been out begging; one returned with a bottle of beer a miner gave her. That helped a little. Now the sisters were out again in the night, going door to door, seeking water.

"This is Adelaide Kearney, Sister," Will said. "She runs the Clover Club."

Sister Carmela drew Adelaide's hand into hers and pressed it. "You and Will Yancey have spared us much grief," she said.

"We'll bring more," Adelaide said. "It's a mile away."

"It's a spring I opened up, Sister, and how it's running free. Where's Slow Eddie?"

"He's down on the trail to Silverton, seeking some water for us."

"We'll show him where to get water," Will said. "Where's Dr. Borden?"

"Treating people."

Sister Carmela carried a tumbler gotten from the Calabash Club around to all of her patients and offered them water again, and again they drank.

"Mr. Yancey says there's plenty of water now," she said. "Our prayers are answered."

She returned to Will and clasped his hand. "You are the instrument of God and the salvation of our ministry here," she said. "You can't know what's happened to us since this morning. The vagrants along Copper Street burst in, took every drop we had, even the little we kept in our apartment. These people have suffered. We had nothing to cool the fever of Mrs. Jacobus, nothing to clean them up, nothing to cook with. . . ." She gazed fondly at them in that dim light. "But our supplications were heard; Our Gracious Lady answered our pleas."

Will Yancey scratched his head. "I don't know about that, but I had a hunch about a seep up on the side of Table Mountain, and starting digging like a badger."

"Who are we to know what inspires us, what voice is in our heart, what strength is at our elbow?" she said. "I thank God for you, and we will remember you."

"Are you moving?" Adelaide asked.

"If we have water, we'll stay until our patients can care for themselves."

"But what if others need you?"

She lifted her head. "We are here. If we have water, we can do the rest."

"The town will come back to life," he said.

She stared, scarcely believing.

"I opened a good spring, and it can be piped here, and it's enough if it isn't wasted. And it's above town, so we won't need water wagons."

"You found the true bonanza then," Sister Carmela said.

"Water is the greatest wealth," he replied. "But I've decided not to keep it."

"Not keep it?"

"At first I thought I'd charge for every gallon. I claimed the land and the spring. It's mine. I could make some money; not a fortune, but I could live comfortably. Then, oh, I don't know. It just didn't seem right."

Sister Carmela waited, but Hard Luck seemed reluctant to talk of it anymore.

One by one, the sisters straggled in. None had water. Isabella had received a bottle of beer. Sister Carmela received it as if it were gold.

"Drink," she said, pointing to the half-empty bucket. "Mr. Yancey has brought us water."

"Oh, that's for people who are desperate," Sister Isabella said.

Sister Carmela handed her a tumbler. "Drink," she said.

The sister did, and again. "I never knew water could mean so much or be so precious," she said.

They heard weary footsteps on the stair, and then Rufus Borden emerged in the gloom. He sat heavily on the nearest empty bed and stared at them all.

Sister Carmela scooped water into a tumbler and handed it to him. He looked drawn. He shook his head. "Save it," he muttered.

"There's more."

Borden stared, and then drank.

"You'll want to explain this gift from heaven," he said.

"There's enough for everyone," Yancey said.

"I've treated a whole family who managed to poison themselves with some mine water they found. I think the girl will not last the night. They had some tins of stewed tomatoes on a shelf, and I told them to eat them, and drink every drop. Maybe they'll live. I've treated a man who got shot in the arm. Fight on the road, when a water wagon showed up. The owner was bringing water up from Sourdough Springs, tried to sell it, and that started a riot. Several people got hurt and most of the water ended up on the road."

Borden looked so drawn that Sister Carmela feared he would slide into a grand mal seizure. That sort of weariness seemed to precede his attacks. But he just sat, slumped down.

Slow Eddie entered, his hands empty. He tried to form words, but words wouldn't come, and Sister Carmela spoke for him.

"You've hunted for water everywhere, and now we have it," she said. "Mr. Yancey found some."

Slow Eddie stared at the bucket, at Yancey.

"I'll need people with buckets," Yancey said. "It's a mile uphill, and some of it's tough walking. But there's all the water this town needs."

They stared at him in wonderment.

"I'll go," said Sister Carmela. "Sister Isabella, you look after our patients. There's still a quart or so."

"But Sister, you're so tired, and it's a long trip," Adelaide said.

But Sister Carmela was transformed by the thought of water. She would carry two buckets. They would find vessels, pots, jars, bottles in the Calabash Club.

"Tell me about this miracle," Borden said.

"I just cleaned out a seep I knew about," Yancey said.

"Cleaned out? He's been prying out rock for days," Adelaide said. "And now there's a good flow, like the old spring."

"That much?"

"Enough to keep this town going. No one need suffer anymore."

The doctor covered his face with his hands, and Carmela saw wetness glinting in the dull light of the coal oil lamp.

Slow Eddie vanished, and soon they heard him rummaging around the dark club downstairs. When he returned he carried another bucket, jars, two large kettles, and some empty whiskey bottles.

They moved into the icy night, the sisters wearing black shawls, Dr. Borden dressed in his buffalo coat, Adelaide Kearney in her cloak, Slow Eddie staggering under a collection of vessels. This night a bright moon lit their path, and made the trip easy. They passed the mines, where armed guards at the commandeered water wagons watched them suspiciously, and then Will Yancey led them up the ridge, and along the steep side of Table Mountain where a trail clung beside an abyss, but Sister Carmela didn't pause. She felt refreshed, like a young girl, for ahead was the hope of a dying city.

They walked up that narrow trail in moonwashed brightness, and then, suddenly, Yancey stopped. They had reached an intimate horseshoe, and there below it, shimmering in the cold light, was a pond, and water was flowing over its lip.

"Yancey! How did you find this?" Borden said.

Hard Luck seemed embarrassed. "Sort of read the rock," he said. "Fill up."

But Sister Carmela summoned Sisters Margaret and Elizabeth to her, and knelt at the pool's edge. She touched the water, felt its coldness on her fingers, and then touched the foreheads of her dear sisters, almost as if this were a baptism, though it wasn't, and lifted water to her lips almost as if this were the Host, though it wasn't.

She uttered one small prayer. "Thanks be to God for this great gift. May it relieve the thirsty, help the suffering, cleanse the bodies and souls of all."

They filled every pail, pot, kettle, bottle, and jar. Off on the slopes they heard an owl hoot.

"Is this where you've been all this time, Yancey?" asked Borden.

"Old cliff house up there," Yancey said. "I did claim it, a hundred sixty acres."

Slow Eddie wanted to speak, so they waited for him to form his words. "You . . . wondered where your life was leading. Now you know, Yancey. . . . This is your gift to the world. You were born to give the world this gift."

"Yes, it will be a gift," Yancey said soberly. "But I expect the syndicate's going to try to take it from us."

Thirty-eight

Alfred Noble huddled in his office chair, a scarf wrapped about his neck, his overcoat tight about him, glaring at the papers before him. The soft light of a single coal-oil lamp lit the old chapel. He reached for his blue bottle and swilled some Wildroot Tonic, but not even that magical potion could lift his desolation.

The windows of the old hospital had all shattered when the spring had been blasted, so the woodstoves in the building did little good. But there was no point in moving the general offices of the Rhode Island Syndicate up to the Minerva Mine again, because the syndicate was about to go out of existence.

Water. Who would have thought it? He generated mighty oaths in his mind to unloose against Gus Moran, his chief of operations, and assorted geologists, for not foreseeing the peril the company was in if it blasted too close to that sole water supply.

He lifted the papers with numb fingers and studied the data again: Without water, the gold and silver buried in the mountain were almost worthless. Unless some miracle of technology came along, it would cost more to extract the ores than they were worth, so long as water had to be pumped from Sourdough Springs five miles away and several thousand feet lower. And without water, there could be no miners. Nor was there any sign of aquifers or springs elsewhere. In short, and this was maddening, he was sitting on a mountain of high-grade gold ore, and a huge supply of low-grade silver, and couldn't make a dime from it.

He sighed. There would be no more twenty-percent dividends, much less the thirty-percent ones, or the real bonanza payouts he had been calculating if he could get a railroad in and the water was present. Not even if capitalists were to ante up for the railroad spur, and other capitalists were to build a water system that would tap some distant source, would the syndicate make any more money.

Worse, if they abandoned the works, the shafts and tunnels would deteriorate rapidly. You cannot simply walk away from a mine and hope to return to it a few years hence without a huge investment in new timbers, pumping out flooded shafts and drifts, and all the rest. Once the syndicate quit, it was all over.

He drummed cold fingers on his waxed desk, wondering what to do. Moran said that there was enough water from the commandeered wagons to keep the dray horses pulling ore wagons the next day; that the high-grade telluride gold already dug out of the tunnel and lifted up the Minerva shaft could all be hauled off. There would be freight wagons available to haul the entire households of the Morans and the Nobles to Silverton, and after that . . . Yancey City would be a parched relic.

But the syndicate was done for. He would have trouble peddling patented claims to large bodies of ore if there was no way to extract them. Experienced mining men would look the place over, and decide that Yancey City was not where they would put their chips.

He felt an icy breeze eddy through the hospital, and drew his scarf tighter. Soon it would be December, and the death of the old year, along with the death of the Rhode Island Syndicate, of which he was the principal owner. The rest were junior partners whose capital was needed to develop the mines and pay the heavy cost of the legal fight to obtain them. Lawyers didn't come cheap, especially the specialist sort who could win an apex suit, and appeals and gifts to certain members of the judiciary didn't come cheap either.

A breeze banged the shutters of the hospital, and the chatter sounded like a death rattle. By tomorrow evening, probably eighty percent of the denizens of Yancey City would be on the road, and the holdouts would depart in the next day or two. Once the labor was gone, the mines would lie useless.

The first flight had consisted largely of the sharpers, gamblers, saloon men, bawds, pickpockets, and their ilk, who suddenly had no prospects in a town without enough water to fix a decent drink. These were the ones without families, without property, who could pick up and go from their rented rooms and never look back. Tomorrow the miners and their families would depart, the lucky few with wagons or even wheelbarrows; most on foot, carrying what they could, or dragging it on improvised sleds.

Grumpily Alfred Noble wondered why fate had chosen to play him so cruel a trick. What had he done to deserve this ignominy? What would he do next, his paper fortune gone, his bank illiquid, his town lots worth pennies, his huge lode of gold beyond reach?

He thought maybe he could unload the worthless mines on some sucker for some last coup. But the very thought was so improbable that he quit thinking it. No investor bought a mine without sending in the geologists, the assayers, the mineralogists, the assessors, and the sharp-pencil boys who calculated the odds.

He smiled broadly, even though there was no one to smile at. Moran had abandoned him to go start packing. The last of the mined high-grade gold was even now rolling downslope, leaving nothing but heaps of carbonate silver with values too low to transport, and an unknown amount of gold still in the ground with no way to extract it.

Moodily he downed another slug of the Wildroot and waited. It seemed to take more and more of the stuff to achieve the euphoria he wanted. Gertrude had discovered its medicinal qualities and was sampling it herself.

Maybe soon they wouldn't be able afford any more Wildroot. Maybe they wouldn't even be able to afford a pair of railroad tickets back to Rhode Island. Maybe they'd end up selling off their furniture in Silverton, for the want of cash. Maybe they would be reduced to . . . ordinary people.

He heard the crash of a door, and hastily dug into his desk for his Smith and Wesson. But it proved to be Moran, looking rumpled in the dull light of the lamp.

"Thought I'd find you here," Moran said. "The ore's gone; there's fifty gallons left to water livestock. After that we're up the creek."

"That's not exactly an expression I would use, Gus."

Moran passed the altar rail without a by-your-leave and parked himself next to Noble.

"How does it look?" Moran asked.

"How do you think? We're in the hole. What did you expect?"

"How much in the hole?"

"We've got fifty-two thousand of milling equipment and unpaid labor costs and construction materials right here, none of it paid for, and the only assets we have are ten grand or so for the ore now on the road."

Moran sighed. "You know what milling equipment sells for? Ten cents on the dollar. It's tough to haul."

"We also owe six and a half thousand in wages, but I don't see any miners around to collect. The bank is busted; it holds mortgages on a pile of worthless houses and stores. There's also a few thousand in teamster invoices. We just got a shipment of powder from DuPont, and there's a heap of timber and firewood invoices and there's some taxes. . . ."

"Bankrupt?"

Noble laughed sardonically.

"How much?"

Right now, even after salvage sales, maybe forty or fifty thousand owing."

"Syndicate's belly-up?"

"Unless we can find a sucker to buy us out."

"There's a lot of gold under there, Alfie."

"Sure, and that's where it's going to stay unless you can figure out how to strike a rock and make water gush out of it."

"Somebody in the Bible did that."

"Yeah, and somebody parted the Red Sea. Water, for God's sake. Wiped out. Why the hell weren't you careful about the blasting, Gus? You could have fired small shots, a foot at a time."

Moran looked affronted. "Now don't be giving me that. Not now. I was told full speed ahead. I was told to finish that bore and hook it to the Minerva drift three shifts a day. You wanted it all done yesterday. So we blew out three feet at a time, and now you're blaming me."

Noble wasn't going to let him get away with that. "You cost us a fortune. You knew that spring was there, not fifty yards away, but you didn't slow down."

Moran was grinning, mockery plain in his face.

"Now the water's draining somewhere, all the way to hell as far as I know."

"Down a fault," Moran said. "Maybe it'll fill up and start flowing from the spring again."

"Yeah, in ten thousand years."

Moran sighed. "All I wanted was a good mine and now it's gone. I traded it to the syndicate for a piece of the pie, and now there's no pie. I'm broke."

Moran reached for the carafe of water on Noble's desk and poured himself a glass. Noble watched malevolently. The water was worth more than the Rhode Island Syndicate.

"Here it is," Moran said, lifting the glass and sipping. "Without it, there's no wealth, no life, no cities, no plants."

"Fancy that. You're a philosopher now instead of a mining man," Noble said.

Moran sipped and smiled and sipped deliberately, sighing, smacking his lips, devilish humor in his face. "Well, what're you going to tell our partners?"

"What's there to say? We're broke. They won't be getting boodle. The assets all turned into ash."

"Yeah, and maybe you can trade assets for debt; trade mines for milling equipment," Moran said.

Noble laughed. "Just see whether Union Steel's going to accept a dry mine for those crushers and stamps out there."

Moran rose. "Yeah, well, I'm going to Chile and try copper," he said. "Maybe you can dig diamonds in Johannesburg."

Those were his last words. Noble watched his production chief vanish into the icy night.

He smiled brightly, full of loathing.

What to do, what to do? He couldn't think. He rose at last, turned down the wick until the lamp blued out, and braved the sharp cold trip up the slope to his house. It was an odd thing, hiking through the night in a doomed city, hiking toward a fancy house he would abandon, hiking toward a wife who'd never liked Yancey City and would be glad to escape.

Noble had heard of large bodies of ore being abandoned, almost always because of flooding. But this was the first time he'd heard of ore being abandoned because there wasn't a drop of water for miles around.

Thirty-nine

When Hard Luck Yancey strolled into town the next morning, he ran smack into Abner Cruikshank.

"Yancey!"

Hard Luck stopped.

"I told you I'd throw you into the pokey if I saw your mug around here."

Yancey nodded. "I came to see Mr. Noble about water."

"There ain't any. This town's clearing out, and I'm not going to let some vagrant like you steal stuff that folks leave behind. It's not yours."

Yancey grinned. "I came to give away some water."

"Give away water! Give away water!" Cruikshank couldn't think of a coherent thing to say.

"So, if you'll let me pass, I'll go talk to Mr. Noble."

"Let you pass? You turn around and git, and if I see you again you'll be in trouble."

"All right, but you take a message to him. Tell him that I found water and it'll be enough for the town."

"You been sipping something strong, Yancey? Lot have, you know. They ain't got water so they're sipping booze."

"You heard me. Tell that to him."

"Like hell I will. He's a busy man and ain't interested

in your schemes. You want me to be part of your confidence game, do you?"

Yancey shrugged. "All right. I'll give water to others, if the syndicate doesn't want it."

"Give? Give?"

"You having trouble thinking today, Abner? That the only word on your tongue? There's enough water to run the mines. Enough for every family. Enough so the company can hire all the miners again."

"I'm taking you in and you can sleep it off, Yancey," Cruikshank said.

Hard Luck was disgusted. "Listen, Abner. Now dammit, you get one thing straight. I found water. If you want it, let me pass. If not, then you'll take the blame for wrecking the town."

The constable jabbed his billy club into Hard Luck's belly. "You're just begging for some time in the pokey, aren't you?" he said. "Found water. Ha!"

Hard Luck saw how it would go. "All right. I'll just leave. It's your funeral."

"Oh, no, you don't! I warned you not to come here. We're going on a little trip to Copper Street."

"Can you give me one good reason?"

For a response, Cruikshank jabbed Yancey in the gut, driving the air out of him. Yancey walked ahead, with the fat constable right behind. They passed a myriad of wagons, and scores of people frantically loading possessions into them. Yancey guessed that the wagons were from Silverton, and that their owners had rushed to Yancey City to make quick money.

It didn't look like a dying city, but surely it was, with the streets teeming with people on the move.

Down on Copper Street things were different. The lowlifes had been first out of town, and this street hung forlorn and silent. Yancey thought to run for the Calabash Club and get Slow Eddie to help him beat off the constable, but Cruikshank sensed it.

"Get in there," he said, roughly shoving Yancey into the small and foul office, and then into a sole, a vomit-caked cell. Yancey heard the door clang behind him. He feared, suddenly, that he would be forgotten there, in the great exodus out of town, and die a miserable death.

There was a slimy bench, and he sat on it, and time slowed down so that every minute seemed like an hour. He was thirsty, and dreamed of that great pool of sweet water. The constable had vanished, and Yancey wondered what was next. He didn't have to wait long. Cruikshank showed up with Alfred Noble himself.

"What's this about water? Make it fast, I'm packing," Noble said, peering through bars, his lips pursed into a perpetual smile.

"Want to give you water," Yancey said, rising.

"Stay away from them bars, and no tricks," the constable yelled.

"What water?"

"I developed a good spring on land I've patented, and I thought you might need it."

Noble laughed, wheezing. "Yancey, I've heard confident men spin stories, but this takes the cake. And how much do you plan to sell this spring for?"

"I thought I'd just give it to the town. You know, people need water. It didn't seem right to sell it."

Noble stared, smiled until his lips were stretched across his face, and chuckled. "What's your angle? Come on now, what do you take me for?"

"You want to go for a walk, Mr. Noble? I'll show it to you."

"That's one way to get out of the hog pen, isn't it, Yancey?" the constable said.

"I'll show you a spring on Table Mountain, above

Yancey City, that's flowing maybe fifteen or twenty gallons a minute of sweet water, and it's not for sale. Life depends on water, so I thought I'd donate it." Yancey waited. "I swear to God I can take you to good water."

Noble's smile faded at last. "I don't know what your angle is, Yancey, maybe some last little game, but you're wasting my time."

"That's it? You don't want the water?"

Noble turned to Cruikshank. "Keep him here until tomorrow. After that, no one will care anyway. And don't give him a drink."

"You leaving? What about the syndicate property?" Yancey asked.

"It's not worth a dime."

"All that gold?"

"All that debt, you mean, Yancey."

"I'll take it if you don't want it. Including the debt."

"You're crazy. There's a pile of debt you'd never get out from under."

"You give me ownership for the price of the debt, and you'll be free from your creditors," Yancey said.

"And what would you do with it?"

"Try to make it work."

Noble stared. "You'd assume all the syndicate's debt? We walk out without owing a cent? And not a drop of water within miles?"

Yancey nodded. "One thing, though. Do you have the authority to convey the property without the consent of your partners?"

"Absolutely, Yancey. I own a majority of the company, and the rest are junior partners without voting rights. I set it up that way. I'll run it; they'll contribute capital and reap their harvest. That was the deal."

"All right, I'll do it. I'll assume all your debt," Yancey said.

"A live sucker, right before my eyes, Yancey. Abner, give me a sheet of paper," Noble said.

Yancey watched the man scratch out two copies of an agreement with the constable's worn and treacherous pen, but eventually he produced a sale agreement, and handed one copy to Yancey.

It was straightforward. As of that date, the Rhode Island Syndicate conveyed all of its mining properties in the Yancey District, along with the Town Lot Company and all its properties, and the bank, and the materials for the mill, to Will Yancey; and Will Yancey agreed to assume all the syndicate's debt and hold the members of the syndicate free from further obligation.

"That suit you, Yancey?"

"Give me the pen and ink and I'll sign both copies."

"Let him out," said Noble.

Cruikshank turned the lock and swung the heavy barred door open. Yancey sat down and signed the copies. Noble signed them. Cruikshank signed the witness line. A witnessed agreement was executed.

Noble pocketed his copy and smiled. "You just saved us fifty grand," he said. "It's all yours to pay off. Union Steel wants payment tomorrow, that's twenty thousand right there. Now, tell me how you were going to work your water game."

"Lots of water," Yancey said. "There for the taking."

Noble laughed brightly, and winked.

That was the last that Yancey saw of Alfred Noble. Hard Luck stepped out upon silent and sullen Copper Street, aware that the sisters and their remaining patients were only a block away. He would soon visit them, and assign them their land and the minerals under it if they wanted it. But there was more urgent business to attend to first.

He climbed the steep grade toward Gold Street, passing grim people overloading wagons, tearful women filling wheelbarrows, miners heaping their possessions on overloaded burros, children staring silently, and great wagons rumbling downslope, away forever from Yancey City. They scarcely noticed the city's founder as he hiked up the grade. They were staring at homes that suddenly had no value, at buildings that had turned to ash, and at the distant valley, trying to plumb an uncertain future. Tomorrow, the winds would pile tumbleweeds against the wooden walls and glass would lie in shards below each hollow window.

He knocked at Adelaide's door, and when it opened at last he found tears in her eyes.

"Adelaide—"

She rushed into his arms. He drew her tight and held her. He felt her melt into him, fierce and warm, her hands catching his hair, even as he wrapped her within an unbreakable circle of love.

She drew him in and hugged him as if life depended on it, and perhaps it did.

He kissed her wet cheeks, and her lips.

"This is no time for tears," he said.

"I thought . . . oh, it doesn't matter what I thought."

"Just say yes, and I will be in heaven."

"Yes, Will, yes," she said.

Forty

Yancey City survived barely two more years before the last of the gold was extracted from the bowels of Table Mountain. The large deposits of low grade silver carbonate ore were not profitable to mine, and were either stockpiled in great mounds beside the old mines, or left underground.

The town never did return to its previous size, but about eight hundred did settle back into their houses, or bought new ones that Hard Luck made available to them for very little.

Hard Luck Yancey and his bride, Adelaide, moved into the stone mansion once occupied by Alfred Noble, and enjoyed being rich. But much of the fun of having all that money was that Hard Luck didn't really need it or care about it. He had won Adelaide when he didn't have a cent, and that was a wonderment and a lesson to him. He ended up giving a lot of it away to people whose luck was harder than his own.

At once, upon acquiring all that property from the Rhode Island syndicate, Hard Luck deeded the flat back to the Sisters of Charity of Leavenworth, and paid them a royalty of half the profit on ore taken from their holdings. Mining continued under the old hospital for many more months. He converted an abandoned dry-goods mercantile on Silver Street into a fine new hospital, and

converted the house next to it into a small convent for
the sisters.

The mill was a sound mining investment, so he completed it and operated it at the head of the adit that cut
under the old hospital grounds. Because no more ore
was ever discovered in the region, no railroad spur was
ever built to Yancey City, and to the last, the concentrate
was hauled off in heavy wagons for processing in other
locales, which limited the profitability of the whole
Yancey District.

Just because she was so happy operating her club,
Adelaide reopened the Clover Club, and always spent
part of each day affectionately serving her miners, and
listening to their tall tales of tommyknockers and other
gremlins in the mines.

The bank didn't fail; with water, the mortgaged properties had value again, and Hard Luck managed to steer
past the shoals of disaster. He knew, though, that Yancey
City, like most mining towns, would not live long, so he
prepared for its demise by reducing outstanding loans,
shortening the duration of others, and switching to cash
assets. In the end, he honored every deposit.

The sisters operated their new hospital for a year and
a half, but as the mines shut down, the hospital was less
and less needed, and in the end Dr. Borden acquired the
building and maintained a small infirmary operated by
himself and a nurse and Slow Eddie, who stayed on. But
for all of those two years, the sisters profited from the
royalties that Hard Luck faithfully sent to the motherhouse in Leavenworth. Eventually, Sister Drill Sergeant
moved herself and her beloved colleagues to Bisbee,
Arizona, to nurse copper miners, and Slow Eddie rejoined them there, along with Dr. Borden.

When Yancey City died, no one missed it, not even
Hard Luck and Adelaide. It was built where no city

should have been, and most of those who had rooted down there during the fat times were glad enough to head for flatter and warmer places. As much as Yancey and Adelaide enjoyed the mansion, they often spent time up at the mysterious old cliff house, where the spring purled fresh sweet water, the true wealth of the world, into a pipe that carried it to Yancey City. It was there that they felt at one with the world.

Hard Luck and Adelaide lived happily in Globe, Arizona, after that, invested in Salt River Valley pecan groves, and lived sweetly together.